SECOND

BETROTHED #6

PENELOPE SKY

Hartwick Publishing

Second

Copyright © 2020 by Penelope Sky

All rights reserved.

No part of this book may be reproduced in any form or by any electronic or mechanical means, including information storage and retrieval systems, without written permission from the author, except for the use of brief quotations in a book review.

CONTENTS

1.	Annabella	1
2.	Damien	11
3.	Annabella	27
4.	Damien	45
5.	Annabella	55
6.	Damien	63
7.	Annabella	71
8.	Damien	79
9.	Annabella	101
10.	Damien	107
11.	Annabella	109
12.	Annabella	125
13.	Damien	133
14.	Annabella	153
15.	Damien	163
16.	Annabella	173
17.	Damien	183
18.	Annabella	195
19.	Damien	203
20.	Annabella	211
21.	Damien	221
22.	Annabella	239
23.	Damien	251
24.	Annabella	255
25.	Damien	259
26.	Annabella	269
27.	Damien	277
28.	Annabella	285
29.	Damien	297
30.	Annabella	301
31.	Damien	309

Their story continues in Forever...   317

1
ANNABELLA

Sofia stepped into my office. "Want to get lunch? It's on me. Well, on the Tuscan Rose."

"Hmm..." I looked away from my computer. "Paperwork or free lunch? What a hard decision."

She chuckled at my sarcasm. "Where do you want to go?"

"You know I'm not picky." I grabbed my coat and walked out of the hotel with Sofia. Christmas was over, and now it was just bleak and cold winter. Liam and I had spent our first month together as husband and wife on good terms, never mentioning Damien again. Being married felt different from living together, but it didn't feel the same as our first marriage. Instead of passionate with unbridled love, it was more comfortable. But that was exactly what I wanted.

"So, how's married life?" Sofia asked. "Still like each other?"

"Yeah. It's nice to leave my apartment and move into my old place. We've fallen into our old routine, where we trade off making dinner and doing the dishes. You know, typical marriage stuff."

"Have you guys thought about trying to have a family again?"

After what happened last time, I was terrified to even bring up the subject. Having a family wasn't on my mind. "I think we'd rather just enjoy each other for a while before considering that."

"Good idea." Her phone rang in her pocket, so she fished it out. "It's Hades. I've got to answer."

"I understand."

"Hey," she said as she answered. "I'm walking to Angelini's for lunch. No, it's not too cold to walk." She rolled her eyes. "You want to join us?" She turned to me to ask if it was okay.

I immediately answered. "Of course."

She turned back to the phone. "I'll see you there in a couple minutes." She hung up and returned the phone to her pocket. "I'm glad you don't mind that Hades tags along."

He was kinda my boss since he also owned the hotel, but he was also a nice guy...as far as I could tell. "I don't mind at all." Sometimes when I was around him, I thought about Damien, but I couldn't let that bother me. It was impossible to avoid Hades, and it wasn't his fault that he reminded me of his best friend. It wasn't like I ever saw Damien in the flesh.

We continued to talk for the rest of the walk. This restaurant was farther away than other choices, but it was the best, so we pushed through the cold until we stepped inside the restaurant. After we checked in with the host, we spotted Hades sitting at the table—with Damien.

Sofia quickly turned to me so they couldn't see her expression. "Shit, I had no idea—"

"It's fine." My heart leaped into my throat and my pulse was manic, but I played it cool. I didn't want to see Damien, but it was impossible to expect to always avoid him. He was bound to show his face at events, birthday parties, stuff like that. I just had to be mature about it, to hold my head high even though he'd rejected me...how many times?

"You sure?" she asked, keeping her voice low.

"Yes. We're both adults. I don't hate him, and I can't imagine why he'd hate me."

"Alright." She squeezed my wrist for support before she headed to the table. She was in front of me, so she blocked my view of the guys.

Hades stood up to greet his wife, his eyes filling with an intense look of love for both her and the little person inside her. His arms wrapped around her, and he gave her a gentle kiss on the lips, greeting her as if he hadn't seen her just a few hours ago.

Now I had a full view of Damien.

He sat in the chair with one ankle resting on the opposite knee, looking like a catch in that tailored suit. He was relaxed, but his ripped body still stretched the crispness of the fabric in the sexiest ways, over his broad shoulders, his thick biceps, even his forearms. Judging by the slight surprise in his eyes, he hadn't expected me to be there. His green eyes only reacted for an instant, a flicker of dilemma, but he quickly covered it, adopting a skilled poker face.

He didn't say anything.

Neither did I.

I didn't want it to be awkward every time we saw each other, to think about the last time we had been in the same room together, when I'd admitted I would leave Liam that instant if Damien still wanted me. It was embarrassing to be so hung up on someone who didn't give a damn about you. But it was over...and it was time to move on.

Damien spoke first. "It's nice to see you, Annabella." He rose from his chair and flattened his tie against his hard chest, the touch reminding me exactly how that felt with my own hand. I used to press my palm against the spot all the time, loving that strong heartbeat in that powerful cage. He moved to the chair across from him and pulled it out for me —like a gentleman.

It was hard for me to say anything because I was floored by his reaction, by the way I was instantly attracted to him even though I'd been married for a month. He'd ripped me apart in my office, so I should hate him...but I didn't. "It's nice to see you too. And thank you." I took off my coat and hung it over the back of the chair before I sat down. I was committed to Liam, so I had to turn off these feelings, especially for my own sake. I didn't want my heart on my sleeve, for it to be obvious there was still a longing deep inside me. I was done embarrassing myself.

Hades did the same for Sofia before he sat across from her.

That meant I was stuck looking at Damien.

Ugh.

I grabbed my menu and buried my nose in it.

It was quiet at the table, the awkwardness setting in for all of us. Hades hadn't known I was coming either, so he probably exchanged a few glances with Sofia to show his regret for not asking if I had come along.

I didn't want it to be tense, so I smashed the silence. "You guys wanna get an appetizer? The arancini? I'm starving."

Sofia went with it. "I'm in."

"I think I'm gonna get some wine too," I said to her. "Unless you're going to write me up or something?"

She chuckled. "I'd be drinking too if I could."

I lifted my gaze and looked Damien straight in the eye. "If I got a bottle, would you want any?" I then turned my gaze to Hades, so he knew I was addressing him too.

Hades answered. "That's a great idea."

Damien stared at me with a focused expression, as if he knew exactly what I was doing. "I'll have a glass. You pick the wine."

When the waitress came over, we ordered, and soon after, we were eating the appetizer and drinking wine. Despite my attempts to make everything feel normal, it grew tense again.

So I spoke to Damien directly. "How have you been?"

He stilled slightly at the question, but he covered the tension in his shoulders by taking a sip of wine. "Busy with work." He didn't give me much detail and didn't ask me anything in return.

"How's your father?" I'd never met him, but I knew he was important to Damien.

He was surprised by the second question. "I'm in the process of moving him in with me."

"Aww...that's sweet." And just like that, I thought Damien was the perfect man again.

"He's a stubborn son of a bitch, so I think this is gonna be an ordeal." He swirled his wine as he stared at the glass.

"Like father, like son," I teased.

He lifted his gaze to look at me, surprised I'd spoken to him so casually.

When I felt like I'd proved my point, that I was over him, I talked to the entire table. The conversation was stiff at first, as if no one understood what was an appropriate thing to say in the situation, but like a train leaving the station, it picked up speed.

SOFIA PICKED UP HER PHONE. "IT'S MY MOTHER."

Hades chewed his food before he responded. "Great..."

She answered. "Hey, Ma. What's up?" She listened to the line before her face started to turn pale.

Hades picked up on her reaction, his eyes narrowing. "What is it?"

"I'll meet you at the doctor's office." She hung up. "She said Andrew has been coughing all morning, and it's getting worse. She thinks he might have a rash or an allergic reaction. She's taking him to the pediatrician now." She got to her feet and grabbed her coat.

Hades turned to Damien. "Can you—"

"I got it." Damien pulled out his chair as he stood up. "Go."

Hades and Sofia left in a rush, abandoning their untouched food and dashing out the door.

Now it was just us…alone.

Our plates were still full because we'd only just gotten our lunch, so it would be weird to box it up and leave because we couldn't stand being together. Neither one of us would cave and blow our pride like that.

Damien pushed in Hades's chair and grabbed his fork to continue eating. He'd ordered a garden salad with extra chicken, avoiding the basket of bread in the center and only allowing himself a single glass of wine.

It was no surprise he was in such great shape when he was so diligent about his diet. No carbs. No fat. Just pure protein with vegetables. It reminded me of the times we got pizza together and he acted like he'd lost all control.

I'd ordered spaghetti because I didn't give a damn about the scale. As long as I was healthy and still getting laid, it didn't matter to me. Why waste time stressing about your body like it was your finances?

Silence continued.

Heavy, painful silence.

I tried to think of something to say, but I was drawing a blank. We didn't have any mutual hobbies, any mutual friends. It wasn't like we both played golf, and saying nothing was better than talking about the weather.

At my reception, Hades had come over and congratulated Liam and me. Then he explained Damien had fallen ill and couldn't attend the wedding, which was bullshit because men like Damien didn't get sick. But I was glad he wasn't there. There were already so many emotions I had to deal with that day. Seeing Damien across the room would have only made it worse.

He chewed a bite and lifted his gaze to stare at me, his dark eyes swirling with several thoughts. When he swallowed his food, he spoke. "How are things with Liam?" He addressed the elephant in the room, the marriage he was venomously opposed to.

I was surprised he'd gone there. "Good."

He took another bite, chewing slowly as he examined the painting on the wall, looking for something to stare at so he wouldn't have to look at me. "I'm sorry I couldn't attend. I was—"

"It's fine." I knew it was an excuse because he didn't want to be there. "I didn't want you there either."

He seemed slightly surprised by my honesty, his eyes flashing in interest. "You'll continue to work at the Tuscan Rose?"

"Would you rather I quit?"

He shook his head. "I want you to do whatever makes you

happy. I just assumed Liam would prefer if you stayed home."

"He would, but I don't care what he wants." I stayed home last time because that was what he wanted, and after he broke my heart, I regretted doing what he asked. This time, I was going to stay busy because it gave me a sense of purpose, gave me some independence.

He pushed his food around with his fork. "Good answer."

"You don't care if you have to see me once in a while?"

He set down his fork and stared at me for a long time, as if the question floored him. "I always enjoy seeing you, Annabella." His eyes lingered for minutes, as if he couldn't look away…because he never wanted to look away.

2

DAMIEN

"No!" My father stormed away from the couch and marched into the kitchen.

"Father—"

"I'd rather die!" He opened the fridge and grabbed a beer.

I turned to Catalina.

She rolled her eyes. "Don't you think you're overreacting right now?"

"You're overreacting." He stepped back into our view. "I don't need your charity. I don't need a babysitter. I'm a grown-ass man." He went to twist off the cap and struggled to get it loose. When it didn't come off, he used his sleeve, but that just created less friction. "I'm perfectly fine living here on my own."

I left the couch and walked to him. I took the beer out of his hand, and with a simple twist, the cap came off. I handed it to him, giving him a pointed look to make sure he understood how wrong he was.

My father barely nodded in gratitude and headed back to the couch.

Catalina shifted to the spot beside him. "Dad, I know this is hard—"

"It's not hard." He pushed her hand away. "I've told you many times I don't need your help. I've got plenty of years left, and I'm fine living on my own."

"But you would be much more comfortable with Damien," she said. "He's got a big place, and Patricia can do so much for you—"

"I don't need a maid." He took a drink.

His apartment was full of dirty dishes, clothes that needed to be washed, and fast-food wrappers that never made it into the garbage can. He lived like a slob, and anytime he needed to find something, he couldn't recall where he put it. "Father, I want you to live with me." I sat in the armchair beside them, doing my best to convince him to leave all this behind. He couldn't be unprotected when I went after Heath. He needed to be in my fortress, where he would be untouched. "I'm gonna need someone I trust to watch my kids while I'm at work." I'd never have a family of my own. Never have a wife. But this was the best way to lure him away from this pigsty.

He turned to me, his interest piqued. "Grandkids?"

I nodded. "I don't want to hire a nanny. How could I trust someone more than you?"

"Are you seeing someone?" he blurted.

"Not exactly." Just random women I picked up at bars and

clubs. "But I'm looking. I'm getting old. I've got to start that family soon."

That was what my father wanted more than anything. "Well, I'll move in then—"

"You're moving in now." I was losing my patience with this old man. Nothing I said could get him to see reason. He didn't understand his life was in jeopardy the longer he stayed here alone. I needed him under my roof for my own peace of mind. "We can argue about this in circles forever, but the outcome will not change. You're packing up your shit and coming with me. Catalina and I have decided this is best, so that's what's happening."

"And I don't get a say?" he asked quietly.

"No." I hated talking to my father this way. When I was young, I used to look up to him as my strong hero. But age had taken its toll on his body and mind, and now he was alone and scared…and prideful. "I'm asking you to live with me because I love you. I want you under my roof so I can keep an eye on you. I'm a very successful man, just as you wanted, so let me share that success with you. We can also spend more time together. And when my family is here, my children will know their grandfather well."

He finally stopped protesting. "I don't want to burden you, son…"

I rested my hand on his. "You aren't, Father. I worry about you here by yourself. By moving in with me, you're easing my concerns. You're helping me sleep at night. You're giving me what I want."

Catalina rubbed his arm. "This is what Mama would want."

"You're sure?" he asked, his voice weak.

"Yes." I gripped his shoulder. "I'm sure, Father."

I walked inside their bedroom. "How's the little guy?"

"Better." Hades poured me a drink and handed it over. "Sofia is putting him to sleep right now."

"What was the problem?" I took the scotch and had a sip.

"Turns out it was an allergy." It was too cold to sit outside, so he walked to the couch in front of the fire. He was in his sweatpants and slippers, right at home despite the fact that he had company.

"To what?" I sat on the other couch and felt the heat from the flames.

"Peanuts."

"Oh, really?"

"Maria let him have a bite of her peanut butter and jelly sandwich…and that triggered it."

"At least you know now."

"Yeah. And his allergy is minor. His throat doesn't close up or anything."

"Good news." I had been at the office alone because Hades hadn't been in for a few days, staying home with Sofia and Andrew to make sure his family was okay. "I'm surprised neither one of you has the same allergy."

"I'm not sure how it works." He stared at the fire for a while before he turned back to me. "Sorry we ditched you. How'd that go?"

I stared into my glass as I remembered the uncomfortable conversation. "Fine."

"That bad, huh?"

"It was going to happen at some point. At least we got it out of the way."

"What did you talk about?"

"I asked her about Liam. She said a few things. But most of the time, we just sat in silence and finished our lunch. She asked if I wanted her to quit so I wouldn't have to see her anymore."

"And what did you say?"

I shook my head. "I told her I didn't mind seeing her... because I don't."

"Really?" he asked, not believing that.

"I don't." I looked him in the eye. "It'll probably always be weird, but I don't want her to change her life because of me. She likes her job, and I know Sofia likes her too. Our past relationship shouldn't haunt us forever."

"But are you fine seeing her every day?"

I stared at him.

"That was the question." He saw my reaction at her wedding, how I couldn't suck it up and plaster on a fake smile. I couldn't keep a straight face and be strong despite my pain.

"Yeah…I'm fine with it."

He didn't seem to buy my answer, but he let it go. "Liam has his first fight this weekend. She'll probably be there."

I thought I would only see Annabella every couple months, not be confronted with her presence on a regular basis. "What does that have to do with me?"

"Because we're going."

"Why?"

"Because he's our client."

"You said he was *your* client," I snapped. "And what does that matter? We don't get involved with our other clients."

"We're getting a big piece of the pie. And Liam is preparing to return to death fighting. We'll be heavily involved in that."

All the anger drained from my face when I heard what he said.

"I know the only reason you don't want to go is because of her," Hades said. "Because you'd be jumping at this opportunity in any other scenario."

I didn't hear what he said. "He said that?"

Hades cocked an eyebrow.

"About death fighting?"

He nodded.

"When?"

"A few weeks ago. Why?"

"Annabella told me he would give it up if she took him back. Now he's trying to do it behind her back?" Would he really do something like that? The second she was his wife, he would throw her wishes out the window?

"Maybe she changed her mind about it."

"No." She never would.

He watched me for a long time. "Damien, whatever the case may be, you need to stay out of it."

"Meaning?"

"Even if he is keeping this a secret from her, it's not your place to tell her."

I would watch his fights, knowing full well he risked his life every night, and say nothing to her?

"It will violate his trust and jeopardize our partnerships. And it'll be a dead giveaway that you were the one fucking his wife. Why else would you tell her?"

Valid point. But I was still disturbed by what I'd learned.

Hades continued to study me. "She's the one who decided to marry him. This is their marriage, their business. Whatever happens is not your concern, so you better leave it alone. You understand me?"

Annabella and I were nothing and had always been nothing. She'd made her choice to marry him, and I stepped aside and let it happen. It was time to move on, not to concern myself with her happiness. "Fine."

After we walked through the casino and took the elevator to the basement, we met with Bosco.

"It's been a long time." He grinned as he shook hands with Hades. "Who do you have your money on?"

"Liam." He dropped his hand. "He's my client."

"Loyalty. Nice." He turned to me and shook my hand. "Nice to see you, Damien. I got some new girls out front."

"I noticed."

He winked. "Nothing gets past you, huh?" He clapped me on the shoulder. "Enjoy yourselves tonight. I've been trying to get Liam back into death fighting. See if you can talk him into it." He walked off with his friend to find a seat in the underground arena.

Hades and I went to the back where the fighters waited for their call. Liam was behind the first door on the left, in his black sweatpants and t-shirt. His muscles were flexed and full like he'd hit the weights just moments ago, but he was visibly calm.

Annabella wasn't. She was in a blue cocktail dress, her curled hair pinned to the back of her head. She was covered in diamonds, like a prized jewel Liam wanted to show off. Her eyes were wet with impending tears, and it was obvious she had just been arguing with him, probably trying to dissuade him from doing this.

"Baby, I'll be fine." He was sitting beside her on the couch, and he rose to his feet to greet us. "My boys." He shook hands with Hades, and his previous beef with me seemed to be forgotten because he shook my hand too. He probably had more important things to focus on other than our bitter exchange. "Could you keep an eye on my woman while I'm in the ring?" He kept his voice low in the hope she wouldn't hear.

Impulsive rage overtook me. I would never let another man protect my wife besides Hades. I'd do it my goddamn self.

Hades answered for me. "Of course."

After we exchanged a few words, Liam left to get ready for his fight.

Hades glanced at me before he silently excused himself.

Annabella didn't look at me, her gaze averted as she struggled with what was about to happen to her husband. The woman was selfless with her heart, caring and loving to people who didn't deserve it—like me. She crossed her arms over her chest and kept her eyes on the floor.

All I wanted to do was comfort her, hold her, cradle her face into my shoulder as I wrapped my arms around her.

But that wasn't my job.

Liam should be here, giving up everything because that was what she wanted.

I slid my hands into my pockets and stepped closer to her.

She quietly sniffled. "Is there something I can help you with, Damien?" Despite her distress, her voice was strong.

I didn't tell her Liam had asked me to babysit her. If he knew the things I'd done to her, he wouldn't let me anywhere near her...especially when she was vulnerable like this. "He'll be fine, Annabella."

She finally lifted her gaze to look me in the eye. "You don't know that."

"He's a big guy who knows what he's doing."

"And so is the other guy…"

Her quiet words got under my skin, and I found myself on the couch beside her.

She stilled when I came close to her, affected by my proximity. She shifted away slightly as if my presence bothered her.

"Ask him to stop."

"It's his career…his passion. That would be like him asking me to quit my job."

"Your job at the hotel isn't dangerous. It's not the same thing. And it shouldn't matter. If it bothers you this much…" He should have walked away from all of it if he wanted to be with her, to sacrifice everything if he wanted to be her husband. And if he couldn't…he should bow out. That was why I left, and it was the right thing to do. I wish Hades were still my partner in our drug business, but I respected his giving it up for his family. "It's not like he needs the money."

She shook her head. "He won't. I've asked."

The sound of the cheering crowd was audible at the announcement of the next fight.

She closed her eyes as if she knew exactly what that meant.

There were a few inches between us, so we weren't touching, but it was the closest I'd been to her since that conversation in her office months ago. I could feel the heat, the electricity, that tingly sensation on the back of my neck. But I wasn't sure if she felt it too. "You want to stay in here until it's over?"

"Yes...but I know I should be out there. I should support him."

"Did you go to his matches before?"

She nodded. "I never liked it, though. But I know it means a lot to him—to see my face in the crowd." She smoothed out her skirt before she rose to her feet, looking amazing in that short dress. The color was perfect on her, the straps crossing over her back and giving the look more elegance. With all those diamonds and her perfect features, she was the prize Liam wanted everyone to know belonged to him.

Couldn't blame him. "I'll take you."

She moved to the door. "I don't need your help, Damien." She opened it and stepped outside.

I walked with her anyway, knowing she would change her mind once she saw the turnout for the fight. It was all vicious men cursing about the bout, pushing one another out of the way to get a better view. There were a few women present, but not many.

One guy didn't notice her because of how small she was and bumped right into her.

"Watch where the fuck you're going." I shoved him in the arm and pushed him back.

She tensed when she realized she was overwhelmed, prey in a room of predators.

I placed my arm around her waist, touching her for the first time in...forever.

And it was there…that same magnificent desire.

I ignored it and guided her through the crowd to a safe place.

She would ordinarily push my hand away or tell me not to touch her, but the fights had clearly changed since the last time she was here, and she was overwhelmed. It was practically a mosh pit.

I got her to one of the stages where Hades was talking with Bosco. Liam and his opponent threw punches and attacked each other in the ring, prepared to fight until someone passed out.

I got her a seat and sat beside her.

Liam had just done a number on his opponent, slamming his fist into his face, his ribs, and then his stomach. Blood spilled from his mouth, either the product of broken teeth or a bleeding stomach.

Annabella crossed her legs and cringed, not impressed by her husband's strength and agility. Fighting wasn't a turn-on for her the way it was for most women. She craved peace, simplicity. When she wanted a man, money and power weren't important to her. It was the soul that mattered.

Instead of watching the fight, I watched her.

Watched her cringe over and over as her husband beat this stranger to a pulp. "There's only about a minute left."

"Is there a timer?" she asked.

"No. But I can tell the guy won't last much longer."

She watched for another thirty seconds, and when Liam got the last hit, she turned back to me. "You called it."

"I've been to a lot of these." Half the men cheered, and the other half shouted with frustration. Some men made a lot of money that night, and some lost a lot. But all the chaos didn't distract me from the woman beside me, the angel in this hell. I felt the same way I did when I had too much to drink, like I couldn't do anything but stare at the fire...and she was the flame.

"Do you bet?"

"Always."

"And did you bet on Liam?"

"I wouldn't bet against my client."

"Even though you don't like him."

I liked him less with every passing moment. "Personally. Not professionally."

Now she stared at me the same way I stared at her, as if she couldn't stop.

Did she have any idea how beautiful she looked tonight? That if I walked away, every man would be on her? That they wouldn't care about that enormous diamond ring on her left hand?

She finally looked at Liam as he stepped out of the ring. He had blood dripping down his nose, but he looked otherwise unharmed. He moved through the crowd and headed to her like he knew where she was.

He may be a strong fighter, but he wasn't very observant.

The man right beside her was thinking about the night we'd shared a pizza on the couch then made love all night. Flashbacks of her small tits, her sweaty body, her succulent lips came rushing back…beautiful.

He wiped his face with a towel. "Told you I would be fine, baby."

"You're covered in blood."

He gave a slight smile. "I like to bleed a little bit." He leaned in and kissed her.

I looked away.

"I'm gonna shower and get ready in my room. Then we'll go."

"Alright." She watched him walk away without following him.

He didn't question me beside her. "You want me to take you back?" She could have left with him now if she wanted to be with him, but it seemed like she preferred to stay behind.

"I'd rather see him after he's cleaned up. I don't like seeing him like that."

That had been the last fight of the night, so the men started to file out and head back to the casino. Hades returned to us. "He fought well. Congratulations." He said the words to Annabella even though she was anything but proud.

"Yes, he did," she said in agreement.

Hades turned to me. "He's been out of the ring for a while. That was a strong return."

That meant more money for us because we took a cut of his

profits to launder. Liam couldn't take so much cash and spend it all. "Yeah."

Hades was in a black t-shirt and jeans, his wedding ring the only piece of jewelry he wore. "I'm gonna head home. Want a ride, or are you going to hit up the casino?"

If I went home, I would just be alone. I'd rather be surrounded by booze, money, and women than be by myself—even though Annabella had given me more comfort during this fight than I'd had in months. "I'm gonna stick around."

Annabella addressed him. "I'm glad Andrew is alright. Sofia told me about that peanut allergy."

"Thank you," Hades said. "He's a strong boy, so he recovered quickly."

"Still...no peanut butter and jelly sandwiches for life." She shook her head. "That's a rough fate."

He chuckled. "If he's anything like his father, he won't eat them anyway." He turned around and walked away.

Annabella turned to me. "I'm glad you guys are friends again."

"Me too."

"You're so much alike."

I shook my head. "No, we aren't. He's the smart, pragmatic one. I'm the irrational and emotional one."

She stared at me with a slightly incredulous look. "By emotional, you mean passionate. And by irrational, you mean spontaneous. You're one of the smartest men I've ever met. Don't ever think otherwise, Damien."

All I could do was stare at her because I didn't know what else to say. I was used to being showered with insults by the people who knew me best, but Annabella had nothing but good things to say about me, had always accepted me for who I was. If the circumstances were different, I would lean in and kiss her.

But the circumstances weren't different. She was married. And even if she weren't, she couldn't be mine anyway. "I'll walk you to his room." I left the chair and stood off to the side, taking my gaze off her so I could shut down all those feelings, bottle all those desires.

She rose to her feet, an hourglass figure in that cocktail dress. "Most of the crowd is gone…I can make it on my own." She spun away without giving me a chance to say goodbye. She seemed to want to get away from me as quickly as I wanted to get away from her.

Instead of walking away myself, I turned my gaze and watched her.

Watched her walk all the way across the room and disappear into the hallway.

And only then did I walk away.

3

ANNABELLA

I grabbed an ice pack from the freezer and walked to where Liam sat at the bar, his empty plate in front of him where his dinner had been moments ago. I placed the ice pack on his temple next to his eye, where the swelling was the most prominent.

He didn't protest. "Baby, I'm fine."

I continued to apply it to the bruised area, the discoloration making me sick.

"And let's not forget how the other guy looked."

I never checked. "Liam." I moved the ice pack a few more places before I lowered the bag.

He sighed because he recognized my tone.

"We're together now. Isn't that what you wanted?"

"Of course." He grabbed the bag out of my hand and tossed it on the counter. "More than anything."

"Then why don't you enjoy it? Let's travel. Let's start a family. Let's not spend our time with you in the ring."

"Baby—"

"It's not like you need the money." Damien's argument came back to me, the only man who seemed to understand how I felt, who knew watching my husband risk his body and life was terrifying.

"I'm thirty, Anna. I can't do this much longer…"

"Then retire now."

"I'm not the kind of man to sit around the house and do nothing all day."

"You won't be doing nothing. You'll be with me…and your family." Why wasn't that enough?

He turned away and sighed. "It's just a few more years, alright?"

"But you could get really hurt—"

"I won't."

"Then why wouldn't you stop now? It'll happen after you get seriously injured anyway. That's the only way you'll consider yourself to be too old."

"Nothing I can't handle."

I grew frustrated and stepped away.

"Baby."

I crossed my arms over my chest and kept my back to him.

"Baby." He got out of the chair and came up behind me, his

arms moving around my waist. "I want to earn more money before I can't anymore."

"We have plenty of money."

"Not to maintain this lifestyle."

I turned around. "Then we'll downgrade. I don't need a mansion or a nice car."

His eyes softened slightly, as if he appreciated the fact that I cared more about his health than his bank account. "It's just a few more years. Please give that to me."

I dropped my gaze.

"Baby. Look at me."

I refused.

He placed his fingers under my chin and lifted my gaze. "I have my wife back. And I have my fighting. My life is perfect right now, and it's the first time I've been happy since you walked out. Let me have that a little longer. Please."

"Why is it so important to you?" My weak voice came out as a whisper.

"I can't explain it." He shook his head. "It makes me feel alive."

"And I don't?"

"Yes…but in a different way."

I COULDN'T SLEEP.

I sat up in bed, with Liam dead asleep beside me, snoring lightly because he was exhausted after his fight. My back was against the propped pillows, and I looked out the frosted windows, seeing the devastating effects of this freezing winter. It was ice-cold.

I wondered if Damien was sleeping alone.

Probably not.

I'd been to the casino before, saw the women dance in cages suspended above the ceiling while the men gambled chips worth a million euro each. Damien said he was going there after the fight, probably to drink, gamble, and fuck.

I shouldn't care.

But I would always care.

He comforted me when my own husband didn't. He stayed by my side and made me feel so much better with just his presence. There was something about the tone of his voice, his choice of words, that made all my muscles relax from their rigid positions. My heart beat slower, and I felt warm despite the cold temperature of the underground arena. The men huddled around the ring weren't gentlemen and didn't care about shoving me with their enormous shoulders, but Damien kept me safe. His hand wrapped around my waist, just the way it used to when he walked me to my door.

And he erased all my problems.

I thought I could be around him and keep up a poker face, but the more I was near him, the harder it was. I wanted to be committed in my marriage, to love only my husband and no one else. But when I'd started to make progress...I saw Damien's handsome face, and all my attempts went to shit.

Could you get over someone if you had to still see them?

Sometimes I wondered if I should quit my job, but apparently, I would still see him at the fights, so there was no escape.

I would just have to try harder.

A week had passed, and my life started to feel normal again.

Liam didn't mention another fight, so we spent our time cooking together and talking in front of the fire. We'd share a bottle of wine, get a little drunk, and have good sex. That was one of the nicest things about Liam; he knew how to fuck. All the other men I went out with had no idea what they were doing, or they just didn't care.

Besides Damien. He was on a whole other level. I thought the sex was good because it was so emotional, like a hurricane and a tsunami combined. A forest fire drenched in gasoline. It was passionate, so good it brought tears to my eyes from time to time. I thought it was because I was so deeply and stupidly in love...and he felt that way too. But he was just good in bed, I guess.

But the longer I wasn't around Damien, the less I thought about him...which was nice. It was a healing process. As if I'd broken my arm, it felt better until I used it again. Then there was a setback, and I lost all that progress and had to start over. Same exact thing. But a broken arm would be much less painful than a broken heart.

I sat in the chair facing Sofia's desk, and we discussed the weekly reports, the things that needed to be addressed for the hotel. It was my job to do paperwork in the office, but I also made my rounds around the hotel, randomly checking cleaned rooms and doing customer surveys of their experience as guests.

Sofia never asked me about Damien anymore, so our relationship seemed to be old news. That was nice because I didn't want to talk about him anyway. "How are things with Liam?" He was my husband now, so that was the only person she should be asking about.

"Good."

"That's it?" she asked, teasing me slightly.

"I'm not happy that he continues to fight, but everything else is good. He looks at me differently, like he can't believe I'm there. He hasn't taken me for granted now that I'm back, as if he still remembers the pain of my absence. So, he loves me pretty hard..."

"That's great," she said. "It's hard to let go of the past sometimes, but it's worth it if you can. His infidelity is unacceptable, but if he's different now...that's all that really matters." She flipped through her papers.

I truly believed it would be different, despite what Damien thought. Our marriage had been solid and honest before tragedy struck us, so it wasn't like Liam was innately unfaithful. He'd just made a bad decision. When I took him back, I forgave him for what he did and gave him a clean slate. "Yeah." When Damien was passionate about fidelity, that Liam shouldn't have cheated in the first place, that real men never did those things, it made me believe in fantasy, made me picture having Damien as mine. But in the end, it was all a lie…because he'd never committed to a woman in his entire life, including me. "Has Hades ever…?" It was a personal question and I probably shouldn't ask, but we'd become good friends over the last few months. It seemed impossible that Hades would ever do something like that, but it seemed as if she spoke from experience.

She pulled her gaze away from her work and considered the question a long time.

Maybe I shouldn't have asked. "Forget I said anything—"

"No, it's okay," she said quickly. "Hades and I actually got divorced at one point, but not because we wanted to. He spent time with other women then, but there was no sex, so it wasn't cheating…but it still hurt. When we got back together, I just let it go. The past has no effect on us now, so it really doesn't matter."

I didn't ask for the specifics. "I've let it go too." I used to wonder who the woman was, if she was a brunette like me, if she was as good in bed as I was. But I'd stopped thinking about it and moved on.

"I think that's—" She suddenly stopped speaking, her hand moving to her stomach.

"Are you okay?"

"Yeah. I just had a weird—" She faltered again.

Now, I started to freak out. "Maybe we should go to the hospital." She was about halfway through her pregnancy, so she might get cramps and other pains, but it could also be more serious. "Did anything like this happen with Andrew?"

"No…"

"Then we should go."

"I'll call Hades and—" This time, she stood up and gripped the desk.

"That will take too long, Sofia. I'll drive you and call him on the way." I pulled her arm over my shoulder and got her out from behind the desk. "It'll be alright. Just keep breathing and stay calm."

Hades got there with amazing speed.

He stormed down the hallway until he found me sitting outside the room. "Where is she? Is she alright? Is the doctor here?" He was in his suit because he'd just left the bank. He was clean and crisp, but that fear in his eyes made him look a little insane.

"I don't have any news." I rose out of the chair. "She just started having pain in the office, and I got here as quickly as I could."

He didn't say another word before he stepped into the room.

I sat back in the chair again, feeling the dread. Seeing Hades worry about Sofia like that was painful to watch. I prayed everything would be alright, that there wouldn't be a miscarriage. They were both so excited for their second child.

I knew what it was like to lose a baby, and no one deserved to experience that.

No one.

Just thinking about it made my eyes water a little. Memories of that awful day were still fresh. I'd felt so connected to the baby inside me before I lost her, and it would be painful for the rest of my life.

I didn't want Sofia to know that kind of pain.

I started to cry. Tears ran down my face, and I closed my eyes to control my breathing, to get everything to calm so the tears would run dry. I focused on something else, the sound of birds in the morning, the smell of a fresh pie on Christmas, and brought myself to normalcy again. But my eyes were still wet...along with my cheeks.

Quick footsteps sounded down the hall, as if someone else was in a hurry.

I lifted my gaze to see.

It was Damien. He must have dropped Hades off at the entrance then found parking afterward. When he saw me sitting on the bench, he stopped midstep, wearing a black suit that looked so delicious on that perfect body. His jawline was sprinkled with a sexy shadow, highlighting those beautiful lips. His eyes were always the best, especially when they were packed with emotion, whether that be anger, desire, or joy. Pain was in his eyes in that moment, like the sight of the remnants of my tears was enough to make him forget why he was there in the first place.

He moved to the seat beside me on the bench, his arm sliding over the back and automatically wrapping around my body. His strong hand gripped my arm, and once he made contact, his cologne came over me, the exact smell that used to be on his sheets and my clothes. His face moved close to mine, holding me like we were still lovers. "Annabella, what's going on?" His voice was quiet so the doctors and nurses who passed in the hallway couldn't overhear us. His fingers dug into the fabric of my coat, and even though it was just one in the afternoon, his breath smelled of scotch. And he called me Annabella...as if nothing had changed in the last few months.

"Sofia has been in there for a while. Hades just went in. I don't have any news..."

He sighed in disappointment before his hand slipped into my hair, his fingers pulling back the strands from my face. It was the same touch he used to give me, and I was transported back in time. I pictured my old apartment, the empty pizza box on the edge of the bed, and his clothes on the floor. Instead of questioning me about my tears, he stared at me hard, his eyes looking into mine like we were making love. He came to the conclusion all on his own because he knew me so well. "I'm so sorry, Annabella." He turned my face into his, and he placed his forehead against mine.

It felt so right that I didn't pull away. I closed my eyes and let him comfort me, let him carry the burden of the past with me. My fingers wrapped around his wrist, and I held on with shaky breaths, feeling so much emotion from so little. Everything about him calmed me, made me think of deep rivers, of the ocean tide as it crashed onto the shore. I thought of low fires burning in the hearth that were hungry for the next log. I thought of the softest sheets that brushed against my skin when I scooted closer to him in the middle of the night.

"Their son will be alright."

I opened my eyes and pulled back slightly to look at him. "How do you know it's a boy?"

His hand slid to the back of my neck, releasing my hair. "Just do."

"And how do you know everything will be alright?"

He was quiet again. "I just do." His thumb moved to my cheek, and he wiped away a tear that still clung to my skin. Then he did the other side, keeping his eyes on me. "I'm sure it's not life-threatening. Easily treatable."

I wanted to fall into those false promises and never leave.

He continued to wipe away my tears until my cheeks were clean and dry. He seemed to realize he'd crossed the line with his affection, so he pulled his touch away and scooted slightly to the left, leaving a few inches between us.

I didn't want him to move.

He leaned forward with his elbows on his knees, his hands together. When someone walked by, he casually lifted his gaze to glance at the person as they passed. His sleeves were slightly pulled back to reveal his watch. His slacks were also pulled up, showing his black socks underneath.

Ugh, he was so hot.

I crossed my legs and looked away, doing my best not to stare. Then we sat in silence, both pretending that we hadn't just collided like two trains.

After fifteen minutes passed, he straightened and leaned against the back of the bench. He crossed one ankle onto the opposite knee, his hands folded together in his lap.

"You don't have to stay here with me."

"I'm not." He adjusted his sleeve under his jacket and continued to look ahead. "I want to make sure Sofia is okay."

"You don't need to get back to the office?"

He shook his head. "I don't give a shit about the office."

Just like that, he squeezed my heart again. He was loyal to the people he loved.

We returned to silence once more.

He was the one person in the world who affected me this deeply, but I couldn't bring myself to say anything. Words were gone because I didn't know how to connect with the man I had connected with so intensely in the past. But maybe that was the reason why...because I didn't want some of him, but all of him.

"Did you change Liam's mind?"

I turned to him, unsure what he was referring to.

"Fighting."

"Oh..." It was weird to think about Liam when I was with Damien. "He said no."

He pulled back his sleeve and looked at the time. "If it makes you feel better, I've been in the fighting game a long time, and serious injuries rarely happen. Fighters respect one another's longevity. It's a sport, not a massacre."

"But it does happen. Fighters lapse into comas and never wake up again. They break their legs and can't walk for a year. They develop internal bleeding that leads to hemorrhaging. Don't pretend fighting is safe. The objective is to knock your opponent out cold."

"Then why did you marry him?" Now his tone was a bit chilly when it was so warm minutes ago. He turned on me, comforting me one moment and then condemning me the next.

I turned to him, provoked by the question. "What kind of question is that?"

"A legitimate one. Why marry a man who fights for a living if you hate it so much? Why marry a man who fucked someone else while you struggled through the hardest thing you've ever had to deal with in your whole life? Why—"

"I told you why, Damien."

He turned away, his jaw tight. "That's not a good enough reason, Annabella. You're one hell of a woman, and you deserve one hell of a man."

"Well, you're the only one-hell-of-a-man I've ever met, and you don't want me." The bitterness came out of my mouth so fast, like a striking snake. I didn't even have time to think about it before I blurted it out of my angry lips.

He pivoted his body toward me. "It's not that I don't—"

Hades and Sofia stepped out of the room.

Our conversation was abandoned because all we cared about was her. We both got to our feet and started firing off questions.

"Everything okay?" I asked.

"What did the doctor say?" Damien asked.

Hades had his arm around Sofia, who had her hand over her stomach. "The baby is safe, and so is Sofia. It was just some cramping. The doctor ran some tests, and everything came back good. We're in the clear."

"Oh good." My hand pressed into my chest with relief. "I'm so happy to hear that…"

"That's great news." Damien gripped his friend's shoulder then patted him on the back before he hugged Sofia and kissed her on the cheek.

I knew Damien could be dark and cold, even with me, but when I saw him interact with Hades and Sofia…he was a whole new man. He'd give his life for either one of them. I could tell just by watching.

Hades started to walk with Sofia. "I'm gonna take her home. You'll figure out your own way?"

"Don't worry about me." Damien lingered behind and started to walk with me.

"I can give you a ride," I offered, even though I didn't want to. Nothing but bad things happened when we were alone together. Or good things…depending on how you looked at it.

Damien nodded in agreement. "Thanks."

I liked having a car, but I didn't care for the model.

Bugatti.

Liam insisted I get it because he wanted the world to know what I was worth, but I thought it was ridiculously extravagant and not me whatsoever. I'd rather sell this car so Liam could retire than continue to drive it around like some kind of royal.

Damien didn't comment on the vehicle. He just sat there quietly…looking out the window.

It was a long drive, even though his office was only fifteen minutes away.

We listened to the radio to pass the time, and every once in a while, he pulled his sleeve back to glance at the time on his nice watch. His hair was styled the way I liked, and his tanned skin peeked out from underneath his cuffs sometimes…beautiful.

I parked in front of the entrance to the bank and waited for him to leave.

He made no move to open the door. He continued to look out the window as if he didn't realize where we were. After a quiet sigh that filled the car, he turned to me, his green eyes packed with so much intensity, it seemed like he might kiss me.

I held his gaze because I didn't know what else to do. I was paralyzed by the look, so weak I couldn't even blink. I didn't want to miss a single word, a single movement he might make. My mind was transported back in time, and I stood naked in front of him, frozen by that exact same gaze. I was entirely his, and no one else could claim me…not even my own husband. Damien already owned every piece of my body, had kissed my most tender places with embraces that still burned. My body was covered with his scars, a map of everywhere he'd been. No matter how many showers I took, I couldn't wash him off. Sometimes, I smelled him on my sheets, smelled him on my clothes, but that simply wasn't possible.

He didn't say anything, and he turned away when he realized he wasn't going to. He opened the door, got out, and walked away. No words were spoken, but a lengthy conversation had just happened between us. The heat from the fire was in the car, making my skin flush and turn pink. The wine we'd already drunk was in my veins, still potent even though it'd been ingested months ago. Memories so sharp they cut us both made us bleed all over the seats.

I watched him walk through the front doors, and when I couldn't see him anymore, I drove away.

I sat at my vanity and fastened the diamond earrings into my lobes. My hair was in loose curls, and all the thick strands were pinned to one side, making my layers fall down one shoulder. I was in a sweetheart-neckline strapless black dress with a diamond hanging down from my throat.

Liam was visible in the mirror, wearing a three-piece suit. "What's this dinner for?"

"You don't have to come." I didn't want to drag Liam to an event he didn't want to be part of. The Tuscan Rose was hosting a charity dinner for the city, and the guest list was expected to be over five hundred. I wasn't working tonight, but I was attending as a guest on behalf of the hotel.

"I didn't say that. Just wondering what it's for." Once his tie was tied, he came up behind me and placed his large hands on my bare shoulders. His fingers gently dug into me, warm and callused.

"Charity."

He leaned down and pressed a kiss to my exposed shoulder. "Like I'm gonna let my beautiful wife go out alone dressed like this." He kissed me again, this time moving to my neck. He smelled my hair before he straightened. He turned away and moved to his dresser, where his wedding ring sat. "And I'm happy to be with you, wherever you are."

We stepped into the crowded ballroom where the attendees wore beautiful gowns and pressed suits. Waiters passed flutes on trays, and guests congregated at the bars for something stronger. Music from the string quartet played, and all the chandeliers were lit with a heavenly glow.

Liam's arm was around my waist. "Beautiful place."

"Yeah…" I didn't expect to see Sofia for a while, not when it was this crowded, but after we got our champagne, I spotted her talking to someone with Hades beside her, her pregnant belly visible in her blue dress. Hades had his arm around her, wearing a dark blue suit like he'd intentionally tried to match her.

We moved toward them just as their previous guest left. "I think this party is a success."

"Me too." Sofia hugged me and looked me up and down. "Wow, you look beautiful."

"Thank you. So do you." I turned to Liam. "Let me introduce my husband. Liam, this is Sofia."

Liam shook her hand. "Pleasure to meet you." He turned to Hades quickly and shook his hand. "Congratulations on the baby. Didn't know you were expecting."

Hades returned the gesture. "It's our second."

"Then I should congratulate you twice," Liam said. "Know what you're having?"

"A boy," Hades answered immediately. "This will be our second son."

"That's great." Liam returned his arm around my waist. "How old is your first boy?" Their conversation faded away when I became distracted.

By the six-foot-three, sexy-as-hell, gorgeous man on the other side of the room. He held a glass of scotch while he spoke to a few gentlemen, his legs long and toned in the black slacks he wore. His black jacket fit his broad shoulders perfectly, and his jawline was clean-shaven, showing that sexy smile that he flashed once in a while. I knew I wasn't the only woman in the room staring at him.

His presence hadn't crossed my mind. I just assumed he wouldn't be there because he had nothing to do with the Tuscan Rose, and it didn't seem like the type of event he would want to attend anyway.

Damn, I was wrong.

4

DAMIEN

I felt her before I saw her.

Like the distinct tingle on the back of your neck when the temperature changes in the room, or the ominous feeling you get in your gut when you feel someone watching you, or the inexplicable intuition you sense when you know something is about to happen...good or bad.

That was exactly what I felt.

And then I saw her.

She wore a skintight black dress with four-inch heels, her sexy hips narrowed into a petite waistline. Her sculpted legs were sexy and tanned, visible from mid-thigh all the way to her toes. Her tits were pressed together and perky in the tight ensemble, and the thing she'd done with her hair was sexy. It was exactly the way I pushed her hair off her face, and it made me wonder if she did that on purpose.

She must have felt the same feeling I did, because she turned my way when she felt my stare. Our eyes locked for seconds, both impossible to read. She was the first one to look away, returning to her conversation with Sofia and Hades...and Liam.

His hand was around her waist, his height and size diminishing hers. He seemed bored with the conversation, so he continued to drink the champagne, getting a new glass far quicker than everyone else.

Get a man's drink, asshole.

I'd known she would be there, but that didn't prepare me for the way she looked, the way she took my breath away just the way she used to when she was naked and riding my dick in the middle of the night.

It'd been a week since I'd seen her at the hospital. She'd given me a ride to the office, and as we sat in front of the entrance, we had the longest and most silent conversation in the world. It was intense...even though I had no idea what she was thinking.

But I knew what I was thinking.

I assumed after the initial tension was broken, she would become a former flame who dulled into a stranger. But it seemed to get more difficult for us to be in the same room together. When I saw her stained cheeks at the hospital, I didn't think twice before I comforted her as if I were her man...and she was my woman. I knew she was worried about Sofia, and that triggered her own painful memories of losing her child. I couldn't explain how I knew that, how I could read her eyes like words on a page, but I could. Knowing she was in pain broke my heart, and I immediately reverted to who we used to be, when I was the man who picked up the pieces of her pain and put them back together.

People continued to come up to me and talk to me, most of them people I knew from the bank. But sometimes, a woman would have the courage to flirt with me, to make small talk as she found an excuse to touch my tie, and then she would slip me her number.

I didn't even have to try.

That should be a good thing, a victorious feeling. But instead, it made me lift my gaze to look at Annabella, to see if she'd noticed what just happened. She was married, so she shouldn't care.

But I wanted her to care.

When I looked at where she'd been a moment before, she was gone. Liam was still there, having an intense conversation with Hades as he made punching moves like he was describing his last fight.

She could be anywhere, and there was no way I would find her. But my body seemed to know exactly where she was, like a silent sonar that could pick up her movements through crowds and walls.

And I spotted her through the cracks of people as she headed outside to the balcony. The doors were closed because it was too cold, but she went out there anyway as if she had an objective.

I finished my scotch and left the empty glass on the table before I followed her.

The second I stepped onto the patio, the vapor left my mouth and evaporated into the dry hair. It was thicker than the smoke from my cigars. My suit was a heavy material so I was immune to the cold, but she only wore a little dress that looked practically like lingerie.

I didn't see her anyway. The patio was large and overlooked the city with lots of seating for guests, but she was nowhere in sight. I walked to the right where the windows disappeared, and I spotted her around the corner where there was a small section of balcony area left. It was out of sight from the building, so it was totally private.

She stood with her hands on the rail, looking out at the lights that shone from the cathedral a few blocks away—where she got married. The wind moved through her hair gently, and her skin was already turning pale because of the cold. Her eyes were lifeless as if she were focused on her thoughts with deep concentration.

I approached her from behind and stripped off my jacket so I could place it around her shoulders. I purposely made my footsteps loud, so she knew she wasn't alone when I came close. But she seemed to know I was there because she didn't flinch as the jacket was placed around her petite shoulders. I pulled it tighter over her body so my body heat would stay close to her skin as long as possible before it escaped.

She pushed her arms through the sleeves then hugged it across her body. "Thank you."

I leaned against the rail with my back to the city, my eyes on the stone wall that comprised the exterior of the ballroom. It was a freezing night, but somehow, I wasn't cold, not even with the loss of my jacket. "This is where Hades and Sofia spoke for the first time."

That seemed to distract her from whatever she was thinking about. "Really?" She turned her head toward me, her curls stretching down one side of her chest. In this light, she looked beautiful, the distant illumination from the cathedral making her eyes glow like she possessed the spirit of an angel.

I nodded. "She was just eighteen, and he was in his twenties."

"I didn't realize he was older than her."

"You would never know, huh?" I slid my hands into my pockets. "But all that booze and cigars will catch up to him soon."

"And they fell in love right then?"

"No. Hades said she was too young for him. But Sofia didn't like that answer, so she grabbed him and kissed him so hard, he never forgot about her."

She smiled.

"And four years later, their paths crossed again…and that's where it all started."

"He loves her so much. I can tell by the way he looks at her."

I nodded. "Yeah…they're soul mates."

Her eyes softened when she looked at me. "You believe in that stuff?"

"More than you'll ever know." I turned my gaze back to the wall as I remembered the last few years, everything Hades did to keep Sofia as his wife. There was nothing he wouldn't have done for her.

"You believe there's one special person out there for everyone?"

"No."

She raised an eyebrow.

"I think some people are soul mates. That's all."

"Any other soul mates you know?"

I shook my head. "He's the only one."

"Why do you think they are meant for each other?"

I would never tell her the story. She would think I was crazy. "I just do."

"Like how you *just* knew the baby would alright?"

"Just like that, actually."

She stared at me for a while before she looked out at the city. "Why do I feel like there's something you aren't telling me?"

How did she know me so well? We were only together for a short time, but she read me in a special way. "Because there is."

She pivoted her body to me this time, looking at me head on.

"But you wouldn't believe me if I told you."

"Try me."

I stared at her pretty face and almost considered it. "Maybe someday."

Her pretty eyes continued to shift back and forth and look into mine, her body covered in the enormous jacket. It was the same way she looked in all my clothes, as if she were wearing a blanket. Her curves were covered and her slender neck was nearly invisible, but she still looked so damn beautiful.

Holy fuck.

I kept my hands in my pockets as I stared at her, noticing the way her big diamonds reflected any little flicker of light. She was a woman who wasn't just sexy in a traditional way, with those long legs and that tight stomach. She had a special glow to her that was unmatched by anyone else. Her beauty was radiant, pure. As I stared at her in that moment, I could honestly say she was the most beautiful woman I'd ever seen.

And I'd let her go.

Regret started to wash over me like waves upon stepping into a cold ocean. She was with a man who didn't deserve her. She was a diamond that had been handed over to a jeweler to be carved into pieces when she deserved to be one magnificent rock.

She held my gaze, her thoughts invisible to me.

I'd give anything to know what she was thinking, to feel her emotions in real time. Did she come out here because that woman gave me her number? Or did she come out here because Liam went into the details of his last victory?

I didn't ask because the answer wouldn't make me feel better. "You look beautiful tonight."

She dropped her gaze for just a moment, the compliment enough to make her cheeks blush with a rosy color that was unmistakable. The cold had pulled her blood away from her extremities to conserve heat, so that reaction was a spike in temperature.

She was the only woman who valued my compliments, who blushed at the simplest words. The only woman who believed in my positive qualities and couldn't see my flaws. She was the only woman who stared at me like this…as if I was the only man she would ever love.

Why did I let her go?

I stepped closer to her, my face coming into close proximity with hers. It was like at the hospital, when I lost my mind as I tried to comfort her. My hand moved on top of hers on the rail, feeling how cold it was in the nighttime air. My palm smothered her hand and brought it back to life with warmth.

My free hand moved into that curtain of hair, and I tilted her face to meet mine. I stared at her for a long time, my eyes shifting back and forth to see hers doing the same. My thumb brushed over her cheek and touched the corner of her lip. I remembered every kiss, every sweet whisper in the middle of the night, and I suddenly felt empty…like I'd just lost all those things.

My hand cupped the back of her head, and I moved in, transfixed by her beauty, intoxicated by the way she stared at me, moved by the memories of our past. I didn't think about Liam or anyone else. All I thought about was her, the woman I hadn't stopped thinking about since the moment she stepped into my office.

And I kissed her.

Her lips were warm and soft, just as I remembered, but they were also now rigid and still. She took a deep breath when she felt me, her body tightening under my grasp.

I kissed her again, feeling that old inferno spark to life at the simplest touch. My chest rumbled with the fire in my heart, and my cold fingertips suddenly felt scalding hot. My hand left hers, and I circled her waist, wanting to pull her into me so I could feel her heartbeat through her clothes.

But I never got the chance.

She pushed me off and stepped back, her fingers moving to her lips like I'd punched her instead of kissed her. She closed her eyes for a moment, self-loathing written on her face. She wiped away my kiss on the jacket before she opened her eyes and looked at me again. There was no desire there anymore. Now, there was just contempt like she hated me. "I'm married."

I felt terrible. Her rejection stung, but the pain in her voice hurt me more.

She stripped off the jacket and threw it at me. "He cheated on me, but I would never do the same. I'm better than that. I'm bigger than that." Ferocity was in her gaze, as if she'd lost all respect for me. "Stop doing this, Damien."

"Doing what?" I asked quietly.

"Using me. You know how I feel about you, and you play me—"

"I'm not playing you." Was that how it seemed? My feelings were one-hundred-percent genuine.

"Yes, you are. What was your plan? Push me up against that wall and fuck me right here? Then pretend like nothing happened?" Her voice was loud and hysterical, as if she didn't give a damn if anyone overheard us.

"Annabella, I didn't have a plan—"

"Fuck you, Damien." She threw down her arms. "You dumped me because you didn't want me. You told me not to marry Liam even though you don't love me. You just want me on your hook. You want me to pine for you because it inflates your ego—"

"That's not true at all."

"Just stay away from me, Damien. I mean it." She held up her hand to keep me back. "You turn me into a person I don't want to be. You make me desperate, irrational—and now you're turning me into a woman who cheats on her husband. That's not who I want to be. That's not who I'm going to be." She turned around and walked off.

"Annabella."

She didn't stop. She went back into the ballroom and left me there.

Alone.

5

ANNABELLA

I hadn't realized love could turn to hate so quickly.

Damien played me for a fool, made me sing like the strings of a violin. He turned me into an imbecile, a stupid woman who would abandon everything for a beautiful man.

I was not falling for it...not this time.

I knew who I was, and I wouldn't falter. I wouldn't abandon my beliefs just because of the pain in my heart. I wouldn't betray the man who loved me. I told Liam I was committed to our marriage, that I wanted to try again. Hooking up with Damien was disrespectful and just wrong.

Damien was an asshole for putting me in that situation. He'd had his chance to be with me, and he declined.

And I wouldn't be his goddamn side chick.

I sat at the vanity and removed my diamond earrings before I unclasped the necklace from around my throat.

Liam was visible in the reflection behind me. He sat on the

edge of the bed and untied his dress shoes before he slipped them off. Then he sat there, staring at me with those intense blue eyes. It wasn't a gaze packed with desire. It was a different look altogether.

I returned his stare, just as prey looked at the predator before they were attacked.

"Did I do something?" His deep voice shattered the silence of the room, quiet but still innately powerful.

I dropped my gaze in shame. "No." I'd been angry with Damien since the event on the balcony. After I'd walked inside, I'd calmed down in the bathroom, but when I found Liam in the crowd, I said I was ready to leave…even though the party had just started. "It wasn't you…"

"Then tell me."

I hadn't decided if I was going to tell Liam what happened, but it seemed wrong to lie about it now. When he was with another woman, he came clean and told me. I didn't appreciate what he did, but I did respect his honesty. He deserved the same from me. "I went to get some air on the balcony… and he joined me."

Confusion came over his face, digesting the equation I'd just thrown at him. When he cracked it, he turned cold again but also angry. "And what did *he* do?" He straightened on the bed, his hands gripping each of his thighs, taking a defensive stance.

I dropped my gaze. "Kissed me."

He wasn't visible, but his reaction was potent, like deadly gas filling the entire room, entering our lungs and making our eyes smart.

"I ended it right away." I lifted my gaze and looked at him. "So, nothing happened."

His hands came together, and he leaned forward, his knuckles resting against his forehead. He was wordless, but his anger was hot, humid like a sauna. It was silent but so loud it blocked out all other noise. "You want to be with him, then?" He kept his pose as if he didn't want to look at me...couldn't bear it.

"No."

He lowered his hands and returned his gaze to the mirror.

"I told him I was married and it wasn't going to happen."

He stared at me with a stoic expression, as if he couldn't believe the words coming out of my mouth.

"I made a commitment to you, Liam. I don't want to have an affair with a man who plays with my heart. And I don't want to leave a marriage to be with a man who would kiss someone's wife."

The relief in his expression was touching, as if that meant the world to him. He straightened his position. "Who is he?"

My heart started to race.

"Anna."

I was pissed at Damien, but I wouldn't feed him to the wolves. "Does it matter? I told him to leave me alone."

"It does matter. Because I'll tell him to leave you alone myself." He cracked his knuckles, the noise loud in our quiet bedroom.

"It's over. Let it go." I took off the rest of my jewelry then pulled the clips from my scalp so my hair would come loose and move across my shoulders. I didn't tell Liam so he would be angry. I did it because it was the right thing to do. I just hoped there wouldn't be long-term consequences for my integrity. "I picked you."

That reminder calmed him down. "I don't deserve you."

I stared at my wedding ring on the vanity.

"Anyone else would think it was fair…"

"That's not the kind of person I am." I looked at his reflection in the mirror.

"I know." He rose to his feet then walked to me, his hands moving to my shoulders. "And that's why I don't deserve you."

I was sitting inside my office when Damien texted me.

I want to talk.

I ignored his message and locked my phone. If I weren't so infatuated with him, I would have seen the signs a long time ago. He would forget our plans all the time and wouldn't even text me back. He would ignore my phone calls because he was in a bad mood. He never gave a damn about me. When he agreed to exclusivity, it was just to ditch the condom. No other reason.

Hours passed, and he texted me again.

Annabella.

I ignored him again.

This time, he didn't wait hours before he texted me again. *Please.*

I finally caved. *Don't text me again. Ever.* I locked the phone.

This time, he called.

Motherfucker. I picked up but got my message across before he could say a word. "Don't call me again. Ever." I hung up.

He called back.

I got so fed up, I turned off the phone altogether.

HE TOOK IT A STEP FURTHER AND WALKED INTO MY OFFICE AT the end of the day.

"You've got to be kidding me..." This time, I wasn't enticed by his appearance in the tight shirt and the jeans that squeezed his sculpted thighs. I didn't notice if he'd shaved or not because I didn't check.

"Annabella." He started to shut the door behind him. "Just listen to me—"

"Get the fuck out, or I'll call Liam."

"You think I'm scared of him?" He approached my desk, his head tilted to the side slightly. "Call him. I don't give a shit."

I didn't call his bluff. Instead, I hit the button on my phone and used the intercom. "Sofia, could you help me with something?"

He groaned in frustration.

Sofia was hesitant but agreed. "Uh, yeah. I'll be right there."

I glared at him. "How this plays out is up to you."

She opened the door and stepped in seconds later, mildly surprised that Damien was in there with the door shut. "What's up?"

I stared at Damien, threatening to throw him under the bus to Sofia, whose opinion actually mattered to him.

She must have picked up on the tension because she glanced back and forth between us.

Damien wasn't afraid of Liam, but he was obviously afraid of Sofia. "I'll let you get back to work..." He let himself out without argument.

I was victorious. "I just need help with these spreadsheets..." I left the chair so she could take my vacated spot.

Sofia stared at me for a few seconds before she sank into the leather chair. "Everything alright?"

"Yeah, I just wasn't sure where to put these invoices." I fished them out of the pile.

"No." She didn't look at the computer. "Everything alright with Damien?"

I decided to keep his secret. "Yeah. He just stopped by to get something for Liam."

She stared at me like she knew I was full of shit, but she let it go. "Alright..."

Days passed, and Damien didn't bother me again.

Maybe he finally got the hint.

I wanted nothing to do with him.

I let my guard down and stopped thinking about him. That kiss on the balcony was the best thing that could have happened to me, because it really made me forget about him, made me break the spell he cast over me. I saw him for what he really was.

A player.

He wanted me to keep wanting him, but he would never want me back.

I tightened my coat around my body and stepped into the parking lot. The days were short in winter, so it was almost dark when I left the office every day. I stepped into the parking lot and made my way to my car.

And Damien came out of nowhere.

He stepped into my path, wearing a leather jacket and dark jeans. His breath escaped as vapor, and he stared at me like he'd marked me as his next target. He blocked my path with his size.

I halted in my tracks, stunned because I hadn't been aware of my surroundings. I was too busy thinking about what to make for dinner and the mound of paperwork I had to take care of in the morning.

He didn't come close to me. "Annabella, I just want to—"

I slapped him. I didn't realize how much I wanted to do it, how much anger was packed deep inside me, until my hand moved on its own. It wasn't a premeditated attack, just an expression of all the pain he caused me.

He turned his head slightly with the hit, but the rest of his body was solid as a mountain. His cheek instantly turned red, and the imprint of my fingers was noticeable almost immediately. He closed his eyes for a second, bottling his rage before he looked at me again.

I moved around him and walked to my car. I didn't apologize or warn him to stay away from me.

Because I'd just made that pretty damn clear.

6

DAMIEN

I finally got my father into my house.

We packed all of his belongings that he couldn't live without and tossed everything else. Most of his furniture was old, dusty, and seriously lacking in structural integrity. We couldn't even donate it, so it was tossed.

His bedroom had a private living room where he could watch TV, and he had his own bathroom with a walk-in shower so he didn't have to worry about tripping. With a maid to do his laundry and wash his sheets, he would be able to ditch that old-man smell in no time.

"It's nice." Catalina looked around the bedroom, seeing the integration of the old and the new. There were picture frames on one of the end tables in the living room, showing photos of Mom and us as kids. "I like it."

My father nodded, but he didn't seem impressed. He still had cold feet about the whole thing.

I clapped him on the shoulder. "I'm really glad you're here,

Father." My dad used to be the strong provider of our family, the person who never needed anyone for anything. Time had passed quicker than he anticipated, and he struggled to accept his age, his lack of strength and youth.

He turned to me, and his eyes slowly narrowed. "Why is your cheek so red?"

I'd headed home right after I'd confronted Annabella in the parking lot...and it didn't go the way I expected. I patted him on the back. "I'm happy we're going to spend more time together."

Catalina grinned. "He got slapped."

I shot her a glare.

"Hard." She fell onto the couch and put up her feet. "I like her. A lot."

My phone started to ring, so I walked off to answer it. It was Hades. "What's up?"

"Want to come over for dinner?"

Our relationship wasn't exactly how it used to be, because most of our friendship had been spent in mutual bachelorhood. But now that he was married, we stopped going to the whorehouses and the strip clubs and did tamer activities... like having dinner with his family. But I loved every invitation because now I had two friends instead of one. "What's on the menu?"

"Like it matters," he said with a chuckle.

"Will there be booze?"

"Always."

"Then I'll be there." I hung up and returned to my family.

Catalina hugged my father goodbye. "I have to get going. I have a late rehearsal tonight." She kissed him on the cheek. "I'm so happy you're here. Damien and I are both so happy." She squeezed both of his hands.

He perked up a bit. "Thank you, sweetheart." He kissed her forehead before he let her go. Anytime he was with my sister, his eyes lit up with happiness. She was the favorite child. He didn't bother hiding it.

I was fine with it.

She walked by me and stuck out her tongue at me. "Bye."

I rolled my eyes. "You're lucky I don't slap you."

"I dare you to try." She flipped me the bird and walked out.

I turned back to my father. "Hades invited me over for dinner. You want to come along?"

He stared at the table with the picture frames before he picked up the one of my mother. "Catalina looks so much like her… Sometimes I feel like she's still here when I look at her." My father had never gotten over my mother's death. He'd never remarried. Didn't even try to date. When she was gone, so was he.

I came up beside him and patted him on the back. "I noticed the same thing."

He set down the picture frame but continued to stare at it.

"Let's go see her tomorrow." We used to go to my mother's grave all the time, but over the years, our trips became less frequent.

He shook his head. "It's alright. It just hurts every time I go."

I pitied my father for being so lost without her. "How about the two of us have dinner together? We can go somewhere, or Patricia can serve it here."

He finally pulled his gaze away from the picture. "Thanks, son. But I just want to be alone tonight…"

Hades took one look at my face and raised an eyebrow. "What the fuck happened to your face?"

I thought the mark would wear off within an hour or two, but she'd hit me so damn hard, it would probably be there until morning. "I ran into a door." I walked past him and saw Andrew on the rug on the hardwood floor, playing with a few toys with a binky in his mouth.

Hades followed me. "You ran into a door? You?" He crossed his arms over his chest and didn't buy it.

I leaned down and tickled Andrew's stomach before I got to my feet again. "What's for dinner?"

"Don't change the subject."

Sofia came out of the bathroom. "Hey—" Her face turned white when she saw the same mark. "Your face—"

"I ran into a door, alright?" I snapped. "Drop it." I walked into the dining room, where the food was already laid out. I poured myself a glass of red wine and took a long drink.

Hades sat across from me. "I didn't know doors had fingers." He poured himself a glass of wine before he swirled it.

Sofia only had water and grabbed a piece of bread from the basket in the center of the table. "I know something is going on between you and Anna. I could feel it when I walked into the office that day." She shot me a look of accusation before she took a bite of her bread.

Maybe coming over here was a bad idea.

"If that was her—" Hades nodded to my cheek "—then damn, she's got one hell of an arm."

"Or she's just really pissed." Sofia took another bite of her bread. "What did you do, Damien?"

"You guys are making a lot of assumptions." I grabbed my silverware and cut into my dinner. It was a chicken dish with flavorful rice and slowly roasted vegetables.

"Then correct those assumptions," Sofia said coldly.

Hades ate but continued to stare at me.

I felt comfortable telling Hades the truth because his moral compass wasn't always pointed north, but Sofia was different. She saw the world in black-and-white, with the exception of her husband's character.

"Well?" she pressed.

I kept eating.

She glared at me. "Damien."

I finally cracked. "I kissed her." Sofia was going to find out eventually, so may as well come clean now.

Hades shook his head slightly, knowing my behavior could compromise his relationship with Liam.

Sofia was outright shocked. "You did what?"

"We were on the balcony during the party, and every time we're together, there's this...chemistry." I could never accurately describe the energy in the air, the hum in my chest, the desperation I felt to have her. "It just happened. Every time I'm around her, it just gets harder and harder, and I caved."

Hades leaned back in his chair, his appetite lost. "Damien..." He dragged his hands down his face in irritation.

"What the hell were you thinking?" she snapped. "She's married—"

"I know, I know." I held up my hand to shut her up. "Like I said, I wasn't thinking. And she turned me down, so nothing happened. She screamed at me for a bit, accusing me of toying with her feelings, keeping her on a hook...shit like that."

Sofia looked at me with sheer disappointment, and Hades shook his head slightly.

"That's not what I'm doing," I said defensively.

Sofia narrowed her eyes. "She told you she loved you, Damien."

"I know, but—"

"Leave the girl alone." Her anger slowly simmered down, but it was still potent. "She's moving on with Liam, and you need to let her do that."

"You think I'm doing this on purpose?" I asked incredulously. "It's completely out of my control. I can't even be in the same room as her without all this shit happening. I can't stop staring at her. I can't stop thinking about her. I just… It's out of my control."

Sofia was unsympathetic. "Then you need to stop being in the same room as her. But first, apologize."

"I've been trying. She won't talk to me. And I want her to know that's not what I'm doing. That I'm not playing games. That I genuinely care about her. That…it's hard for me." I sank into my chair and was swallowed by the self-loathing.

"I'll talk to her," Sofia said. "Apologize and move on."

Hades stared at me. "Did she tell Liam?"

I shook my head. "I have no idea. But I doubt it…because we'd know by now."

7
ANNABELLA

Sofia stepped into my office. "You got a minute?"

"You're my boss. I have more than a minute." I shut my laptop so she could have my full attention.

She chuckled. "Good answer." She sat at the edge of my desk and took a deep breath before she continued. "So, Damien told me everything that happened…"

He did?

"And he would really like the opportunity to apologize."

Now I know why he told her. "I can't believe he asked you to help him…"

"I saw how red his face was. You hit him pretty damn hard."

It felt good in the moment, but I'd quickly regretted it.

"That could only mean you're really upset about the whole thing…and I doubt it's all because of the kiss."

I dropped my gaze.

"Will you talk to him?"

"Do I have a choice?"

"You always have a choice, Anna." She slid off the desk. "I think it's good that you both clear the air. Maybe it'll allow both of you to move on…on good terms. I know it's hard for you to be around each other, but for as long as you continue to work here, it's gonna happen. He's my husband's best friend. He's gonna show his face from time to time. You could never speak ever again, but I don't think that's the best choice for either of you." She crossed her arms over her chest.

It'd been over a week since that crazy night. My anger had dipped after I hit him, but the pain was still there.

"So?"

"I have to decide right now?"

"He's standing outside…so that would help."

My heart started to race, my pulse quick in my neck and my wrists. A distinctive pain rushed through my chest, a drop of adrenaline and anxiety at the same time. I sighed as I got to my feet, not prepared for this at all. "Fine."

"Alright." Sofia opened the door and walked out. Her whispers were audible down the hallway, probably telling Damien he had my full attention.

I came around the desk with my arms crossed over my chest, feeling my heart beat strong in my body. I was nervous when I shouldn't be, weak when I should be strong.

This man had no power over me anymore, so I shouldn't feel anything at all.

Then he walked inside, in a leather jacket and jeans. The shirt underneath his jacket was olive green, and the watch on his wrist was black instead of shiny and silver. His eyes grabbed mine, and he closed the door behind him.

Now my heart was racing like a Bugatti on the Autobahn.

I leaned against the desk and stared at him coldly, waiting for an apology that wouldn't make me feel better. This was something we could never bury, something we would never be mature enough to forget. We were both irrational when we had to deal with the other.

He stepped closer to me and slid his hands into the front pockets of his jeans, as if he needed some time to think of what to say...even though he'd been chasing me down for almost two weeks. "Annabella." He took a breath after he said my name, like that single word was too much for him. "I want to apologize for what I did, but I also want to explain why I did what I did. It's not because I'm playing you, keeping you on my hook and taking advantage of your feelings. This isn't a game to me. You've never been a game to me."

I wanted to believe him, but I couldn't.

As if he could read my thoughts, he said, "You don't believe me."

My arms tightened over my chest.

"Anytime we're close to each other, I feel this..." With a closed fist, he pressed his hand against his chest, right in the center. "I can't even explain it. It's this need to get close to you, to touch you like you're mine. When I ended things, I thought it would be easy for me to walk away. But I've never really been able to walk away. When I see you with Liam, I don't like it...and not just because he's not good enough for you. I'm jealous. I'm hurt."

"If that were true—"

"Let me finish." He slowly lowered his hand.

I turned quiet even though I shouldn't obey.

"It's hard for me. It's as hard for me as it is for you."

I wanted to argue, but I kept my mouth shut.

"I'm sorry I kissed you. When we were on the balcony, I forgot about the party inside, I forgot about Liam inside, I forgot about everything. All I could do was feel...feel the woman beside me. I wanted you, and I let my inhibitions go down the drain. But you don't understand how I look at you, how I think you're stunning each and every time I see you."

How could he say all these romantic things but not want to be with me?

"I'm not using you. I'm not taking advantage of you. I'm not playing you. I never told you this, but I didn't end things because I wanted to..."

My eyes narrowed.

"I did it because I had to." He pulled his hands out of his pockets and let them hang by his sides, his shoulders rigid and tight. He stared at me with sincerity in his eyes, his voice softer than it'd ever been. "The Skull King took my father and was going to execute him because of something I did. It was a punishment. And the only reason my father is alive right now is because Hades got to him before they pulled the trigger. My life is always in jeopardy, but that's never been important to me. But my family…the people I care about…I can't handle that. And when I imagined him taking you…it terrified me. So, the next time I saw you, I broke it off."

That information should comfort me, but it didn't. It made me regret what I'd lost even more, that I could still have the man I really wanted if he'd just told me the truth. "You should have told me, Damien…"

He lowered his gaze.

"This whole time, I've been living in the past, wondering if you ever felt anything for me when it seemed like you did, and it would have prevented a lot of heartbreak. And that was *my* decision to stay or leave. I should have been the one to decide if I could tolerate the risk…because I would have stayed."

He lifted his gaze again, touched by my words. "That's exactly why I didn't tell you, Annabella."

When I took my next breath, I felt the pain all the way into my lungs.

"I would never put you in danger. You deserve more than that." His eyes were focused on me, shining like emeralds.

"Then walk away…" That was the easiest decision, to abandon the dangers altogether.

He was quiet for a long time as he considered the suggestion. "Hades left the business for his wife. That was the right decision for him because he loves her...and they're supposed to be together. But that's not me... That's not us."

I understood what he was saying, and it hurt. He didn't love me...and he was saying it as gently as possible.

He was quiet for a long time, his eyes focused on the painting on the wall. The tension rose and filled the room with suffocating heat. When he turned back to me, he spoke again. "It's not easy for me to be around you because my feelings haven't changed. When I look at you, it still feels like you're mine. When I see tears on your face, I want to be the one to fix them. When I see a man hold you, I want to be the one who has my hands on you. I bowed out because I wasn't willing to abandon my work for you, and it pisses me off that Liam won't stop fighting when that's what you want. If a man is going to have a wife, she's his number one commitment. She gets whatever she wants. And if you can't handle the responsibility, then don't marry her."

He spoke so passionately about marriage, and I knew he got his opinions from Hades and Sofia...and that made me wish I were married to him now. I wanted a man who committed, who would put his wife first, not second. I still wished he was the man I came home to every day.

"I couldn't let you continue thinking I was using you... because that's not true. But I hope I didn't just make this worse." He sighed and rubbed the back of his head, his fingers brushing through the soft strands I used to fist every night.

"There's risk with everything we do, Damien. Any man who has money is dangerous. Liam has enemies that could hurt me to get back at him. Even the bank is dangerous if you piss off the wrong person. I wish you had talked to me about this because I don't care about the risk. I would rather be happy and live on the edge than have a dull and safe life."

He didn't know what to say.

I lowered my gaze because it was too hard to look at him. "I have no idea how this happened, how I fell in love with you so quickly. We saw each other for, what? Two months?" I asked incredulously. "Liam and I were happy together and I loved him so much, so I didn't expect to feel that way about someone for a really long time…and then I met you. And it was passionate, deep, and just so quick. I can't even explain it." I'd gone over our relationship a million times and still hadn't uncovered any answers. "But it doesn't matter now because I married Liam…and I'm committed to making that relationship work. I wish you had told me the truth when I could have done something about it, but you didn't. So, we both need to move on…" I didn't want to let Damien go, even now. Sometimes I forgot about the wedding ring on my left hand even though it was so damn heavy. But I had to remember that Damien was already gone, that the past couldn't be changed, that he still didn't love me. So, none of it mattered anyway.

He said nothing for a long time, just staring at me. "Yes…we do."

If we had a real chance to be together, to date for a year or two, maybe Damien would have fallen in love with me and left his business. But that opportunity was stolen from us, and that would always haunt me. "Friends?" I extended my right hand.

He stared at it for a while before he sighed. "I'm not sure we can be friends, Annabella." He came closer to me and placed his right hand in mine. Instead of shaking it like two colleagues, he fanned his fingers across my wrist so he could feel my pulse. His thumb brushed over the web of my palm, and he came closer to me, our bodies coming so near that we could hear each other breathe. His eyes looked into mine, so damn beautiful that it hurt. "But I can try…"

8

DAMIEN

I SAT IN MY OFFICE AND WORKED ON THE STACK OF PAPERWORK Hades had dropped on my desk a few minutes ago. We may have buried the hatchet, but Hades still lost his temper whenever we had to do paperwork. My work was never good enough, and he didn't hesitate to tell me that, accompanied by a string of profanities.

My assistant spoke. "Your next appointment is here."

I looked at the mountain of paperwork and sighed. I had too much shit to do today, and I didn't want to waste time on my clients. But it was too late to cancel, and my clients were the kind of people you didn't want to piss off. "Who is it?"

"Conway Barsetti."

At least I liked the guy. "Send him in." I stacked the papers and placed them on the edge of my desk.

A moment later, Conway Barsetti walked inside, wearing jeans, a long-sleeved shirt, and a casual blazer on top. A black wedding ring was on his left hand, and he looked so much like his father, they could be brothers. He smiled as he extended his hand. "Damien."

I grabbed him with a tight grip. "It's been a while. Business going well?"

"It's always going well." He stepped to the side and revealed the woman he was with. A beautiful brunette with thick lashes and bright blue eyes. She was tall, and in that tight dress, she had curves in all the right places. She wasn't his wife, so I assumed it was one of his models. "Let me introduce you to Charlotte."

She stared at me for a few seconds before a slight smile stretched across her lips. "Nice to meet you." She had a French accent.

I shook her hand. "Damien. Pleasure is all mine."

Conway sat in one of the leather armchairs, and Charlotte did the same.

I relaxed in my chair and drummed my fingers on the surface of the wood. "How's your father?"

"The same," Conway answered. "He took my son to the zoo today."

"He's a good grandfather?" I asked.

"Better grandfather than father," he said with a chuckle. "He never took me to the zoo."

I smiled because I knew he was kidding. "What are we doing today? Moving money around? Buying another piece of real estate?"

"Actually, I'm here on behalf of Charlotte," he explained.

"She's been in my lineup for the last year and has gained immense popularity. Now she's a rich woman and doesn't know what to do with all her cash. That's where you come in."

I turned to her. "I can make all your problems go away."

She smiled. "I can tell."

"You'll take her on as a client?" Conway asked.

I wasn't taking new clients unless they were billionaires, but Conway was a friend, so I would make an exception. "Sure."

"Great." Conway rose to his feet. "I'll let you talk specifics." He gave me a nod before he walked out.

"Tell your wife I said hi."

"Will do." He shut the door behind him.

I turned back to Charlotte and got down to business. "I can launder a lot of money for you since Conway is your client. He can pay some of your salary in cash since I know his books so well. You have a good boss."

"Yeah, he's great." She crossed her legs and pulled her hair over one shoulder. "He spoke highly of you."

"Well, I'm the best," I said with a smile. "I earned that reputation."

She smiled back. "I'm sure you've earned your reputation in other ways too."

AFTER WE FINISHED WITH OUR MEETING, I WALKED TO MY

office door and opened it. "We're gonna make a lot of money together." I turned to her and slid my hands into my pockets as I waited for her to walk out.

She grabbed her purse and stepped up to me. "I'm sure we will." She opened her bag and grabbed a business card sitting inside. She turned it over, wrote down her number, and handed it back to me. "Maybe we can go out for a drink and talk about it more." She was the most famous lingerie model in this country, and she was the one who put the moves on me.

It was incredibly flattering. I took the card from her hand and slid it into my pocket. "I'll call you."

When she got what she wanted, she smiled. Then she flipped her hair over her shoulder and walked out, strutting down my hallway like it was the runway instead of a stuffy bank.

My eyes moved to her ass in the short dress, and I watched her hips shake. But then I was distracted by something else.

Heath leaned against the wall with his hands in his pockets, and he watched her go with the same interest. He whistled under his breath as he watched her walk, staring at her ass like it was a billboard on a freeway. "Damn." He walked up to me and finally turned his gaze on me. "Can I get a copy of that?"

It was annoying when he stopped by my office at the lab, but it was far more annoying when he showed up here. I stepped inside my office. "Don't show your face here again."

He closed the door behind him and followed me. "What?" He stood in a t-shirt despite the freezing temperatures outside, ink up and down his muscled arms. "It's a bank. There's money here."

"This business has nothing to do with our business. Do it again, and you won't get paid." It really didn't matter where he showed his face. It would piss me off, no matter what. But Hades was in this office, and I didn't want my drug business anywhere near him. I went to my chair behind my desk.

He sank into the chair where Charlotte had just been sitting, his knees apart and his thick arms on the armrests. He glanced around my office and took in the bookshelves and artwork. "Pretty snazzy place."

"Did you hear what I said?"

His eyes shifted back to me, his smile fading away.

"Don't come here again." I didn't care about the threat in his eyes, the malicious expression on his face. If killing him wouldn't start a full war, I would pull out my pistol and shoot him right now. "You have my number. You know my other place of business. You even know where I live. No need to come here."

He sat there in silence, watching me with those arctic blue eyes. He was so still, it didn't seem like he was breathing.

"I've been cooperative, Heath. But don't test me." It was stupid to provoke him when things seemed to have smoothed over, but I didn't want him anywhere near Hades. Sometimes Sofia stopped by and brought Andrew. This place was supposed to be safe.

"Don't test me either."

I held his gaze and didn't back down. "Hades is my partner, and he left the drug business. So, I don't want you near him or his family." Maybe that admission would make him understand. Hades and I were finally friends again, but I knew that could disappear in an instant if he thought his family was at risk.

Heath retained his coldness. "You're trying to protect your boy."

"If you want this to be a long-lasting relationship, respect my wishes."

"We both know I wouldn't be here right now if you behaved like a good little boy in the first place."

I was seriously tempted to grab the pistol and shoot him.

As if he could read my mind, he grinned. "There better be six bullets in the clip. Because it's gonna take that many to stop me." It was as if he had X-ray vision, piercing right through the wood to where I stashed my ammo. He leaned forward. "Give me my money, and I'll be on my way."

"I don't have it."

He cocked an eyebrow. "Choose your words carefully, Damien."

"I don't keep it here. Meet me tonight at the lab. I'll have it for you then."

He continued to stare at me.

"If you want your money every month, that's where you should go."

"But I like keeping you on your toes. It's fun." He rose to his feet. "And pissing you off is fun too."

I knew this was payback for the stunt I pulled, and he wouldn't let it go for a very long time. He would continue to push me around like a punching bag until I was thoroughly humiliated.

"I don't want to go to war with you, Heath."

He straightened and crossed his arms over his chest.

"But I will if you come near the people I care about—including Hades." I rose to my feet so my height could match his. "If you want to keep getting paid for no work, do as I say." Hades was my family, the brother I'd never had. I would jump on a grenade to save his life. I would take a bullet to save his wife, because if he loved her, then so did I. I'd never truly understood loyalty until I lost my best friend. "You understand me?"

Heath was silent.

I knew he wanted me to remain under his thumb, to keep me as his prisoner because he got a kick out of it. If he pushed me too hard, that would all go to shit. All he did was give a slight nod in agreement before he opened the door and walked out.

Hades had been just about to walk inside...because I had the worst timing in the world.

Heath stopped and stared at him, his gaze frozen and fiery at the same time. Hades was the reason his plan had backfired, and he obviously hadn't forgotten that. He looked him up and down subtly before he walked off.

Hades wore the same focused expression, unafraid of the giant monster who had just occupied our halls. He watched

Heath walk away before he turned his gaze on me—livid. He stormed into my office. "What the fuck—"

"I told him never to come here again. This place is off-limits. That you have nothing to do with the other business, so he shouldn't be here. He understood, and it won't happen again."

Hades didn't argue with me, but he still looked angry.

"I would never put you or your family in danger."

He slid his hands into his pockets.

"Alright?"

He sighed and finally nodded. "If I see him here again, I walk."

I knew it wasn't an idle threat. He wouldn't do anything to jeopardize the quiet life he'd committed himself to. He had enough money to pack up and disappear forever. "It won't happen again."

He finally grabbed the papers he'd dropped off earlier. "Why aren't these filled out?"

"Because Conway Barsetti stopped by."

"How is he?" He tossed them back onto my desk.

"Same."

"What did he need?"

"Nothing. He actually brought one of his models. She needs financial help." I pulled the business card out of my pocket and held it up so he could see her number written in her feminine writing. "She gave me her number."

"I'm surprised she agreed to go out with you."

"I didn't even ask her."

He smiled slightly. "So…are things good with Anna?"

The mention of her name immediately destroyed my mood. I slipped the card back into my pocket. "We talked…and we're friends."

"Friends with benefits?" he teased.

"No." I leaned against the desk and crossed my ankles. "I apologized for the situation I put her in…and told her why I broke it off with her."

With his hands resting in his pockets, Hades stared at me with his brown eyes, absorbing everything I said while giving nothing away. Whenever he listened, he exuded such a focused level of concentration that he reminded me of a wild animal about to kill its prey. "What did she say?"

"That she wished I told her the truth…because she doesn't care about the risk."

"Then you were right."

I nodded. "Yeah…"

"And you parted on good terms?"

"She said she wants to be friends. I told her I would try."

"Good. She and Sofia have become good friends, so I don't think she's going to disappear from our lives."

"Yeah…" My existence would be much easier if I never had to see her again, but the idea of her really being gone…was unsettling. I guess I always wanted to have eyes on her, to make sure she didn't need help because her piece-of-shit husband was too oblivious to notice.

"You gonna call her?"

My thoughts drifted far away, to that dark balcony when it was just the two of us and I forgot she wasn't mine anymore. If she wanted to have an affair with me, would I say yes? I could have her, and no one would ever know…including my enemies. Maybe it was better that she had stronger morals than I did because I would get myself in a world of trouble. "What?" I didn't register what he'd just said.

He nodded to my pocket. "Are you going to call the model?"

"Oh…I guess."

"You were a lot more excited about her a moment ago."

That was before I started thinking about Annabella. Women had come and gone since she'd been in my bed, but my thoughts were solely on her. She was the only person who kept my attention after the sex was over, the only woman I ditched a condom for. "Just got a lot on my mind."

Hades knew what I was thinking before I did. "Forget about Anna, alright?"

"I have."

"No, you haven't." He called me out on my bullshit all the time, whether it was about my personal life or my numbers. "And you need to. That model seems like exactly your type, so call her, fuck her, and move on."

I'd already made my peace with my decision, and Annabella seemed to as well. It was time to stop living in the past, to stop looking at her like I had every right to fist that hair like a leash. "Got it."

He pressed his hand against the stack of papers on my desk. "And get this shit done within an hour."

"I'm about to take lunch."

He pulled his hand away and gave me a vicious look, like a gargoyle haunting an old cathedral.

"Or I'll take my lunch in here…"

I LAY IN BED AND READ THE TEXT ON MY PHONE. *MEET ME AT the bar in fifteen*. It was from Hades.

The sound of the running shower came from the bathroom, and the fire burned in the hearth. There were a couple of empty bottles of wine scattered around, and I'd had enough to drink that I really didn't need more booze. *Why?*

He never texted back…in typical Hades fashion.

Charlotte stepped out of the shower with a white towel around her lithe body. Her dry brown hair cascaded over her shoulders, and she instantly dropped the towel next to my bed and pulled on her panties that had been left on the floor. She arched her back as she moved, as if she was on the runway.

I watched her because…you know, how could I not?

She sauntered to the bed, her eyes focused on me like she wasn't satisfied with my performance for that evening. "Has anyone told you that you have the prettiest eyes?" She straddled my hips on top of the sheets, her tits in my face.

More times than I could count. "No."

"Well, you do." Her palms planted against my stomach, and she started to pull the sheets down. It'd been a week since I'd called her, and she ended up in my bed several times throughout that time. She was the one who texted me for more, unapologetic about using me. But she was so greedy with my body that I wondered if she wanted more.

I steadied the sheets. "I have to go."

She pouted her lips. "Right now?"

"Unfortunately." I knew her panties were on, so she had probably intended to suck my dick, which she was very good at.

"And where are you running off to?"

"A bar. I have a business meeting—best way to describe it."

"Then I can come along."

I glanced at the time on my phone. "It's almost eleven."

"So?" She wiggled her body on my lap. "If I'm with you, then you can't go home with someone else." She was confident about her desirability, knowing she was one of the sexiest women in the country. So, if she was on my arm, I wouldn't notice anyone else.

"Why do you care if I go home with someone else? You can have any man you want."

She moved on top of me, crawling like a kitten. Then she pressed her full lips against mine and gave me a soft kiss, a gentle moan coming from her lips. "I know. And you're the man I want."

CHARLOTTE HAD HER HAND ON MY THIGH, AND WHEN A DROP of scotch caught in the corner of my mouth, she wiped it away with her finger and placed it into her mouth for a taste. She was all over me, cuddled into my side like we hadn't even slept together yet.

Hades slid into the spot in the booth across from me, a glass in his hand. He glanced at both of us but didn't comment on the ridiculous PDA. When he and Sofia first got together, I had been subjected to their make-out sessions and ass-grabs. He glanced at Charlotte before he gave me a pointed stare.

"She wanted to come along," I explained without actually hearing his question.

Hades addressed her. "Hades. Nice to meet you."

"Hi." She waved with her fingers. "Are you guys friends?"

"Yes," I said. "And business partners. He owns the other half of the bank."

"Interesting." She glanced at his left hand. "You're married."

Hades nodded. "And I have a son."

"Aww," she said. "How old is he?"

"His first birthday is on Saturday."

Like all women, she turned into a baby-loving freak. "Do you have a picture?"

Slightly annoyed, he reached into his pocket and pulled out his phone so he could show her pictures.

"Aww." She swiped through a few, gradually more impressed with my nephew's cuteness.

Hades turned his glare on me. "Damien, we're here for business."

I shrugged. "You're the one who told me to move on."

"Oh my god, he's adorable!" Oblivious to our conversation, she kept swiping through the photo album.

Hades continued his look of annoyance. "I meant on your own time."

"What are we here for?" I asked, bypassing the subject.

I got my answer a moment later when Liam walked into the bar. In a gray hoodie, he was noticeable because of his size. His arms stretched the cotton of the sweater, and he headed to the bar to grab a drink. A few girls glanced his way, and I was happy to see he didn't look at them. I shifted my gaze back to Hades, miffed that I had to spend my evening with the man I despised.

Hades read my mind. "We're moving on, remember?"

Liam approached the table and set down his drink. "Hades." He shook his hand while standing up, then did the same to me. "Damien."

I took his hand, but the touch still made my muscles tighten in dislike.

Charlotte put down the phone. "Hey, I'm Char." She extended her hand to shake his.

Liam hesitated before he reciprocated. "Liam." He scooted into the round booth.

"Hades was just showing me adorable pictures of his son." Charlotte returned the phone. "What's his name?"

"Andrew." Hades slipped the phone back into his pocket. "And I'm expecting another."

"How sweet," she said. "What are you having?"

"Another boy," he answered, his voice dark because he was irritated we were discussing pussy shit in front of a client. He gave me that look that told me I needed to get rid of her.

I took the hint. "Char, the men are gonna talk about a few things. Could you grab yourself a drink?"

Instead of being offended, she rolled with it. "Sure." She rubbed my arm then leaned in and kissed me on the mouth like she was saying goodbye forever. To take it to a whole other level, she rubbed her palm across my crotch like she was saying goodbye to my dick before she scooted out of the booth and headed to the bar.

Hades didn't say anything, but he shook his head slightly, even though he would have had a completely different reaction if he were single. When we were both bachelors, he would pull the same shit all the time. Guess his memory wasn't that great.

Liam turned to me. "Is she that lingerie model?"

I was perturbed he recognized her. "Yeah."

"Conway Barsetti is our client," Hades interjected, like he was afraid I'd say something stupid. "He introduced them."

"Wow," Liam said with a chuckle. "That's a nice perk."

My eyes narrowed. "What the—"

"What do you think about starting the death matches?" Hades covered up my outburst with an entirely different question, masking my anger by taking the conversation in a new direction.

Liam turned to him and didn't seem to notice my fury. "Let's do it."

Now, I was mad again—for a whole new reason.

Liam's fingers rested on the rim of his glass, and he gave it a gentle swirl. "I've thought about it a lot, and I'm never going to make as much money unless I go back to that level. And regular matches are boring. My adrenaline doesn't rise at all. There's not that rush, not like when my life is on the line and I take someone else's."

I'd killed people because I had to, not because I wanted to. When he said it like that, he sounded like a psychopath, like Maddox or the Skull King. If Annabella heard him say that, would she be with him right now?

Hades didn't blink an eye over it. "Great. What if we set up the first match two weeks from now? Will you be ready?"

Liam held his gaze for a long time as he considered it. His other hand rested on the table, and he was wearing his wedding ring. "Yeah. Let's do it."

What?

"We'll make the arrangements," Hades said. "But we need to talk about money now. We need a strategic plan when this kind of cash starts rolling in." He glanced at me to make sure I would keep my mouth shut about the whole thing.

I did...but it was the hardest thing I've ever had to do.

Did he intend to do this behind Annabella's back? Keep it a fucking secret?

Shouldn't I tell her?

But I couldn't...not if I wanted to keep my neck and my relationship with Hades.

Hades pulled out his phone when it vibrated. He glanced at the screen, and his eyebrows immediately furrowed like the call was important. "It's my wife. I have to take this." He slid out of the booth and answered. "Baby, everything alright?"

I knew it was her because no other call would make him leave a meeting like that.

Now, it was just Liam and me.

He turned his gaze to me, holding his third drink. "So, how long have you been seeing her?"

I didn't want to talk about my personal life, but I had nothing else to talk about. Business had been handled. "A week."

He nodded. "Nice. Can't do much better, right?"

Annabella was better. "Happily married?" I asked, slightly sarcastic.

"Yeah." The mention of Annabella changed his attitude instantly, making him softer. "It's been great. We were apart for a long time, and it feels right now that she's back. Things aren't perfect, but…at least she's mine again."

"Why aren't they perfect?"

He stared into his glass for a long time, and the only reason he answered was probably because it was empty. "She was hung up on her ex for a while… That's been rough."

I was shocked she'd told him that. "Then why do you want to be with her if she's into someone else?"

He leaned forward, his elbows on the table. "I love her. And I'm the one who fucked everything up. It serves me right…"

If he spoke this way about her, then why the hell was he going back to death fighting? I knew I should keep my mouth shut, but I couldn't. I would always care about her, and if she rejected me because she was committed to their marriage, then she deserved to have him just as committed. So, I did something really stupid…something that would bite me in the ass in a few minutes. "If you love her, you shouldn't do this, Liam."

He raised his head and looked at me, clearly surprised I would say something that contradicted my own self-interest.

"I was with her at the match. She hates it when you fight. Imagine how she'll feel when she finds out about this."

"She doesn't have to know."

I was about to lose my shit. "So, your plan is to lie to her?"

"I'll tell her not to come to my matches. I know she hates it anyway."

"So, you could die at any moment, and your wife has no idea?" I asked incredulously. "You realize how stupid that is?"

He must have been pretty buzzed because he didn't scream at me. He just stared at me, like he didn't know what to say.

"You would do that to her? After everything you did to get her back? Why would you gamble the most important thing in your life for this?"

He sighed. "I just wish I could have both."

"Well, you can't," I snapped. "You need to either be honest with Annabella, or don't do it at all."

"I know she'll just say no—"

I slammed my hand down on the table. "Then you have your answer."

He turned back to me.

"Be the husband she deserves, Liam."

Seconds passed as if he was seriously considering what I said. He grabbed his glass so he could have the last few drops. When there wasn't a single splash left, he turned the glass over.

Hades came back to the table when his conversation was finished.

"Everything alright with Sofia?" I asked, my attention diverting to her well-being.

"She's fine," Hades answered. "She just wants me home."

"Is she okay?" I repeated.

"Just had a nightmare." He didn't elaborate because he didn't need to. I knew exactly what her nightmares were about. He turned back to Liam. "Everything is set up, so hit the gym. I'll handle everything—"

"I've changed my mind." Liam stared straight ahead, his eyes filled with regret for what he had to do. "I need to talk to my wife about all this…"

Hades snapped his neck so hard when he turned back to me. His eyes bored into mine, so satanic, he really looked like the devil. He fell back into the leather cushion of the booth, so furious that his tanned skin was turning red. He knew I was responsible—no doubt in his mind.

My decision was officially biting me in the ass.

"I should go." Liam threw his cash on the table. "I'll let you know what she says…" He disappeared from the table and walked out of the bar.

Hades didn't say goodbye because he was too busy staring at me with two bullets for eyes. "What the fuck did I say?" His hand tightened into a fist like he was about to punch a hole through the solid wood table. "I told you to stay out of it—"

"You told me not to tell her. I didn't."

Both of his hands moved to his scalp, and he fisted his hair before he dropped his arms. "Do you realize how much money you lost us?"

"I don't care." I didn't want to rock the boat with Hades when we'd only moved past our problems a few months ago, but I couldn't control my impulses. Annabella deserved a man who would do anything for her, who would be honest with her. If she wanted Liam, then I would just have to turn him into the man she wanted.

"She's. Not. Yours."

"I know, but—"

"No but," he snapped. "It's not our place to interfere in their marriage. If she finds out and wants to leave, then she can leave. It's not like Liam beats her or keeps her hostage."

"But if he dies in a match, do you have any idea what that will do to her?"

He sighed so loud, it was a quiet scream. "I don't give a shit what it will do to her. She means nothing to me—as she should mean nothing to you."

"We're friends, and friends look out for one another."

"You aren't looking out for her. You're manipulating her husband like a puppet."

I didn't have an argument that he would understand. What I did was stupid and illogical, but I didn't care. "Maybe she'll agree when he talks to her."

He shook his head slightly. "Come on, Damien. We both know that's not going to happen."

"Then we'll find another client. We'll make money some other way—"

"He's the best fighter in this fucking city." He slammed his forefinger into the wood.

"And we'll still represent him for the regular fights—"

"No one gives a shit about those fights. And don't you want

Liam to be dead? Think about it. With him out of the way, you could have another fling, or whatever the fuck you had. All your problems are solved."

I'd be lying if I said the thought hadn't crossed my mind. "But it would hurt her…and I don't want her to get hurt."

When Hades officially gave up, he leaned back into the booth and stared across the room. His drink was untouched because a smooth glass of scotch couldn't wash away his rage. "I don't know what to do with you…"

"We still have him as a client, and he's still fighting. So, nothing has changed."

"And if your business isn't growing, then it's slowing. Those are your words, Damien."

"Just let it go." The damage was done, so it was time to move on.

"You want me to let it go?" He pointed his finger into his chest. "No, asshole. You're the one who needs to just let it go."

9

ANNABELLA

Weeks passed after my conversation with Damien, and I didn't hear from him. I was so angry with him for what he did, but after we talked, my rage evaporated like a pot of boiling water. I blew off all my steam...and then let it go. Knowing I did mean something to him made me feel better...but also worse.

But now that door was closed forever, and it was time to move on.

So, that was what I did.

Next time I saw him, I would be calm about it, practically indifferent. I would try to look at him as just a friend...not the sexy hunk who used to be in my bed.

After I finished work, I drove home. When I woke up that morning, Liam was still in bed because he was out late the night before. He said he had business to take care of, and since I was giving him a clean slate, I believed what he said.

I left my coat by the door, relieved to be in the warm house after feeling the cold weather against my skin. My boots were pulled off, and I left my purse and keys on the table in the walkway.

Liam was in the kitchen, the sound of him moving pots and pans on the stove reaching the entry. "Baby?"

One of the things I loved about Liam was his work ethic. Sometimes he cooked dinner, sometimes he did the dishes, and sometimes he did the laundry. I never had to ask him. He didn't expect me to do it because I was the woman in the relationship. It had always been that way, even when we were married the first time. "What are you making?" I turned the corner and saw him scoop the pasta onto two plates. "Ooh...chicken parmesan."

"Hungry?"

"You know I'm always hungry."

He set the pot back on the stove then kissed me, his arm resting across the deep curve in my back as he pulled me in. "One of the things I love about you." He kissed my forehead before he pulled away. He carried the plates to the main dining table, where he almost never sat.

I sat across from him and placed the cloth napkin in my lap. "Looks good."

He was already eating, cutting into his breaded chicken and placing a large bite in his mouth. He was in one of his gray t-shirts, his loungewear. He leaned over the plate and continued to demolish his food. "How was your day?"

"Good. Same as always. Yours?"

"I worked out and did some laundry."

"What time did you get home last night?"

"Two, I think." He wiped his mouth with a napkin and kept eating.

"And how was that?" I tried not to pry, but I was curious why he needed to go out so late.

"I met Damien and Hades at a bar to talk about business."

The mention of his name made my heart race a little, but I forced my pulse to calm down. "Why did you need to meet so late?"

"Because we have a business idea, and they wanted to discuss it right away."

"Oh?" Now I was attached to Damien in many ways, and I would probably continue to see him for the foreseeable future.

"You'll never guess who Damien is seeing."

The sentence made me go rigid, and I couldn't hide it at all. I gripped my fork and stopped eating, suddenly sick.

"I don't know her last name, but her name is Charlotte. She's the biggest model for Barsetti Lingerie. I've seen her on billboards and in shop windows for a few years now. I've never seen Damien with a woman before, and I was starting to wonder if he was gay."

He was definitely not gay. "And they are serious?"

"No idea. But she was all over him like he was god's gift to women or something." He chuckled then kept eating.

Of course, she was...because he was god's gift to women. I didn't want to hear about Damien's personal life anymore, so I changed the subject. "What was the business they had in mind?"

It must have been serious because he stopped eating. He placed his silverware on the plate, covered in marinara sauce. "They suggested I go back to death fighting."

My heart spiraled down to my feet—for two reasons. "They encouraged you to do that?"

He nodded.

Would Damien do that to me? He told me I should ask Liam to quit fighting altogether, and then he turned around and told my husband to do something that could claim his life. "Both of them?" I just couldn't believe it. Maybe Hades would do that because it was just business, but would Damien stab me in the back like that?

"Yeah."

If Damien were sitting there with a model dragging her tongue across his neck, then he must be on board with it. That hurt in a way I couldn't explain. We'd agreed to be friends, but would friends do that to each other? "And you said no, right?"

He stared at me for a long time, his eyes shifting back and forth as he looked into mine. "I said I had to ask you first."

Dinner was forgotten, and my rage kicked in. "You already know what my answer is going to be, Liam. Why even bother?"

He sighed quietly. "Baby—"

"Don't fucking *baby* me," I hissed. "No. My answer will

always be no. Why would you even want to do something like that? Put me through something like that?"

He didn't match my emotion and stayed calm. "Baby, I only have a few years left, and this is what I'm passionate about—"

"Killing people?" I asked incredulously.

"It's not about killing people—"

"When you asked me to be yours again, you said you would do anything for me. When you asked me to marry you, you said you would be the best husband you could be, that you wouldn't fuck this up again. So why—"

"I meant that—"

"Shut your fucking mouth. I'm talking."

His eyes filled with anger, but he didn't talk back.

"Why would you risk our happiness for that? You wanted me back for so long, so why don't you spend your time with me? We could travel, we could join a bowling league, whatever the hell you want. What is with this impulsive need to fight? You threatened to go back to death fighting if I didn't take you back. Now you have me, and yet, you want to go back anyway."

He stared at me in silence. "Can I talk? Or do you want me to continue to shut my mouth?" he asked sarcastically.

"If you're going to be an asshole, then yes, keep your goddamn mouth shut." I got to my feet and slammed my plate down onto the floor, where it shattered into a million little pieces. I marched to the front door, put my boots back on, and then grabbed my purse.

"Anna." Liam came down the hallway when he realized I wasn't storming off to my bedroom. "Where the fuck do you think you're going?"

"Out." I flung the front door open.

He grabbed me by the wrist, twisted it, and then pushed me back against the wall.

I was caught off guard by the rough way he handled me, treating me like an opponent in the ring. I stared at him in shock. He'd grabbed me before, in sexual ways in the bedroom, possessively. But that wasn't how he grabbed me now.

He seemed to understand he'd crossed a line because he pulled his hand away and stepped back.

I was so livid that I slapped him across the face. It wasn't the way I hit Damien, violent and passionate. It was just full of rage, full of disappointment. My palm stung with the hit because I'd never hit him before.

He turned with the strike and clenched his jaw. He stepped back and rubbed his cheek, his eyes diverted because he couldn't look at me. He was too enraged to say a word, to try to stop me from leaving. He turned and walked away, like being close to me was dangerous for both of us. He walked into the bedroom and slammed the door so hard, the door cracked off the hinges.

I walked out and did the same—but the door didn't break.

10

DAMIEN

CHARLOTTE WAS ASLEEP BESIDE ME, THE SHEETS WRAPPED around her naked body. She was stuck to me like glue, calling me all the time because she claimed she needed my body on top of hers. I was lonely, so I never said no. If it wasn't her, it would just be someone else, so what difference did it make?

Hades called me. The phone vibrated on the nightstand.

I grabbed it and headed into the hallway so I wouldn't wake my guest. "What happened?"

"Security at the Tuscan Rose contacted Sofia."

"Okay..."

"Anna checked in thirty minutes ago. Paid for a room."

I stilled at his words and stared at the windows that lined the hallway. It was dark outside, and since I was on the top floor, I didn't get any glare from the streetlights outside.

"Since you enjoy sticking your nose in her business, I thought you should know."

Liam must have asked her if he could return to death fighting. And she gave her answer…loud and clear. "Thanks…"

"Are you gonna go down there?"

That was my first impulse. Grab my coat and leave. But being in a hotel room with her alone… Nothing good could come from that. "I don't know…"

"I can take Sofia instead."

They were good friends, but the idea of someone else comforting her didn't feel right. I wanted to be there for her, to be the friend I said I would be. "I'll go."

There was a really long pause. "Are you sure?"

"Yes."

"Damien—"

"Nothing is gonna happen." I wouldn't do anything stupid again.

Hades let it go. "Alright. Good luck."

11

ANNABELLA

I ordered room service and ate it in bed.

Liam didn't try to call me. He probably knew I wouldn't answer if he did. It was best if we both cooled off and took some time apart. When I came to the Tuscan Rose, I didn't know where else to go. I didn't have a friend I could call to crash on their couch. Sofia came into my mind, but she was pregnant and happy with her husband. I didn't want to interrupt their night. So, I came to my second home, the place where I spent forty hours every week.

A knock sounded on the door.

I quickly turned off the TV and stilled. It must be the maid for turndown service because no one had any idea where I went. Liam was strong, not smart, so he wouldn't have figured it out. I quickly put on a robe because it would take too long to get back into my skirt and blouse, and I opened the door.

And came face-to-face with Damien.

I stared at him blankly because I thought I was dreaming for a moment. There was no way he was on the doorstep of my hotel room at ten in the evening. He must be a staff member who looked just like him.

But he wore the same jeans, same shirt, and the same leather jacket I'd seen him in before.

His eyes shifted back and forth as he looked at me, studying the surprise on my face. "Hades told me you checked in to the hotel."

So, it was him. "And how did he know that?"

"He knows everything that happens in this hotel."

I released my grip on the door and stepped back slightly. "That doesn't explain why you're here." My breath probably smelled like the burger and fries I'd just devoured, along with the ice cream sundae. There might even be fudge on my face, but there was no way to check now. I was always uneasy when I was around him, but even more so now that I was caught off guard, wearing a heavy hotel robe.

"I wanted to check on you."

My own husband didn't try to check on me. He hadn't called or texted. "Well, I'm fine…"

He stared at me like he didn't buy the lie. He invited himself inside and let the door shut behind him. He glanced around the room and slid his hands into his pockets. "You and Liam aren't getting along…"

"Something like that." I moved to the small table with two chairs near the window and took a seat. My clothes were on the floor, and my boots had been kicked across the room. I didn't have any makeup on either.

He sat in the other chair.

"He told me about the death fighting." I could barely look at Damien because I knew he was behind it. This fight had been caused by him…indirectly.

"I surmised."

I crossed my legs and stared at the other wall, uncomfortable that we were alone together with a bed just a few feet away. There was no reason to be scared because Damien would never try to do anything again, but my thoughts went into the gutter on their own. "I lost my temper and screamed at him a bit…"

"Understandable."

"I just don't understand him…" I propped my chin on my closed knuckles and kept my gaze away from him. "He wanted me back so much, yet I don't feel like enough for him. He says it's his passion in life and I'm the one holding him back, but he was the one who said he would go back to it if I didn't take him back…and now he's trying to do it anyway."

Damien was quiet for a long time. "Men want to provide for their families. They want respect, pride, credibility…something to make them look good in front of the people they care about. Hades doesn't work at the bank because he needs the money. He does it because he wants to do *something* to feel productive."

"But Hades isn't risking his life."

"I know," he said calmly. "But there are a lot of women who would like a man like Liam, a man so strong he'd kill a man with his bare hands. A man who's built like a brick house and earns millions with his strength. He probably just—"

"I loved him when he had nothing. I loved him when he was nothing. He doesn't have to prove anything to me. If he wants a stupid bimbo to be impressed with the size of his biceps, he shouldn't have married me."

"That's not what I'm saying, Annabella."

I closed my eyes when he said my full name. He was the only person who ever called me that, and he said it the exact same way every time.

"He's a man...and that's how he knows how to be a man. That's it."

"Well, he has to choose."

"He'll choose you. No doubt."

I opened my eyes again but wouldn't look at him. "I don't know... We both got so angry. I threw a plate on the floor and marched to the front door. He grabbed me and pushed me against a wall. I slapped him and walked out. He didn't exactly fight for me."

"He pushed you?" Now his tone was totally different, full of unmistakable threat.

"No. Not really. He just handled me in a way he's never done before. He grabbed my wrist and pinned me to the wall. It was different..." I could tell Liam regretted it the moment it happened. "After I slapped him, he walked into the bedroom. He took himself away from the situation because he knew he was too angry to stay."

Now Damien was quiet.

"I haven't heard from him…"

"I want you to tell me if he ever hurts you."

I finally had the courage to face him. I saw those green eyes that used to look into mine every day. They were more beautiful when he was provoked, when he had adrenaline and emotion in his veins. "He would never hurt me."

He stared at me with the same intensity.

"He just was upset…more upset than I've ever seen him. Fighting is so important to him… I don't get it." I turned my body to face Damien head on, my legs under the table. "And after everything we've been through, I don't know why he would do anything that might rip us apart. I told him I would give him everything, and I feel like he's not doing the same."

Damien leaned back in the chair and stared at me with his focused gaze. His hands rested on his thighs, and he slowly let the breath escape his lungs, his chest falling once his lungs were empty. That jacket looked nice on his shoulders, and the scruff along his jaw was thicker than it'd ever been. Did he stare at everyone like this? Or was it just me? "When we were in the bar, women were giving him the eye. Lots of them. He didn't look at them once."

I knew how attracted other women were to my husband. I knew they didn't care about his wedding ring. He could fuck them while wearing it, they cared that little. "You hate him. So why are you trying to help him?" Damien was furious when I took Liam back and had nothing but bad things to say about his character. But now he'd completely flipped.

He still hadn't blinked since I'd faced him. "Because you said you were committed to this relationship, that you were determined to make it work. I want this to work...because it's important to you. You deserve a man who deserves you. I want Liam to deserve you." He finally blinked, taking a deep breath as he did it.

I didn't know what to say. It was a sweet thing to say, a selfless thing to say. When Damien said he would try to be my friend, he clearly meant it. He wanted me to be happy...even if it wasn't with him. I didn't understand why he suggested death fighting to Liam in the first place if he meant that, but I let it go. The silence was too loud for me to ignore, but I let it linger.

He continued to stare at me, hold my gaze like he was unafraid of the intimacy between our eyes. He eventually sat forward, his elbows moving to the surface of the table. He watched me with his green eyes.

"So...you're dating a supermodel?"

He didn't hesitate at my question even though it was probably awkward to be put on the spot like that. "I wouldn't call it that...but yeah." Our conversation about Liam was over, so he could walk out at any time, but he continued to stay.

I'd felt a jolt of jealousy when Liam told me. "Liam said she was all over you at the bar."

He didn't respond.

"We're friends, right?" I whispered, surprised he didn't give me a single detail.

"I don't divulge details about the women I'm seeing."

Liam made it sound like she was obsessed with Damien, like she couldn't keep her hands off him for a second. She worshiped him, marked his body with her lips so everyone would know she was his. I'd be doing the same thing if he were still mine…so how could I blame her? "Really? Not even to Hades?"

He shook his head.

"You're best friends."

"If it's at a whorehouse or something, we'll talk about it. But if it's a woman one of us is actually seeing, we don't swap details. Plus, she's kinda famous, and I'm not gonna share intimate details that she probably wants to remain private."

I hadn't expected him to say that, and that made me like him so much more. "So, you've never told Hades anything about me?"

He shook his head. "I mean, I said the sex was good, but that was it."

"And he doesn't tell you anything about Sofia?"

He gave a quiet laugh. "No. He doesn't want another guy thinking about his wife naked."

"That's sweet."

"We're assholes on the streets, but not in the bedroom." His hands came together, and he rubbed one of his knuckles, like it was sore from punching something earlier in the day.

I stared at his hands, remembering the way they felt on my body. "You don't have to stay here with me. I'm not going home until after work tomorrow, so it's not like I'm doing anything stupid."

"I don't mind sticking around. It's not like I have plans."

"Not even with the model?"

His eyes hesitated for a moment. "I call her Charlotte. And no..." He rose from his seat and walked to the minibar. He opened up a bottle of scotch and poured it into a coffee mug before he returned to the chair. "I'll tell Hades the bill is on him."

I chuckled. "I'm sure he'll love that."

He drank from his glass then pushed it toward me.

I grabbed it and brought it to my lips for a drink before I pushed it back to him.

"So, other than the situation with Liam, how's life?"

I shrugged. "Fine. My life isn't too interesting."

"So, then it's not fine. It should always be interesting."

"Well, I'm not a billionaire banker by day and a drug lord by night."

He chuckled. "Good point. I'm always living on the edge."

"How's your father?"

"Good." He turned serious at the question. "He moved in with me a few weeks ago."

"Really?" I asked, surprised he would have a roommate. "How's that?"

"It was such a pain in the ass to get him in there. He fought Catalina and me every step of the way."

"Catalina?"

"My sister."

"Ooh…pretty name."

"It's a pretty name for an unpretty girl."

I rolled my eyes because I knew he was teasing. "Why was he so resistant?"

"Because he doesn't want to be a burden. He refuses to accept his old age and lives in the past…like he's still ripe in his youth. He just has a lot of pride. When I was young, my father used to be strong and authoritative. He took care of everything for the family, worked hard, and stayed in shape. It's just hard for him to accept his brittle bones, his atrophied muscles, and his aged brain cells."

"That's sweet of you to offer."

"It was the only solution to keep him safe. He hardly ever leaves the house, so he'll be untouchable in there. As long as he's alive, he'll always be a liability for me."

Because Damien continued to live a life of crime. "What about your sister? Isn't she a liability?"

"Yes. But she would never let me protect her. She's far too independent. I couldn't talk sense to her if I had a gun pointed to her head. She and I don't spend a lot of time together, so I think most people don't know I even have a sister, which is good."

"Does Hades know?"

"Yeah, but he's my partner."

"Is it hard running things without him?" When we were together, we didn't have honest conversations like this. He kept his life a secret from me, and I didn't share details about mine either. But now that we were friends, we could say whatever we wanted.

He took a drink. "It was a lot easier having him around because it was two sets of hands rather than one. But I can manage by myself. I miss the company sometimes, but I see him every day at the bank so it's fine."

"You ever talk to him about the other business?"

"No. He wants no part of it. The Skull King came to my office the other day to demand his payment, which crossed a line. I got him out of there, but Hades was definitely pissed. I promised it wouldn't happen again."

"Why would he come to your office?"

"Piss me off."

"Is it smart to piss someone off before asking for money?" I asked, genuinely confused by the protocol.

He turned quiet as his eyes filled with his thoughts. "No. And he'll pay for it later."

The threat was undeniable, and I could feel how much he meant his words. The air around him hummed with life, packed with rage that was audible without him uttering a sound. "Are you going to kill him?"

"Yes."

"Then why are you paying him?"

"Stalling until it's the right time."

I got more of an insight into his life, the kind of stuff he had to deal with. He moved his father into his home to keep him safe, and he made risky moves against his enemies. And his enemies didn't hesitate to show up unannounced at his place of business. It was dangerous…but it still wouldn't have changed my mind.

He finished his drink and pushed the empty cup away. Talking about the Skull King clearly made him angry because he changed the subject. "What did you order?"

I stared at him blankly.

He glanced at the plates scattered on the bed.

"Oh…" My cheeks filled with embarrassment. "Burger, fries, and a sundae."

"Nice." His smile returned.

"Don't judge me."

"I'm not," he said with a laugh. "I've seen you destroy a pizza."

"But I split that with you. With this, I demolished it all by myself."

"So?"

"So," I said. "I'll never have the figure of a model if I eat like that." I didn't realize how jealous I was of Charlotte until I'd brought her up three different times.

"A woman at any size can have the figure of a model. And you definitely do."

I rolled my eyes to be sarcastic, but his words did mean a lot to me. His lady friend was probably a double zero with perfect hair, perfect skin, perfect everything, but he still made me feel like I could somehow compare. "Thanks…"

His phone vibrated in his pocket, so he pulled it out and glanced at the screen. He quickly typed a message and returned it to his jeans.

I wanted to ask who it was, but I knew it wouldn't be appropriate.

As if nothing had happened, he changed the subject. "Want to watch a movie?"

"You don't have work or something?" Or a sex appointment with a model?

"No. Quiet night." He pushed out of the chair and moved to the couch that hugged the wall. He took a seat and grabbed the remote.

Still in my robe, I sat beside him, keeping several feet between us. This was the last thing I'd expected to do tonight. Liam and I had screamed at each other, and I stormed out. But now, I was in a good mood…a really good mood.

He turned on the TV. "My favorite movie is on."

"*Scarface*?" I asked. "Really?"

"What?" he asked, turning to me.

"It's just so on the nose."

He shrugged. "Hades and I have watched this movie so many times. It's so good."

"I've never seen it."

"Fuck, we gotta watch it now." He turned off the lamp beside him and put his feet on the table.

I grabbed the blanket from the back of the couch and pulled it over my legs. The light from the TV cloaked us both, the flashing lights dancing across our faces. It reminded me of the nights we would sit in front of the fire together. We would talk about anything…or say nothing at all. It felt right, and I wished it felt wrong. I wished it were tense and awkward, that it would be so uncomfortable that he would leave. After our last conversation, I'd assumed it would take a long time for us to bounce back from that. Guess not.

"You've got to be kidding me." His frustrated voice shattered me from sleep.

My head was against the couch, and my eyes were closed. When they opened, I saw the credits playing over the screen and could hear the climactic music.

"You fell asleep?" he asked incredulously. "During the greatest motion picture of all time?"

I rubbed my fingers against my tired eyes and yawned. "No… just closed my eyes for a bit."

"Traitor." He got to his feet and cleared the dirty dishes off my bed.

"What are you doing?" I was repulsed by him cleaning my mess, the plate with a huge pile of ketchup where I dunked my fries, the lettuce that had been pulled off the burger because I didn't like any vegetables on my meat sandwich, and the clear bowl of melted ice cream and the leftover cherry I never ate.

"You're gonna sleep in this?" He set the plates on the tray then grabbed the cherry out of the bowl. He bit the fruit off the stem before tossing the remains onto the tray. He carried everything to the table and set it down.

I was humiliated that he'd not only witnessed my pigsty but cleaned it up too. At least he didn't wipe off the crumbs. I pulled off the blanket and got to my feet.

He walked up to me and crossed his arms over his chest, wide awake even though it was almost two in the morning. "Please tell me you watched at least half of it. What was the last thing you remember?"

"Uh…" I couldn't remember any of it at all, but I knew the most iconic scene in the movie from pop culture. "When he has the gun and shoots everyone…"

His eyes narrowed in disappointment. "Goddammit. You know what, we'll watch it again sometime. And I'll make sure you stay awake." His phone vibrated in his pocket, the noise audible, so he grabbed it, checked the screen, and quickly slid it back into his pocket.

I wondered if it was Charlotte, but I didn't dare ask.

"I'll let you get some sleep." He grabbed the remote off the couch and turned off the TV before he walked to the door.

I walked behind him, watching that strong back stretch the material of his jacket. He had wide shoulders that led to muscular arms, and while he wasn't bulky like Liam, he was lean and cut. I'd always liked Liam's strength, but once I tried something new, I realized I liked that better.

He turned around before he opened the door. "Call me if you need anything."

I wished I could. I wished I could call him for all my problems.

He didn't cross the threshold and disappear. His eyes were glued to my face, and he studied every reaction I made, the slight shift of my eyes, the way I subtly pressed my lips together when I was uneasy.

The atmosphere suddenly became heavy with intensity, and we no longer had the TV on for background noise. Now it was just quiet, quiet enough to hear each other breathe. How long would it be like this? Or would it always be like that?

"Can I hug you?" he asked quietly, his deep voice making my tummy tighten. "Or should I just go?"

Was I a terrible person because I wanted him to hold me? Because I wanted to feel those strong arms wrap around me and suffocate me? Because I wanted to smell his cologne? Because I wanted his clothes to smell like me in the hope Charlotte would notice? Yes, I was a terrible person.

When I didn't answer, he opened the door to leave.

Instinctively, my hand reached for his forearm, feeling the hardness because he was all muscle and bone. My fingers couldn't close around his arm because he dwarfed my size, even if he was on the lean side. I tugged him toward me.

He moved with the pull instantly, like he'd been waiting for me to do just that. His arms circled my shoulders, and he rested his chin on the top of my skull. His hard chest pressed against mine, his clothes smothering me with the sexy smell of his cologne and body soap. His grip tightened as he squeezed me, and he held me far too long for a simple hug.

My cheek rested against his chest, and I closed my eyes as my arms held him around the waist. Did it always feel this good? I'd had this every single day, so it was no wonder I lost my mind. The hardness of his chest was distinct, a special feeling I had never noticed on another man. His narrow waist was solid, my hands touching the strong muscles of his lower back. I could feel his chiseled abs because those were just as much of a concrete wall as his chest.

Seconds turned into minutes…and then a lifetime.

His hands eventually glided down to my waist, his fingers stroking my frame through the softness of the cotton. He gave me a gentle squeeze, feeling my body intimately, the way he used to. After a deep sigh, he pulled away. "Goodnight, baby."

I stilled at the nickname. He hadn't called me that in a long time, and it rolled off his tongue like it was just yesterday when the endearment last left his lips.

He opened the door and stepped into the hallway. He clearly had no idea what he'd just said, didn't even notice the error of his ways. It was so natural to him that nothing felt out of the ordinary.

"Goodnight, Damien…"

12

ANNABELLA

I wore the same outfit I'd worn yesterday because I didn't have a change of clothes. I couldn't stand wearing makeup to bed, so I washed my face and went to work rocking the natural look.

Sofia came into my office, and since she noticed every little detail, she knew I was in my clothes from yesterday. "Never went home?"

I shook my head. "I came downstairs and went straight to work."

"So, you and Liam haven't made up yet?"

He still hadn't texted me. If I didn't go home after work tonight like I usually did, he would probably start chasing me down. "No. He gave me some space."

She sat on the edge of my desk. "That's good. We all need time to clear our head sometimes." She didn't ask what our fight was about, but she was obviously curious. "Hades and I don't argue much anymore, but if he wanted to leave, I wouldn't stop him…even though I'd want to."

I couldn't picture them fighting. Hades was the most dedicated man I'd ever met. He looked at his wife like she was sent from heaven. Even if she'd done something, he probably wouldn't give a damn. "We were having dinner last night, and Liam asked if he could return to death fighting. The conversation turned sour, and I lost my temper…dishes broke…and I bailed."

"Death fighting?"

I guess Hades didn't talk about his work much. "Liam is a professional fighter. That's how he made his fortune. Death fighting is when two fighters fight to the death. There's a lot more money on the table, a lot more glory. He did it a couple of times until I asked him to stop. Now, he wants to go back…and I got upset."

"That's intense."

"Yeah…" I ran my fingers through my hair and sighed. "I just don't get it. He finally has me back, so why would he want to gamble his life like that?"

She shook her head. "You're asking the wrong person. When I first met Hades, I never understood his obsession with the underworld. Our hotel was overrun with the mob and gangsters, and it didn't make him blink an eye. He was already rich, so why continue a life full of death and risk? But…it's a man thing."

"But he stopped."

"Only because of our family. If it were just me, he would probably keep doing it."

"Then maybe we need some kids…"

She chuckled. "It'll definitely change him."

"Yeah." But I wasn't sure if I could have children. After my miscarriage, I was too afraid to do further fertility tests.

"Liam agreed, right?"

"No…not technically." The conversation never got that far. "But my answer is final, and he won't talk me out of it. It's hard enough for me to watch him fight normally. Adding his life on the line…I can't live like that, like every day is his last."

She nodded. "I'm sure it'll be fine. He loves you, so he'll do as you ask."

"Yeah…" Sometimes I wondered if he enjoyed his single life more than he let on. Because he could do whatever he wanted, stay out as late as he wanted. Now, he was used to that but being forced into the confines of marriage. He forgot there were two of us now, not just one. He was probably used to the stupid bimbos who agreed with whatever he said, who were turned on by the scars and old broken bones. That wasn't me. I wanted him healthy, even if that meant we were living in my old, shitty apartment. I could be just as vicious as him in the ring—just with my words.

Sofia slid off the desk. "Let me know how it goes."

"I will."

She walked out of my office, her hand on her stomach.

She didn't ask about Damien, so I assumed she had no idea he spent most of the evening in my hotel room. We had deep conversations, watched a movie, and then hugged on the doorstep like it was the last time we would see each other. I was glad he came over and cheered me up, but his visit also bothered me. Our relationship was easy, natural. Why couldn't Liam and I be that way? Why was it so hard for us to be what we used to be?

When I came home and hung up my coat, the house was dead quiet. There was no sound of Liam making dinner in the kitchen. His heavy footsteps weren't loud against the hardwood floor as he walked around.

It didn't seem like he was home.

I slipped off my boots and set my purse on the entry table before I stepped farther into the house. I stopped at the doorway that led to the kitchen and dining room. The kitchen island was empty, and there were no pans on the stove. Most of the lights were off, and it was getting dark because the sun was almost gone. When I turned to the dining table, I saw him sitting there, like a monster in the dark, rigid and quiet. He didn't look at me, his head slightly down as he slouched in the chair.

I stared at him for a few seconds before I flicked on the lights.

He didn't move.

I slowly walked toward him, seeing the dead look in his eyes. His hands were together in his lap, and his large mass was completely relaxed. I stopped at the head of the table and stared at him.

He finally lifted his gaze and looked at me. "Sit." He didn't need to raise his voice to issue a command. There was a silent authority to his presence, innate leadership in his voice.

The only reason I obeyed was because this conversation was necessary. I sat in the chair across from him and crossed my arms over my chest. I'd had a day to cool off and I was much calmer than I was before, but sitting here where we'd screamed at each other reminded me why I was so mad in the first place.

He continued to stare at me. "Where were you last night?"

I cocked an eyebrow. "Not a strong way to start an apology."

"Why won't you answer the question?"

My anger deepened. "Where were you last night?"

"Here." His tone was clipped. "Alone."

I started to wonder if he knew something I didn't. "I stayed at the Tuscan Rose."

He must have wondered if I went somewhere else, because that answer made him calm a bit.

"Doubting my fidelity is not the best route to take, Liam. You're the cheater. Not me."

He inhaled a deep breath, and his eyes turned hostile.

"I could have cheated, and I didn't. And I've had many, many opportunities." Damien was in my hotel room last night, and we had the perfect chance to screw all night long. Instead, we talked and watched a movie. I loved Damien, but I resisted the urge to take off my clothes and bounce on his dick. Wasn't that hard, so I didn't know why Liam faltered in the first place.

The guilt flushed into his gaze, and his anger faded. "I'm sorry." His sincerity was obvious in his tone. "I know I fucked up. And I guess I'm afraid I'm gonna push you...and then you're gonna run off to him." He dropped his gaze. "Just the idea of you being with someone else kills me inside." His hand moved to his chest, right over his heart, and made a fist. "Even when we weren't married, it cut me to the bone." He dropped his hand. "I knew exactly how you felt when I betrayed you...and it fucking hurts."

Liam's speech went straight to my heart, made me remember why I loved him. "When I married you, I promised to love you, to be committed to you, until death parts us. I'm in this for the long haul. Sometimes I think you don't feel the same way..."

"Of course, I do," he whispered.

"Then why would you try to go back to death fighting?"

"My desire to fight has nothing to do with my love for you."

"But it hurts me...and if you love me, you shouldn't want to hurt me."

"I don't *want* to, Anna. I just...want both."

"Not gonna happen. You have to choose."

He shook his head slightly. "You know I'll always choose you. I just wish you would—"

"No." I held my ground. "There's nothing you could ever say to change my mind. I will never allow my husband to risk his life for money. You either accept my decision or walk away. Because this is a condition for this marriage."

He stared at me for a long time, clearly disappointed but not combative. "Alright."

I released the air in my lungs when I got the answer I wanted. "We should spend our time working on this marriage, Liam. It's still too delicate for you to make rash decisions like that."

"I know…"

I rested my case and turned quiet. I got what I wanted and finally found peace.

"You're the most important thing in my life, Anna. I'm sorry I made you doubt that. But my desire to fight is completely unrelated to my feelings for you. I just want you to know that…in case that wasn't clear."

I gave a slight nod.

"Because I love you…more than life itself." Emotion was in his eyes, his heart and soul shining through in complete transparency.

And it touched my heart, body, and soul. "I know. I love you too."

He took a deep breath at my words. "I'm sorry about…what happened." He couldn't look me in the eye, as if he was too ashamed to meet my gaze. "It won't happen again."

"I know." Perhaps I forgave him too quickly, but it was hard to stay angry when he seemed so apologetic.

"I guess I'm so afraid to lose you again that...I can't think clearly."

I could see the way Liam loved me, even if his desire to return to the ring contradicted it. I could feel it when he looked at me, see it when I looked into his eyes. Our old relationship used to be so passionate and deep, and those memories still influenced us now...even though things were totally different.

"It was wrong for me to accuse you of anything...and I'm sorry for that too."

"I understand."

"I guess I'm just jealous. I have you back, but I still feel like I'm sharing you with this other guy. Not physically, but emotionally. I know it's all my fault because that never would have happened if I hadn't...fucked up my life. The only reason you're mine is because he didn't love you, and I'm afraid he'll realize his mistake, realize what he lost, and he'll change his mind...and I'll lose you again."

"You don't have to worry about that, Liam." Damien's feelings were clear, and we'd moved on from our past. Now, we were friends, and that's all we would ever be. "Even if that did happen, I wouldn't leave you for him."

He lifted his gaze to look at me. "Why?"

"Because I made a promise to you...and I keep my promises."

13

DAMIEN

Hades knocked on my open door. "Coming tonight?"

I stood at my desk and read the portfolio my assistant had placed in front of me. "Wouldn't miss it." I closed it and tossed it aside.

"Bringing your lady friend?"

"No." Charlotte had texted me a few times when I was with Annabella, and I didn't lie about my whereabouts. I told her I was comforting a friend, but I never said that friend was a woman…or someone I'd already slept with. I didn't feel like I needed to explain anything to her, even if she was sleeping in my bed and woke up to discover my absence. She seemed to grow suspicious about the incident, but her response wasn't to question me. Instead, she was more affectionate with me, slipping into my bed every night so I wouldn't have time to be with someone else. She was digging her claws into me deep so I couldn't get away.

"Because you can bring her if you want. You've been seeing her awhile."

"I'm not *seeing* her."

"Whatever," he said. "Offer is on the table."

"Thanks." When he didn't walk away, I lifted my gaze to meet his again. "Yeah?"

"What happened with Anna the other night?"

I never told him, and when he didn't ask, I assumed he forgot. Turned out, he was waiting for me to make the first move. He was probably pushing Charlotte so I would forget about Annabella for good. "We watched *Scarface*."

He cocked an eyebrow. "You watched *our* favorite movie with someone else?"

"It was on TV, so I just left it on. Don't get jealous."

"I'm not jealous," he said defensively. "Just surprised you'd watch that with her."

"Well, she slept through half of it, so she didn't watch much." I'd teased her about it, but in reality, I knew exactly when she fell asleep…and had decided to watch her instead of the film. "And then I left."

"That's it?" he asked, not easily convinced.

"You think I went over there and fucked her, then took off?" I asked incredulously. "We're just friends now. If you and Sofia had a fight and you were an ass to her, I'd do the same thing with her. I watched like twenty movies with her when I was bedridden."

His suspicion disappeared. "Alright. Anna will be there too."

Did that mean I'd have to see Liam's stupid fucking face?

He answered my question. "I don't think he's coming."

"Good."

"So, what happened between Liam and Anna? Did you successfully sabotage our business plan?" His voice dripped with annoyance.

I was glad Liam took my advice and asked her, because even though she was pissed at him, it would have been a million times worse if he'd done it behind her back. That would hurt her so much more. Liam didn't handle greed well, and when he had an opportunity to be the biggest and baddest fighter in the game, he lost sight of the prize he already had. His wife. I knew he loved her... but I had to steer him in the right direction. When I saw the way he ignored every woman in the room at the bar, even though there was no way for Annabella to know about it, I knew he wasn't the jerk I thought he was. "She was upset Liam wanted to return to death fighting. But I'm sure they worked it out."

"And we lost a great revenue stream," he said bitterly. "Good job."

I grew frustrated with his resentment. "Asshole, Anna is friends with Sofia. She works for your company. She's important to your best friend. Instead of seeing her as some insignificant victim, you should see her for what she is—a friend. You should be loyal to her too."

His anger flared. "I'm loyal to very few people, Damien. You know that better than anyone. I didn't ask for this woman to be in my life. The only reason she's here is because you asked Sofia to give her a job—"

"Sofia offered. I never asked. And what does it matter? She's in our lives now. Who cares how she got there?"

He sighed and turned away slightly. "Liam was my client long before she was our friend. I'm not turning my back on our mutual self-interest just because you got involved with his wife. You need to be impartial too, because the details of their relationship are none of our business. To top it off, Liam has absolutely no idea of your relationship, and he would feel much differently about Anna spending time with you if he knew. You're lucky I keep my mouth shut." He turned to walk out. "Just keep that in mind."

I PULLED THROUGH THE PRIVATE GATE OF HIS PROPERTY AND parked. Just when I shut off the engine, my phone rang.

It was Charlotte.

I sighed when I spotted her name on the screen. Sleeping with the sexiest model in the country, and arguably the world, wasn't something to complain about. She wore her heart on her sleeve and wanted me fiercely, so it was a great compliment, but it was also exhausting. I should just ignore her, but then she'd probably text me all night. I answered. "Hey, Char."

"Babe, what are you doing tonight?" She had a deep and seductive voice, like she could be a voice actor if she didn't want to wear a thong on a runway for a living. She was possessive right from the get-go.

"I just pulled up to Hades's place. He's having a birthday party for his son."

"Oh, that's cute." She went quiet, as if she wanted me to extend her an invite. "Need company?"

"No. It's just a few people."

"Oh…" Her disappointment was loud. "I'd really like to spend time with your friends."

I knew Anna was a bit uncomfortable about Charlotte, based on the kind of questions she'd asked me. I didn't want the two women in the same room together if I could help it…just the way I didn't want to see Liam kiss her in front of me. "Char, this isn't a relationship. I'm sorry if I gave you the wrong impression—"

"I know what it is, Damien. You've made yourself clear. But I don't accept that. I want more…and I'm going to get it."

Her ambition was pretty hot. The sexiest model in Barsetti Lingerie was determined to have me. "Char—"

"You're going to repeat yourself, and I'm going to do the same. So, let's not." She was used to getting what she wanted, judging by the confidence in her voice. A man had never turned her down—and I wouldn't be the first. "Text me when you get home. I'm coming over." She hung up without waiting for me to agree.

I shoved the phone into my pocket and stared out the windshield for a moment. I would have ditched her weeks ago if she didn't impress me. After Annabella, I was in a dark place, and I just wanted someone to share my long nights. It didn't matter if it was the same person over and over. It was better than being alone, imagining her sleeping next to that jackass.

I headed inside and greeted Helena in the entryway before I

approached the dining room. Hades had a big place, but he hardly used the other living spaces besides his bedroom. But tonight, he occupied the main dining room, where his mother-in-law joined them.

The first person I saw was Annabella.

She sat at the table and held Andrew under his arms so he could stand on her thighs. She supported him and smiled down at him, her eyes so affectionate, it seemed like they might burst. "Andrew, you're so cute." When she helped him walk up and down her legs, she made him laugh. "You like that, huh?" She continued to play with him.

I stared from the entryway, transfixed by that gorgeous smile. Whenever she was happy, her joy reached every corner of the room, erasing the shadows. Her long hair was pulled over one shoulder, large curls everywhere. She wore a long-sleeved pink sweater, her eyelashes thick and her cheeks rosy. I was bedding the most desirable woman in the country, but she never made me halt like this.

I felt a pair of eyes on me, and I shifted my gaze to Hades.

He was staring at me like he really was the god of the underworld.

I brushed it off and announced my presence. "Happy Birthday."

Sofia was the first one to jump to her feet. She held her large stomach as she waddled to me, having that same pregnant glow as she did with Andrew. She turned her stomach so she could hug me. "I'm so glad you're here."

I kissed her on the cheek. "Me too." I'd thought Sofia was sexy when I first met her, but our friendship turned into something deeper, as if she was another sister to me. But it was deeper than what I had with Catalina because we chose to be close. We didn't have to be. "Thank you for including me."

She patted me on the shoulder. "Wouldn't be the same without you."

Maria came next, who looked very similar to her daughter. "It's been so long since I last saw you. How are you?" She hugged me and kissed me on the cheek.

"Great. What about you?"

"I have another grandchild on the way—so I'm really great." She rubbed my arm and walked away.

Annabella continued to hold Andrew, but she lifted her gaze to look at me, her eyes showing a level of bliss that didn't match anyone else's. She picked up Andrew as she got to her feet, carrying him as she walked to me.

I should look at my nephew, but all I could do was stare at her. Shining brighter than the sun, smiling like it was the happiest day of her life, giving off so much heat it felt like summer...she was hypnotizing. When I'd gone to her hotel, she was in a somber mood, so she wasn't so irresistible, but seeing her happy, that was my weakness.

She held Andrew out to me, oblivious to the hard way I stared at her. "He's such a big boy. Hold him."

When my hands touched his skin, I finally focused on the little person about to rest in my arms. Both of my arms circled him, and I held him upright, noting his density, how much he'd grown since the last time I saw him. I finally looked into his face, seeing a perfect blend of both his parents. "Happy Birthday, Andrew."

He smiled up and me and reached out to touch my nose.

I let him do whatever the hell he wanted.

Annabella smiled as she watched us both, like she thought the two of us were the cutest thing she'd ever seen. Then her eyes filled with a slight look of sadness as dark thoughts weighed on her mind. She grabbed his sock-covered foot and gave it a little squeeze.

No one else noticed, but I did. "It'll happen for you someday... I know it will."

She lifted her gaze, slightly surprised I could read her so well.

I held Andrew with one arm and circled her waist to hug her slightly, to give her comfort.

Her smile came back, and she gave a tiny nod. "How do you do that?"

I had no fucking clue. "I don't know..." My fingers brushed against the soft fabric of her sweater before I pulled my hand back, not wanting my touch to linger until it became inappropriate.

But I did know. All those nights together, touching, kissing, moving together wordlessly...I understood her emotions, could read her thoughts as they danced across her eyes. It wasn't just passion, but something deeper. I could feel her... it was the only way I could explain it.

Hades walked up to us, like he was purposely interrupting the moment. "You didn't bring a gift?" He took Andrew from my arms and held him with one arm, taking his son like he'd done it a million times.

I shut my eyes. "Fuck…"

"Watch the language, asshole," Hades countered.

Annabella chuckled at his hypocrisy before she walked away to talk to Sofia.

Hades bounced Andrew up and down a bit because he liked it, and whenever he glanced at his son, he looked like a proud father who thought his son was the most amazing kid in the world. But when his eyes turned back to me, he was the same cold man I'd always known. There were only two people who received different looks from him—his wife and his kid.

"I'll make it up to him."

"Better be good." He glanced at Annabella before he turned back to me, as if he was telling me to tread carefully. We'd known each other so long, we could have entire conversations without saying a word.

I lowered my voice. "She lost her baby, so it's just hard for her. Trying to make her feel better."

Hades dropped his suspicion. "You wanna eat?"

"That's the only reason why I'm here—besides this guy." I squeezed his foot the way Annabella just had.

Hades gave me a glare with his eyes, but a subtle smile was on his lips. "Whatever, asshole."

After we sang happy birthday, Andrew smashed his fists into the cake, wiping it all over his face and getting it on his father's clothes. He giggled then smacked his hand right onto Hades's nose, getting white frosting everywhere.

Sofia tried not to laugh, but it was impossible.

Annabella didn't care. "Wow, he got you good."

Hades stilled before he grabbed a napkin and wiped the mess off his face. "You're lucky you're so damn cute, Andrew."

Andrew grabbed more cake and smeared it across his father's face.

Of course, Hades did nothing…wrapped around his finger.

Sofia grabbed some cake and did the same, smearing it all over Hades. "Good job, Andrew."

Hades just took it, letting his family ruin his clothes and smearing it across his forehead and getting it stuck in his hair.

Annabella continued to laugh, sitting beside me with her legs crossed.

I made a really stupid decision and wiped my finger into the remaining frosting on my plate and wiped it down her cheek.

She turned to me, her eyes annoyed but also filled with laughter. "How dare you?" She grabbed a handful of cake and pushed it right into my cheek.

"I just did a little spot," I said with a laugh. I grabbed a napkin and wiped it away.

She grabbed another handful and wiped it across my lips.

I licked it away. "Well, I don't have a problem with that."

She chuckled as she looked at me, leaving the streak of white frosting on her cheek. She seemed to forget about it instantly.

My thumb moved to her cheek, and I gently wiped it away, my skin directly against hers. I could feel her softness, like I was stroking a fallen rose petal. I got all the frosting on my thumb, taking my time so I could draw the touch out as long as possible. Then I brought it close to me, about to lick it off, but I realized that would be incredibly inappropriate. I wiped it on my napkin instead.

Her smile faltered for a moment, as if she knew what I was really going to do before I changed my mind. Then she turned away and didn't look at me again.

"When is he gonna be here?" I walked beside Sofia down the stairs as we headed to the entryway.

"Just two more months. He'll be here, wiping frosting all over his father's face." She gripped the rail and held her stomach as she moved.

"I hope they gang up on him."

"Oh, they will," she said with a chuckle. "Me included."

We reached the entryway, where Annabella was still talking to Maria.

I'd hoped she'd be gone by now.

"How's Charlotte?" Sofia asked, even though she'd never met her.

I didn't want to talk about her, especially not in front of Annabella. Charlotte wasn't my girlfriend, even though I'd been seeing her for a while now. "Fine." That was all I gave her.

"Maybe the four of us should go to dinner sometime."

Now we were in earshot. "Uh...maybe." That wasn't going to happen.

Annabella hugged Maria goodbye before she turned to Sofia. "Thanks for inviting me. Your son is adorable."

"Thank you," Sofia said. "But I don't think Hades agrees right now."

Hades took Andrew away to give him a bath before putting him down for a nap. He'd destroyed his clothes with the frosting and got it everywhere, in his hair and all over his arms. I said goodbye to Maria. "See you later."

She kissed me goodbye. "When are you going to start a family, Damien?"

I hated that question, and it seemed like only older people asked me stuff like that. Maybe I should introduce her to my father. "After the mess Hades had to clean up, maybe never." I made a joke out of it instead of telling the truth—that I wasn't interested in a family.

She laughed and let the conversation drop.

Annabella said goodbye and walked out with me.

We stepped into the parking area surrounded by the gate,

and after Sofia waved goodbye, we were alone together. Winter was almost over, so some warmth was returning to the air. Her Bugatti was in one spot, my car on the opposite side of the area.

I should just wave goodbye and walk to my ride, but I didn't. I walked with her to her car like a gentleman...but I wasn't a gentleman. I was only doing it because of the way I felt about her, to be close to her for a few more seconds before we parted. We didn't see each other often, so I didn't know when our paths would cross again...even though I would be better off if they didn't at all.

She got her keys out of her purse and clicked the button so the doors would unlock. Then she turned to me, her gaze serious now that we were alone together. Our conversations were never casual and easy. They were always so complicated, so deep, that it was impossible just to say goodbye and walk off.

Why the fuck was it so hard?

She stared at me in silence, as if she wished she could come up with something good to say. We were both lighthearted just a second ago, making jokes with Sofia and Maria. But now it was like that had never happened. We were instantly transported back in time, back to when we spent the evening together in her hotel room.

"How'd it go with Liam?" I didn't want to talk about him, to acknowledge he existed, but the whole reason I went to her room that night was to check on her. It would be odd to pretend it never happened, to act like I didn't care when I did.

"He apologized...for everything."

That was all he was good for...fucking apologies.

"Said he wouldn't fight."

"Good." I wanted him to be what she deserved. I didn't understand why that was so hard for him. His wife was the most stunning woman on the planet. Why did he want to make his knuckles bloody when he could be home with her?

She gripped the strap of her bag, her other arm crossing over her chest. "Fighting will always be his passion, no matter how rich he is, but he understands why I don't want him to do it. I think the matter is settled."

It should have been settled a long time ago.

"So, you and Hades can move on to another candidate. There're a lot of other good fighters out there."

I'd moved on a long time ago. Hades was the one who hadn't...but I didn't tell her that. "Yeah." I moved past her and opened the door for her. It was hard to stand there when the wind subtly moved through her hair, when the cold air made her nipples harden under her sweater. I could still feel her little nipple in my mouth, remember every groove of each one that was permanently imprinted on my tongue.

She hesitated instead of getting inside the car.

I knew there was something else on her mind.

"What is it, Annabella?"

She dropped her gaze for a moment. "I was thinking about what you said...that it would happen for me someday. Did you mean that?"

She didn't talk about it much, but it was obvious that losing her child still haunted her. That it would always haunt her. And being around Andrew and a pregnant Sofia made her question her fertility, made her wonder if she was less of a woman. I couldn't give her concrete evidence, but she still wanted me to comfort her.

I assumed Liam never tried. He only thought about himself, how it affected him, even though she was the one who'd had life growing inside her. She knew the moment it was gone. "Of course."

She lifted her gaze. "I never went to a fertility specialist because I'm scared—"

"You will have children, baby." I wanted to chase away all those fears, hold her until all the pain was gone. "Miscarriages are common. It's not you. There's nothing you could have done." I hadn't known anything about pregnancy and childbirth until I'd researched all of it. And the only reason I did that was because she told me what had happened to her...so I cared. "Just because it happened once doesn't mean it'll happen again. And even if it does, you have other options. You will find a way." I wasn't her husband so I would never be the father of her children, but I was talking to her like I was. This wasn't my problem to solve. I wasn't the person who should comfort her. But I did it anyway.

She inhaled a breath of relief as if that was what she wanted to hear, that I had successfully consoled her. "You're right."

"Of course I am. I'm always right." I lightened the mood so she could drive away with a smile on her face.

And then she smiled...and that made me smile.

HE WAS HARD TO TRACK.

He never stayed in one place too long, never used the same number for long. That was why he was the best—because even his clients couldn't track him down. Charlotte was asleep in my bed, so I stepped outside onto the cold balcony, my naked chest unaffected by the icy breeze. I rested my arm on the stone wall and looked at the city, quiet ringing in my ear.

He picked up after a few rings. "Who the fuck is this?" Deep and low, his unmistakable voice came over the phone, packed with hostility and rage.

"You're hard to track down."

He was silent for a long time, as if he was trying to recognize my voice. "That's the way I like it. Now answer me."

"Damien."

He was quiet again, like that name meant nothing to him. "I don't do that anymore."

I refused his answer. "Things change."

"Not for me. Don't call me again."

"Bones."

He didn't hang up.

"You're the only one who can pull this off. And I have twenty duffel bags stuffed with cash with your name written on each one."

His answer was the same. "I don't do that anymore."

"Why the fuck not?"

"Don't call me again." He hung up.

I listened to the line go dead. "Fuck." I shoved the phone into my pocket and ran my hand through the back of my hair. Hiring the most skilled hit man in the world was my best option to get rid of Heath. It was quick and anonymous. The Skull Kings would suspect me but would never be able to prove it because Bones could have been hired by anyone. But my brilliant plan just went out the window.

I knew Conway Barsetti had a closer relationship to him based on what he'd said in passing, but I didn't know the nature of the connection. I assumed he used him for protection for his models, something of that nature. So I called him next, ignoring the late hour.

He answered after a couple rings. "Do you always call your clients at two in the morning?"

"Only the ones I like."

He sighed into the phone. "What is it, Damien? The government better be seizing my assets right now."

"You said you were a night owl. That you designed your best work after midnight."

"That was before I got married. Now I've got a kid and another one on the way...things change. And you're lucky you didn't wake up my wife when you called because she would have thrown my phone in the toilet."

"She sounds lovely..."

He chuckled. "She just likes her sleep. She doesn't get a lot of it as a full-time mother."

"Maybe you need to step up."

"I bring home the bacon. That's my job. Anyway, what the hell do you want?"

"I just got off the phone with Bones. Tried to hire him for a job, and he said he was out of the game."

Conway suddenly became stern. "Yeah, he retired a while ago."

"Well, I need him to do this for me. There's no one else who can take care of it."

He was quiet.

"I know you're close to him. Ask him on my behalf. If money is the issue, I can give him whatever he wants." I needed to get rid of the Skull King at all costs. Any amount of money was a small price to pay.

"Money isn't the problem. He's just out of the game."

"Conway, come on—"

"The answer is no." His response was firm, his tone suddenly turning cold despite our long history. "I'm sorry I can't help you." He hung up.

I let out a quiet growl before I shoved my phone into my pocket. I wasn't used to hearing the word no, not getting what I wanted. If only I could convince him to handle this, most of my problems would be solved.

I just needed to see Bones face-to-face...then I could convince him.

But how?

Charlotte must have heard my heated conversation, and she came outside in my t-shirt, her makeup a mess because of how sweaty we both got when we fucked. She came into my side and linked her arm through mine. Her face was tucked into my neck, and she pressed a subtle kiss against my warm skin. "What's wrong, Damien?"

I kept my eyes on the city. "Nothing."

She moved closer into me, placing her body between me and the stone wall. She ran her hand up my chest and sprinkled kisses along my jawline. "Then let's go to bed. I miss you..." Her hand moved to the back of my hair, and she forced my chin to tilt so she could kiss me. She was demanding of my attention, like she didn't get enough of it every night.

I almost caved until I remembered something. I was bedding the woman who worked with Conway every day. She could actually help me with this, could get me to change his mind. "I want you to do something for me."

"Anything." She kissed the corner of my mouth and fisted my hair, smelling of perfume and sweat mixed together.

"I want you to get Conway and his wife to have dinner with us."

"Why?" She pulled away and looked at me.

"I need him to do something for me...but he's being stubborn."

Both of her hands slipped into my hair, and she stared at my lips like she couldn't wait to kiss me again. "Consider it done."

14

ANNABELLA

Liam and I fell into our old routine. I'd come home from work, and he would have dinner on the table. He spent the day training and doing stuff around the house, so when I came home, he spent all his time with me. We'd watch a movie before bed, and then we would be together under the sheets, the sex good the way it used to be.

I refused to think about Damien when I was with my husband. I wanted to get over him and move on with my life. But when I was at work, he popped into my mind. When I saw Hades stop by Sofia's office, I thought about him. Whenever Liam wasn't around, I couldn't control myself.

I set my purse on the table and shed my coat when I heard Liam speaking.

"Alright." His deep voice traveled to me down the hallway. "See you then."

I turned the corner and joined him in the kitchen. "See who when?"

He pulled a pan out of the oven and set it on the kitchen island. It was baked chicken slathered in balsamic marinade. Noodles were in the pot on the stove. "I invited Hades and Damien to dinner, to make up for…" He pulled off his oven mitts and never finished the sentence. "So, we're going out tomorrow."

"Oh." I always felt awkward when Liam and Damien were in the same room together. It was obvious Damien despised him because he could barely hide it. I was surprised Liam hadn't noticed. I also felt guilty for continuing to keep Damien's identity a secret. If Liam knew Damien was the man I loved, he wouldn't continue their business relationship. He had the right to know who he was dealing with, but I also knew it would complicate everything…and might get Damien killed. "Just the three of you?"

"No. The wives too." He came around the kitchen island and kissed me, his hand gripping my lower back.

Instead of enjoying the kiss, I thought of Charlotte. Would Damien bring her?

He noticed the way I flinched. "Everything okay?"

"Yeah…I'm just surprised you want to have dinner with them."

"They're good guys. I've had my problems with Damien, but we moved on." He turned away and grabbed two plates so he could prepare dinner. "We had an entire business plan built around my return to the ring, and I just want to make up for that."

I'd only been around both Damien and Liam once—and we didn't speak. Damien stayed on the opposite side of the ballroom because he was just as uncomfortable. Now I had to sit with both of them, let Liam touch me in front of him, watch Charlotte stick her tongue down his throat... It was going to be terrible.

HADES AND SOFIA ARRIVED, AND WE EXCHANGED HUGS AND handshakes. We sat at a square table, and I was disappointed when Hades and Sofia chose the chairs directly beside us rather than across from us.

That meant Damien would sit there—right in my line of sight.

"Where's Damien?" Liam asked.

"Late," Hades answered. "Always late."

"We were late too," Sofia said. "So, he's just later."

Hades placed his arm around her chair. "Shh, baby."

She gave him a playful glare. "Did you just shh me?"

"What are you going to do about it?" he asked, enjoying the rise he got out of her.

"Oh, I'll show you what I'm gonna do...later." She grabbed the bottle of water in the middle of the table and poured herself a glass.

I could barely focus on their conversation because I was so tense. Would Damien bring Charlotte? He wouldn't, right? He would know how awkward that would make everything, so he would avoid it. And he said it wasn't serious.

Liam moved his hand to mine under the table. "Want some more wine, Anna?"

"Uh…" My eyes flicked to the entry, and I saw a gorgeous woman step inside. In a short cocktail dress, toned physique, and with beautiful long hair, she looked like model material. And then Damien walked in behind her. "Yes, I'll take some." I pushed the glass close to him because I would need every drop.

Once the host directed Damien to our table, he headed our way, in the lead.

Charlotte moved behind him, and she sped up in her heels so she could slide her hand into his, gripping his palm like reins.

I shouldn't care. I was married to Liam, so Damien's personal life shouldn't bother me. He was sleeping with this gorgeous woman, but I was sleeping with a gorgeous man, one who loved me. I forced myself to be indifferent, to let it go.

Damien reached the table and looked at everyone but me, as if he knew this was awkward. "Charlotte, this is Sofia."

"So nice to meet you." Charlotte came to her chair and shook her hand.

"You too," Sofia said politely.

Damien turned to me next, a slight look of dread in his eyes. "And this is Annabella…"

Charlotte moved to me next, ignoring the frown on my face as she smiled wide. She extended her hand. "Hello. I love your dress." She seemed to be trying hard to impress us because she thought it mattered to Damien. That meant she had no idea that Damien used to be mine, that I wanted him to be mine forever. If she knew, she wouldn't want to touch me.

"Thank you." I shook her hand and quickly pulled away.

She seemed to pick up on my dismay because her smile faltered. She turned away, suspicion written on her face. And because my luck was terrible, she sat in the chair directly across from me.

Now I had to stare at this stunning model all night.

God, this was going to suck.

Charlotte was all over him.

It almost seemed purposeful, as if she wanted me to know I had lost and she had won. But if she didn't know about me, then this was just who she was…a woman smitten with her man. Anytime she laughed, she pressed her hand into his chest to steady herself, and whenever Damien spoke, she stared at him with a gaze so focused, it was like she was listening to a lecture. She hung on every word, finding Damien to be the most amazing man to walk this earth.

It hurt to watch.

Damien didn't return the affection, keeping his still position as he focused on the conversation. He didn't look at me or try to talk to me. When she grabbed his hand on the table, he didn't squeeze her hand the way she squeezed his.

Liam had his arm around my chair, oblivious to the pain I was in.

"I'm going to use the restroom." She grabbed Damien's shirt and pulled him close. She kissed him on the mouth, a long kiss that was inappropriate for the situation. But she didn't care...because she wanted the world to know he was hers.

I couldn't keep a straight face because the sight of him kissing her made me feel like shit. I remembered those kisses, remembered grabbing him in the exact same way. When he was mine, I got lost just the way she did...falling so hard. I wanted him every second of every minute because no amount of time was ever enough. I dropped my gaze because the torture was too much, the flashback of memories painful.

I felt her look at me, felt her blue eyes pierce my face. So, I turned back to her.

The stare lasted just a few seconds before she walked away. But that look was purposeful, like she was looking for something specific.

Very specific.

At the end of the meal, Liam and Hades went to the restroom, and since Sofia had to pee all the time, she joined them. Charlotte tagged along too, leaving Damien and me alone at the table.

Somehow, this was worse.

The tab had been paid, and the receipt lay in the leather folder in front of us. Empty wine bottles were scattered across the table, and our glasses were empty.

Damien didn't look at me.

I didn't look at him.

Silence stretched, and the conversations at the other tables were suddenly loud because there was nothing else to focus on. I hadn't enjoyed my dinner because I felt sick the entire time. If it wouldn't be obvious that I had a problem with Charlotte, I would have asked Liam to take me home. I couldn't do that, so I sat there and suffered.

Damien finally turned his chin my way. "I didn't want to bring her—"

"You don't have to explain anything, Damien. It's fine. Really."

He continued to watch me. "I know she acts like we're serious, but we aren't—"

"It doesn't matter. She's very beautiful, and if you're happy… I'm happy for you." I had to force the words out, to take the high road with as much dignity as I could muster. It killed me to stare at a woman so beautiful, the kind of beauty I could never compete with. It killed me to see her cherish him just the way I used to. She didn't take him for granted, knew he was one hell of a catch. He pleased her every night, and she wouldn't let him go without a fight. It was like watching a little movie of our time together, because she loved him just the way I'd loved him. But she got to keep him…and I didn't.

"Annabella." His voice softened, packed with pain. "She said she would do a favor for me…if I brought her tonight."

"What kind of favor?" I asked.

"I need her to get close to someone. I'm trying to hire a hit man to take out the Skull King, but he said no. So now I'm trying to find another way to convince him. It's complicated..."

"I'm surprised she would make a demand like that." She should help him because she wanted to, not make it conditional. That was manipulative and selfish.

He shrugged. "She knows what she wants, and she's willing to do anything to get it."

I knew that feeling all too well. I would have done anything to keep Damien. Charlotte caught the same disease I had... and went insane.

"I just don't want you to get the wrong idea...because she doesn't mean anything to me."

I was married to Liam and I loved him, so he didn't have to say that to me. He didn't have to console me when he was free to do whatever he wanted. "Whether she does or doesn't, it's okay. Really, it's okay..." It wasn't okay, but I did my best to make it seem that way, to convince myself that was the truth...even though it was obviously a lie.

I sat at my vanity and pulled off my wedding ring. Then I unfastened my earrings and set the diamonds on the surface.

Liam undressed behind me, his reflection visible in the mirror. "Damien's a lucky bastard, huh?" Shirtless, he sat on the edge of the bed then slipped off his shoes. Tattoos were on his skin, but not thick enough to cover all the muscles of his body.

I inhaled a deep breath, irked by my own husband's admiration of her. "Yes, she's beautiful." She'd made Hades laugh a few times, and she was so gorgeous that she seemed like a hologram. Was I stupid for thinking Damien could ever feel the way I did? He was used to supermodels being hung up on him, and I was no supermodel.

He stilled and stared at me. "That's not what I meant."

I rolled my eyes. "Yes, it is. And that's fine…" I wasn't jealous of other women because I'd never hated my appearance. I'd always been comfortable in my own skin, confident in what I had to offer the world. But I was jealous of what she had.

"I think he's lucky because he has a woman who's all over him all the time." He stared at my reflection in the mirror. "I wish you were all over me like that…" His hand rested on his thighs as he looked at me, the top of his jeans open. "You used to be that way, and I miss it."

My eyes dropped to my earrings.

"I know I'm the reason you aren't that way anymore, but that doesn't make me miss it less."

15

DAMIEN

Patricia had the fire ready before I walked inside. The flames heated the bedroom, and I immediately made myself a scotch before I moved to the couch in front of the TV. The wine at dinner wasn't enough to make me feel like less of an asshole.

Charlotte slipped off her heels near my bed then unzipped the back of her dress. "I'm glad I got to meet your friends. They were nice."

They weren't my friends. Hades was the only one, but she already knew him.

In her strapless bra and panties, she walked toward me. With her hands on her hips, she stared at me.

When her gaze didn't disappear, I stopped looking into my drink so I could see her face.

Her expression was cold, as if she were angry about something. In the period of time I'd known her, she'd never gotten upset about anything. When I resisted her affection, she just tried harder. "She's still in love with you."

My expression remained stoic, but my heart raced in my chest. I didn't play dumb or deny her assumptions. But I felt like shit. Because if Charlotte noticed it...then it was really obvious how terrible Annabella felt.

"When did you stop seeing each other?"

I didn't answer her question. "I don't owe you an explanation. As I've said a million times..." I left my drink on the table and rose to my feet to regard her head on. "I'm not your man. You aren't my woman. This is just sex—that's fucking it."

Her eyes blinked in sadness, but she still held her angry expression. "You aren't over her either."

My arms rested by my sides and I considered denying the claim, but I didn't. Because I knew it was a lie...and I didn't want to start lying now. I still missed Annabella, still felt incomplete without her. Every time I caused her pain, I wanted to put a bullet in my head. I'd never cared about someone else more than myself before. It was a first.

She crossed her arms over her chest. "That's fine. I'll make you get over her."

Charlotte asked to have dinner with Conway and his wife, Sapphire, and she took me as her date. That was the trade she'd requested. If she took me out, then I had to do the same for her. I did it because it was necessary, but after seeing Annabella's reaction, I questioned whether it was worth it.

Too late now.

Conway was with his wife at the table, her stomach large just the way Sofia's was. They were engaged in conversation, his fingers moving through her hair as they whispered quietly together.

Charlotte arrived at the table first. "You guys are so cute." She leaned down and hugged Sapphire. "How's that baby?"

"Ornery," Sapphire joked. "Likes to kick a lot."

Charlotte moved to Conway next, and instead of hugging him, she shook his hand, probably because he was her boss. "Thanks for having dinner with me."

"Of course," Conway said. "I'm always here if you need anything."

When Charlotte stepped out of the way, Conway finally saw me. His eyes narrowed and he immediately sighed, disappointed that he'd been ambushed like this. "Should have known…" He rose to his feet and faced me head on. "Damien."

I extended my hand. "Would you rather me call at two in the morning?"

He gave me that same scowl. "I suppose not." He shook my hand before he stepped back.

"Nice to see you, Sapphire." I gave her shoulder a squeeze before I moved into the chair across from her husband.

Sapphire and Charlotte immediately engaged in conversation, talking about the baby on the way.

I grabbed the bottle of wine and filled my empty glass.

Conway was rigid in his seat, one hand resting on the table as his fingers drummed against the surface. His head was slightly tilted, and he examined me with a defensive expression, ready for whatever I threw his way.

"Come on, Conway." I broke the ice by addressing the subject we were both thinking about.

"Come on, what?" he asked coldly.

"I've done a lot for you. Solved a lot of problems."

"And I paid you handsomely for that." His fingers stopped drumming. "We're even, in my opinion."

"But we're friends, aren't we?"

He looked away for a second, clearly annoyed. "He said no, Damien. What do you expect me to do?"

"Just put me in a room with him. I can change his mind."

He released a sarcastic chuckle. "Trust me, you can't."

"You don't know what I'm capable of."

"But I know what he's capable of—and he'll never agree."

"How about you let me worry about that? Just tell me where he lives."

His eyes turned cold. "Never."

I didn't understand why Conway was so loyal to him. "Just

get me in a room with him. Let's meet for dinner or something—"

"It's not going to change anything."

"You never know."

He shook his head slightly. "There are a lot of other guys you can hire—"

"We both know he's the best. I don't want less than the best, not for this. There can't be any mistakes."

"Then why don't you do it yourself?" he asked, grabbing his glass and taking a drink.

"Too complicated." When I glanced at the girls, they were still absorbed in their conversation, talking about baby clothes and schools. "He has a special way of simplifying everything."

Conway shook his head again, his eyes looking defeated. "He's been out of the game awhile. He's probably rusty anyway."

I laughed because we both knew that was bullshit. "Conway, do this for me, and I'll owe you one, alright? That could really help you down the road, redeemable at your convenience."

He sighed loudly. "I don't need help. But I suspect you aren't going to let this go…"

"No."

He crossed his arms over his chest for a long time and stared at me. "Fine. I'll arrange a meeting."

"Thank you—"

"But he's going to say no. You're wasting your time, Damien. And he's gonna be in a bad mood because he has to meet you at all."

"So, you're going to tell him?"

He nodded. "I'm not gonna mislead him. He'll meet you because I asked him to. But there's nothing in this world that will convince him to say yes."

"Why are you so close?" They had nothing in common. Conway designed and sold lingerie, and Bones killed people for money. They didn't have the same interests…unless women counted.

Conway stared at me with his hard eyes but never answered. "I'll get you the meeting."

A FEW NIGHTS LATER, I SAT ALONE IN THE BAR.

It was half past two, and the bar stayed open just for me. A glass of scotch was in front of me, and Charlotte was waiting for me at home. She'd pissed me off, but then she dropped to her knees and sucked me off, so I let it go.

It was my second drink, and when I glanced at my watch and saw the time, I wondered if he was coming at all.

Then the front door opened.

It'd been years since I'd last seen Bones in the flesh. He was a large man covered in tattoos, the ink covering most of his fair skin. He had bright-colored eyes, but they were somehow demonic.

He looked the same.

He stopped in the doorway and stared at me, his gaze unforgiving and potently hostile. After a pause, he walked past the empty tables and approached me, wearing a gray t-shirt even though it was still cold outside.

His left hand had a tattooed wedding ring.

His presence was heavy, filling the air in the room with inherent danger. He didn't need to say a word to issue a threat. He didn't need to pull a gun to kill someone else. He had the spirit of an emperor, someone who ruled with an iron fist.

He left an empty stool between us when he sat down. He tapped his knuckles against the bar and spoke in a deep voice. "Scotch. On the rocks. Make it a double."

The bartender gave him what he wanted without speaking. When we both had drinks, he excused himself to the back room, knowing this conversation was private. The bar wasn't owned by either of us, but we ran it like it was.

Bones downed the whole thing in a single gulp before he wiped his lips with the back of his forearm. "No."

"Bones—"

"The answer is no, asshole." He pushed the empty glass away and stared me down, one arm resting on the granite surface. "It's not about the money. It's not about the connection. I'm out of the game, and I'm not coming back in for anything. You think getting Conway to stick his neck out for you impresses me? Bitch, nothing impresses me." He turned the glass over and slammed it down, so it made a distinctive thud.

It looked like Conway was right. "The Skull King took my father—"

"That's who you want me to kill?" he asked incredulously. "Even if I were in the game, I wouldn't take the job."

"Why?"

"I made a truce with them a few years ago. My hands are tied."

"Why did you agree to a truce?"

He stared at me coldly, like he wouldn't answer.

He was more vicious than I remembered, which was odd considering he'd been retired for years.

"You want something to get done?" he whispered. "Do it yourself."

"I would. But if I fail…he'll kill everyone I care about."

"That's exactly why I don't do this shit anymore." His thick arms stretched the sleeves of his t-shirt, his biceps and triceps huge.

I thought I could change his mind, but seeing him in person made me realize it wasn't possible. He wasn't the same person I used to know. "Alright. I'm disappointed…but I get it."

He still wore the same scowl.

"You were the best. You could fetch any price you wanted. Why did you get out of the game?"

He held up his left hand, where his tattooed wedding ring was noticeable. "I told you I got married." He lowered his hand again. "I have a son. And I'm gonna have another kid soon. I'm not going to risk my life killing people, when I only risk my life to protect my family." He rose from the stool. "You're paying for my drink since you've wasted my time." He turned to walk away.

"Why are you and Conway so loyal to each other?" The type of closeness reminded me of Hades and me, and we'd been friends for over a decade. We were business partners, worked together on a daily basis. But I didn't see the connection between them.

Bones stopped and remained still a long time, his powerful back stretching the fabric of his t-shirt. He considered the question at his leisure, and when he thought it was worth a response, he turned around. "His sister is my wife."

I couldn't hide my surprise. "You're married to a Barsetti?"

His eyes narrowed. "Yes."

"She must be a handful." I knew the Barsetti family pretty well. Crow and Cane were stubborn and difficult, and Conway was similar to his father in that regard. I could only imagine how Crow's daughter had turned out.

"She is." He turned around to walk out. "But that's exactly how I like her."

16

ANNABELLA

Sofia stepped into my office. "How are you doing?"

"Good. Weddings are being booked for the spring, and our calendar is almost completely blocked off..." I had my wedding planner on the desk, and newly engaged couples were calling left and right.

"Hades and I got married here, actually," she said. "But that's not what I meant. I was referring to the dinner the other night...didn't realize Damien was bringing his lady friend."

It was like a rusty knife to the stomach. I bled until the wound closed, but then it became infected...so it never really healed. "It was no big deal." I brushed it off and pretended not to care, because that was exactly how I should feel. I was married to Liam, and despite our problems, I should be thinking about him, not someone else. "I'm married...and he's seeing someone else. It's not like I didn't already know that."

Sofia watched me with suspicion, her arms crossed over her chest. "At least you have a good attitude about it."

"What did you think of her?"

She shrugged. "She was fine. She was nice, participated in the conversation, but she was a little possessive of Damien. It was like she knew exactly who you were or something, but I doubt Damien told her. I mean, Hades usually touches me in public, but he's not so over-the-top about it."

"Yeah…she was definitely marking her territory."

"Damien said it's just a fling, so I think she's trying to change his mind."

I didn't want to think about her anymore. Damien's personal life was none of my business, and I didn't want to spend another second thinking about that model groping him under the table. "Maybe." I turned back to the binder. "I'll let you know when I have the final schedule."

She ignored what I said. "Damien and Hades are stopping by to pick me up for lunch. You wanna join?"

Now I knew why she'd bombarded me with questions. She wanted to see if I could handle being in the same room as Damien after that god-awful dinner. "Depends. Will that leech be there?" She'd kissed his neck multiple times throughout dinner, especially during dessert.

She chuckled. "No."

I was hungry and didn't bring lunch. Also, it was a nice day because the weather was starting to clear up. "Sure. Why not?" We left the office and stepped into the hallway.

Damien and Hades walked side by side down the hallway, both wearing suits with shiny watches on their wrists. Hades was in black, and Damien was in dark blue. They were both beautiful men, with dark hair and tanned skin that appeared above their collared shirts. Tall, muscular, and with an innate darkness to them both, they affected the air around them wherever they went. They were engaged in conversation, not noticing us at the end of the hallway.

"He's married to Crow's daughter?" Hades asked. "That's pretty unbelievable."

"I don't understand why Conway kept it a secret," Damien replied. "He could have just told me."

"It's probably to protect his family," Hades said. "The country's best assassin mixed his blood with Barsetti blood? Someone could use that against them. Conway was being loyal by protecting his sister."

"I guess."

"If Bones said it was out of the question, what are you going to do?"

Damien never answered the question because his eyes settled on me, and it was as if nothing else mattered. He took me in without blinking, looking into my eyes as if he were searching for something only he could see. He continued walking until he was right in front of me, his hands in his pockets.

I assumed they were discussing the thing Damien had mentioned to me the other night, that Charlotte got him a meeting with someone in exchange for bringing her to dinner with us. I didn't get the feeling he was going to say anything, so I spoke. "Hey."

He responded. "Hey." It didn't seem like he'd expected to see me even though my office was just a few feet away. He probably assumed I declined the lunch invitation because I couldn't stand to be in the same room as him.

Hades wrapped his arms around Sofia and kissed her, oblivious to the two of us. His hand moved to her stomach, and they shared a few quiet whispers, a pair of lovers who had a connection only they got to enjoy.

Damien kept his eyes on me and didn't even greet Sofia. "Joining us?"

I nodded. "Forgot my lunch today."

"I'm sure whatever we're having is better than the leftover pizza you brought," he teased.

"I haven't had pizza since…" I let the words trail off and disappear into the air. Liam was committed to a healthy diet to stay in shape, so we always cooked all our meals. I noticed I'd dropped the pounds I'd gained living alone very quickly. Now I fit into my old clothes without issue.

Damien knew what I was going to say, and for just an instant, his gaze dropped. "Then let's go to a pizzeria. I know it's your favorite."

"I shouldn't eat that, but I can't resist."

Damien turned to Hades and Sofia when they broke apart. "Pizza okay?"

"I'm not eating that garbage," Hades said.

"Ooh…pizza sounds good." Now Sofia rubbed her stomach like she was hungry.

Hades changed his tune immediately. "Alright, pizza it is."

He took his wife by the hand and guided her down the hallway.

I watched them go, unable to resist their cuteness. "He's a pushover, isn't he?"

Damien started to walk with me. "The biggest one I've ever met."

We left the hotel and walked to the restaurant. It was still cold outside, but not as freezing as it used to be. "So, did you get that meeting you wanted?"

He was close to my side as he walked beside me, his hands in the pockets of his suit. "Yes."

"And how did that go?"

"Not the way I wanted, unfortunately."

I didn't ask specifics because I knew he would tell me on his own.

"I tried to hire the best hit man to take care of my problem. He said no…so I asked for a favor to get into a room with him. That conversation went nowhere…and he still said no. So, I have to find another solution."

"Why don't you kill the guy yourself?"

"Because I'd have to deal with all his cronies afterward. If it remains anonymous, they won't be able to identify the culprit. If I make the wrong move, he'll go after my father again…my sister…maybe even Hades. It's just too risky."

"I'm surprised Charlotte has those connections."

"She doesn't," he said, tensing at the mention of her name.

"Her boss knows the hit man. She brought me to dinner with him."

That was why she wanted to come to dinner with us. It made sense. "Now what?"

He shrugged. "Not sure. Hades and I used to be at the top of the food chain, but our enemies are growing stronger. Our last foe nearly destroyed us, and the Skull King is more complicated. He has his hands in every aspect of the city... it's frustrating."

I wondered if Liam had a similar relationship to him. "I could ask Liam to help you..."

He turned to me, surprised. "What do you mean?"

"I'm not sure what business Liam has with him, but I know they have a relationship."

"Probably collects his royalties from fighting."

Liam didn't share the details with me. "If Liam does something, the Skull King will never see him coming. Just an idea..."

Damien considered it for a long time, staring at me until he faced forward again. "No. But thank you for the offer." His jawline was covered with a thick shadow, but the sharpness of his jaw was still impressive. Cords of veins ran up his neck, and his handsome face was beautiful at this angle.

I didn't push it because I really didn't understand the underworld. I only brushed the surface. "I'm sure you'll figure it out."

"Yeah...maybe." When we arrived at the restaurant, he opened the door for me before he walked in behind me.

Hades and Sofia already had a table, and they shared a single menu.

When Damien reached the table, he pulled out the chair for me.

I hesitated before I sat down, enjoying the way he treated me even though Liam did the exact same thing. When Charlotte had come to the table, he didn't do it for her…and I distinctly remembered that. He only did it for me.

"We're splitting a pizza," Hades said. "Or should we get a bigger size and split it four ways?"

Damien sat down and smoothed his tie. "I thought you didn't eat garbage?"

Hades shot him a glare. "Just answer the question."

"I'll eat anything, so that's fine with me," I said.

Damien shrugged. "I'm not picky either. Let the pregnant woman decide."

"Alright," Sofia said. "Let's get a super large Margherita pizza."

"Super large?" Hades asked playfully. "You mean extra-large?"

"Whatever." She tossed the menu aside. "Just feed me."

Hades chuckled. "Alright, baby."

AT THE END OF THE MEAL, HADES'S PHONE RANG. He glanced at the screen and took the call. "Yes?" He listened to the line for a while before he hung up. "I've got to head back to the office. One of my big clients needs my help."

"Who?" Damien asked.

"Caruso."

Damien nodded. "I'll walk the girls back."

"I'll take Sofia." He rose from the chair. "You can pay the bill."

Damien gave a slight grin. "Jackass."

"Take the leftovers to the office, please." Sofia grabbed her coat and put it over her shoulders. "We'll leave it in the fridge and eat it tomorrow."

"Good idea," I said. "I'll ask for a box."

They said goodbye and left.

Now Damien and I were alone together...for the millionth time. There were other people in the restaurant, but we still felt completely alone, unsupervised. It was tense again, and my thoughts went to places they shouldn't.

I cleared my throat and waved down the waiter. "Could I have a box? And the bill too?"

He nodded and walked away.

My legs were crossed under the table and Damien was directly beside me, so I didn't have to stare at his face. I could force a meaningless conversation, but I was tired of doing that. It never masked reality.

He stared straight ahead for a while. "How are you?"

"Good. You?"

"Miserable," he said quietly.

I turned in his direction so I could see the side of his face. "Why is that?"

He shrugged. "I just am."

"Well, Liam thinks you're a lucky bastard having a woman like Charlotte all over you…" Her beauty made me insecure. So did her paycheck. She was one of the highest-paid models in the world. I brought home a mediocre salary. Those things never mattered before…but now that I was jealous, they bothered me.

He turned to me, his green eyes focused intently on mine. "He's the lucky bastard, Annabella." He held my gaze for a long time, his body so rigid, it seemed like he wasn't breathing.

I couldn't handle his intensity for a moment longer, so I turned away.

The waiter brought the pizza box and the tab. Just so I had something to do, I grabbed the box and prepared to put the leftover slices away.

But Damien grabbed my hand under the table, his fingers interlocking with mine before they rested on my thigh. He gave me a gentle squeeze, but instead of pulling away afterward, he continued to hold me in place.

I didn't fight him. I felt the warmth from his skin, felt the calluses on his fingertips and palm. Touching him reminded me of the way those fingertips felt against my cheek, reminded me of the way they felt on my tits when he squeezed them. We would sit together on the couch, and he would do the same thing, hold my hand like we were young people in love. Now, the touch meant more than it ever did when we were together. It was hotter, stronger, and more beautiful.

He pulled my hand to his thigh and held it there, his thumb gently stroking my skin. His head was tilted down, and he stared at our joined hands. "When I'm with her, I think about you. I see the way men stare at her, and it's the way I stare at you. She chases away the loneliness because I can't have the woman I actually want. She makes you insecure, but you're the one who makes her furious. When we came home from dinner, she said, without preamble, that you're still in love with me...and I'm not over you. She could see it even though I never mentioned you. I don't understand how she can see so much, but Liam doesn't notice what's right in front of his face. Instead of watching other people, he should be watching you...and only you." His thumb stopped brushing mine, and he pulled away. "Liam is the luckiest motherfucker in the world...and I hate that he has no idea that he is."

17

DAMIEN

Hades and I walked side by side into the casino. Suits meant nothing in a place like this, full of demonic billionaires who didn't need fancy clothes to show off the cash in their wallets. I was in a long-sleeved shirt, while Hades wore a gray blazer.

Hades passed a topless woman as she tried to take his drink order. He ignored her as if she didn't exist.

Annabella and I hadn't spoken since that moment in the pizza parlor. I lost my mind and did something stupid… holding her hand and saying a bunch of romantic bullshit. I never told Hades because I knew he would give me a black eye for being a dumbass. I knew I would see her tonight because Liam was fighting, and I dreaded that interaction.

It was the first time I didn't want to see her.

We headed into the industrial elevator and descended to the basement where the underground arena was located. It was far away from everything else, so the sound of moving chips and flipping cards wouldn't be overpowered by the loud screams from the audience.

Hades glanced at me. "What's with the bad mood?"

"What bad mood?"

He turned to me, his eyebrow cocked.

"I'm always in a bad mood."

He let the conversation die.

We stepped into the room, surrounded by hungry men who wanted to see blood spilled. The crowd would double in size once the death fights began. The earlier fights were basically the opening act.

"You see Liam?" Hades glanced around the room, searching for our client.

I didn't bother to look. "No."

When we didn't see him, we entered his changing room.

He sat at the desk and took a shot of booze. He swallowed it then wiped his mouth with the back of his forearm. "About time you showed up."

My eyes immediately searched for Annabella—but she wasn't there.

"Should you be drinking like that before a match?" Hades grabbed the bottle and tightened the cap before he returned it to the cabinet.

"Takes the edge off." He got to his feet and pulled his shirt over his head. "Helps with the pain too."

My curiosity got the best of me. "Where's Annabella?" She wasn't sitting in the stands alone, right?

He turned to me, his eyebrow slightly raised, probably because I used her full name when no one else ever did. But he was too stupid to be suspicious, to notice that another man stared at his wife the way he did. "She didn't want to come."

That explained his foul mood. But I was glad she wasn't here because it was no place for a woman. She was gorgeous, so most of the men there fantasized about pinning her to the mattress, choking her around the neck, and fucking her like they bought her. But he was too stupid to see the world around him.

The door opened, and the ring announcer poked his head in. "You're up, Liam."

"Alright." He hopped in place and shook out his wrists to warm up. "Wish me luck, boys."

Hades clapped him on the shoulder. "You don't need any luck."

I didn't say a word to him.

We followed him to the ring and took our seats. The buzzer went off, and the fighters began the battle.

Hades looked straight ahead as he spoke to me. "You could at least pretend you like the guy."

I shook my head. "Not possible."

"What happened?"

I decided not to tell him the full story. "Annabella told me Liam thinks I'm a lucky bastard for having Charlotte…"

"And?" Hades watched the blows come from left and right, even though he knew how this fight was gonna end.

"Why does he care about the woman in my bed when Anna is in his?"

He leaned forward, and his arms rested on his thighs. "I guess I should never leave the two of you alone…"

"Probably not." Anytime we were alone together, it just got worse and worse.

He gave me an incredulous look when I answered honestly.

I didn't apologize for it.

We stopped talking and watched the rest of the match. It was over in twenty minutes, with Liam emerging as the victor. The crowd cheered, money changed hands, and he stepped out of the arena.

We met him at the perimeter. Hades clapped him on the back. "Good fight."

I was quiet.

Liam wiped the sweat from his face with the towel that was handed to him. "Too easy." The sound of the next match was loud, the buzzer going off before the fighters lunged at each other.

"Easy, huh?" A large man blocked our path, shirtless and in his black shorts. He was muscular, matching Liam's size. The grimace on his face showed his hatred for Liam, like he already knew him. "Maybe it wouldn't be so easy if you didn't take pussy matches."

Liam must have known exactly who he was because he didn't ask for identification. After he'd stepped out of the ring, he'd relaxed because his fight was over, but now, he immediately dropped the towel and adopted his aggressive posture, ready to have another match right on the spot. "You want me to kill you so you don't have to lose your next fight. Pathetic." He walked up to his opponent, his shoulders squared and the muscles of his arms flexed.

"I don't lose my fights, asshole. Because if I do, I die. That's a lot more than you can say." He dropped his gaze and spat on Liam's bare feet.

Liam was rigid, his frenzied eyes showing his heated thoughts. He processed his next move, considering all the possibilities. But pragmatism set in, and he walked around his opponent and took the high road.

I knew this asshole was trying to bait Liam into a death match, and I was relieved Liam didn't cave. Hades and I walked with him.

"Wow," the fighter said after us. "Look at that pussy run."

I kept walking, but I quickly realized I was on my own. I turned around.

Liam faced off with him, giving in to the heckles. "If you don't want to die in this crowd, I suggest you shut your mouth."

The fighter grinned, a few teeth missing. "You'll fight me here but not in the ring because you're a pussy." He spat again. "The only reason you're the reigning champion is because you're scared shitless to get back in that ring. Hold on to that belt all you want—but it don't mean shit."

I grabbed Liam by the arm and tried to tug him away.

He spun out of my grasp so fast.

"You want me dead? Then let's go." He slammed his closed fists together, his knuckles clanking.

I stared at Liam and saw all his pragmatism disappear.

Liam stared back at him for several seconds, taking his time before he answered. "Fine. No mercy."

The other fighter grinned wider when he got what he wanted. "I'll put us at the top of the schedule." He walked away with his cronies.

What the fuck just happened?

Liam headed to his dressing room.

Hades said nothing because he got what he wanted.

"We can't let this happen." I walked beside Hades while Liam pushed everyone out of the way in front of us.

Hades gave me a cold look. "This isn't our lives, Damien. We're spectators."

"But he was manipulated—"

"He was manipulated because he wanted to be." He looked forward again. "I have to make arrangements now. I only have ten minutes." He looked at his watch. "Stay with Liam." He turned to the left and pushed through the crowd.

Jesus Fucking Christ.

I went into the dressing room.

Liam took another drink then poured a bottle of water over his head to cool off.

"What the fuck are you doing?" He and Annabella just talked about this weeks ago. He forgot all of that just because someone talked some shit. "Your wife said no, and you permanently retired."

"She's not here." He grabbed a towel and wiped the water from his wet hair and face. "She doesn't need to know."

"And if you die—"

"I won't." He looked at himself in the mirror, still forming beads of sweat on his forehead despite the quick shower he'd just taken.

"Liam, you're high on adrenaline right now, but your body is exhausted because you just completed a match. This is the worst possible time to do this. You're aren't fully rested."

"I'll be fine."

"You aren't invincible, asshole."

He turned to me, his eyes narrowed. "You think I'm gonna let that fucker talk to me like that?"

"Who gives a shit what he says? He's baiting you because he knows it'll work. And you have a life outside of this ring—and she's sitting at home right now." I slammed my fist down on the desk. "Call this off. Now."

"No." He pushed my arm off his desk.

I couldn't let this happen. "Liam—"

"I said no." He gave me a hard expression, like he might hit me if I kept pushing him. "This is exactly what you want, so why do you care?"

I inhaled a deep breath and silenced my words. I was tempted to tell him the truth just to distract him from this fight. When he knew I'd fucked his wife and still wanted to fuck his wife, he would come after me instead. The death fight would be forgotten. But I didn't say a word.

He turned away. "Give me a few minutes." He opened the drawer to his desk, pulling out two syringes filled with pain meds. He was about to inject himself, so he'd be able to ignore the aches in his bones and fight to his full capability.

I stormed out of the room and stood in the hallway, both of my hands gripping my skull because I didn't know what the fuck to do. Reason wouldn't change Liam's mind, and Hades wouldn't help me fix this. There was only person who could stop this.

Annabella.

I knew I should stay out of it, that Liam would probably win and this wouldn't be a problem at all.

But what if he didn't?

And Annabella lost him?

I wanted her to be a divorcée—but not a widow. If she lost him, she would be devastated. Regardless of the status of their current relationship, they'd been together a long time, had a happy marriage at one point. If he died…it would kill her.

I couldn't let that happen.

I moved into a different hallway and made the call.

She answered almost immediately. "Damien?" I never called her, so she knew this was unusual. She also knew I was probably with Liam right now, so there was concern in her voice, as if she was anticipating something terrible had happened. "What's wrong?"

I hadn't even said a word, and she could read my mood. "Liam finished his fight. But then another fighter provoked him. In ten minutes, he's going back into the ring—but this time for a death match."

She was speechless.

"I tried to talk him out of it, but he won't listen. The only way he's gonna stop—"

"I'm on my way."

I STOOD OUTSIDE AND CHECKED MY WATCH. I ASKED THEM TO put him as the second match just to buy us some time, but even then, it was cutting it close. She had to drive across the city and get here first.

Her Bugatti rounded the corner, and she sped to where I stood, slamming on the brakes and skidding until she burned rubber. The car came to a halt and she jumped out, leaving the expensive Bugatti right at the curb.

She ran to me.

I grabbed her hand and pulled her into the private entryway. We were in the casino immediately, running past the men at the tables and the topless waitresses. We had to slow down to take the elevator, and that took nearly a full minute.

She stood beside me, breathing hard and visibly anxious. Her arms were crossed over her chest, and she rubbed herself like she was cold. She turned one way then another, as if she couldn't stand still.

I stared at her, knowing I'd made the right decision.

The doors opened, and the sound of a fight reached our ears.

"God, we're too late," she yelled.

"No." The buzzer went off when one of the fighters collapsed, his skull caved in. "But Liam is next." I grabbed her hand again and pulled her through the crowd, keeping the assholes off her until I made it to the other side of the room. I took the stairs first and saw Liam pacing with Hades beside him.

I stepped aside so Annabella could get through.

Annabella walked up to him, her ferocity so much stronger than his. "What the fuck are you doing?"

He froze at the sound of her voice. He looked up and saw her, shocked that she was there at all. His body was still pumped with adrenaline, so his muscles were thick and ready to create bone-cracking force. "Anna—"

"You told me you wouldn't do this, and the second I turn my back—"

He came close to her and lowered his voice. "That's not how it happened, okay? Keep it down. Otherwise, you'll embarrass me."

"Oh, I'll embarrass you?" she hissed.

Hades turned to me, and the look he gave me was terrifying.

I ignored him and turned back to Annabella.

Liam flared his nostrils and sighed. "I've committed to this. I'll be—"

"You committed to this." She raised her left hand where her ring was. "I gave you a choice, and now you're going back on your decision." She grabbed her ring and pulled it off. "So, I'm going back on mine." She prepared to throw it on the floor, where it would probably get kicked away and disappear in the cracks.

He grabbed her with lightning speed, his entire hand covering hers so the ring was safe in his grasp. He still looked livid, like he was the one who had the right to be angry. "Fine." He opened her hand and retrieved the ring before he shoved it back on her left hand. "Fine." He finally let her go, breathing hard like he wanted to scream.

Her anger disappeared. Her eyes filled with sadness, and she looked at him like he'd still betrayed her. "You may as well fight, Liam. Because I don't think our marriage will survive this anyway…"

His anger was erased by her words. Now his eyes fell in despair, and all the muscles in his body relaxed. His lungs deflated as life had left his veins. He was impossible to understand, because he clearly loved her…he just couldn't control himself.

She turned around and walked off.

I waited for him to go after her. Because if he didn't, I would.

He made the right decision. "Cancel it." He gave the order without looking at either of us, and then he took off.

I could feel Hades staring at me, feel the vibration of his glare like an avalanche about to crash down. Instead of being too angry to speak, he turned away and walked to the ring announcer to fix the mess I'd just made.

18

ANNABELLA

I TOOK OFF IN MY BUGATTI AND LEFT HIM STANDING AT THE curb in nothing but his shorts. I sped through the streets with the music off, furious about what had just happened. The second I wasn't there to keep him in line, he snuck around behind my back.

Just like when he cheated on me.

Maybe Liam wasn't the person he used to be. Or maybe he'd always been this way…but I was too stupid to notice.

I went home and grabbed a bag to pack my things. My first impulse was to go to Damien's place, but that was the last place I should go right now. I would just go back to the Tuscan Rose, where Liam wouldn't follow me.

I shoved my clothes into the bag and left my ring on the vanity—exactly where I'd left it the first time I'd walked out on him. I was in the middle of the hallway when the front door opened.

Liam shut it behind himself, wearing his black sweatpants

and a gray t-shirt. He was too big of an obstacle to get around, so I was stuck. He stood near the entry table and stared at me, as if daring me to try to get past him. His eyes moved to the bag in my hand. "I'm not letting you leave."

"You're gonna fight me to the death, then?" I snapped.

He walked closer to me, his heavy footfalls echoing against the hardwood floor. His blue eyes were on me, looking at me like an opponent in the ring. He was ready to fight, ready to do whatever he could to get me to stay. "I want to talk." He stopped in front of me, giving me a few feet of space.

"I'm done talking to you, Liam. It doesn't matter anyway, because you turn around and do whatever the fuck you want—"

"Listen." He held up his hand to silence me. "I listened to what you said and had no intention of getting back in the ring. But one of the fighters got under my skin…and got the best of me."

I crossed my arms over my chest, the strap of the bag hanging off my elbow. "Just the way that woman got under your skin?"

He inhaled a deep breath as the shame filled his eyes.

"The way that woman got the best of you?"

"It's not the same thing, and you know it," he said quietly, forcing himself to keep his voice down. "I'm not sneaking around with another woman—"

"This is worse."

His expression fell.

"Because this could kill you, Liam. You hurt me so much when you cheated on me, but at least you weren't in danger. You were going to put your life on the line without even telling me. What if you'd died? I would have had no warning. The last thing I would have known was you lied to me, broke my trust, and got killed for it. And I'm just supposed to live with that?"

The shame grew.

"I don't trust you…"

His eyes dropped to the floor. "Baby, please—"

"Don't 'baby, please' me." I pushed my hand into his chest so I could get around him.

He wouldn't budge. He stuck his hand against the wall so I couldn't escape his mass. "I told you I'm not letting you leave."

"Then I'll call the cops."

"They won't do anything."

"Then I'll call Damien." I quickly realized what I'd said and tried to cover it. "Hades…Sofia. You want me to do that?"

He kept his hand up. "I want to talk about this with you. Because I love you… you know how fucking much I love you." His eyes burned into mine with sincerity, with passion. "I can't explain myself in a way you'll understand. But I'm a man. And when a man talks shit to me, I can't just look the other way and let it go. Maybe that makes me a stupid brute, but that's who I am. I didn't go there with any premeditation. It just happened…and I wasn't thinking. I'm sorry." He stared into my eyes and hoped to see forgiveness.

"Liam, I made my position very clear—"

"I know." He bowed his head. "It won't happen again. I promise."

"You promised last time…"

"Well, I'm making you a new promise now…not to let my anger get the best of me."

It surprised me how easily he could wear me down. "What was your plan? To win that fight and never tell me about it?"

He shrugged. "I honestly didn't think that far. But yeah, I guess. I wasn't going to start doing it regularly. It was just that one time. I wasn't sneaking around behind your back with this huge lie."

"Still not right, Liam. It doesn't matter if it's one fight or a hundred…"

"I know." He slowly lowered his hand, letting me pass if I wanted to. "I'm sorry, and it won't happen again."

I wanted to believe him, and I felt stupid for actually starting to.

He watched me with intense focus. "Baby, please…"

I sighed and bowed my head.

He reached for the strap on my elbow and slowly pulled it free, taking the bag away from me and dropping it on the floor behind him. When he got what he wanted, he moved closer into me and cupped my face, making me lift my gaze to meet his. "Don't leave me. I know you aren't in love with me again yet, but I'm so in love with you…and I can't lose you. I know I should be building our trust, making you feel safe with me, and I keep fucking it up left and right." He rested his head against mine and closed his eyes. "Please."

I felt weak at his touch, felt the sincerity of his voice all the way into my soul. I loved this man, but he was right, it wasn't in the way that I used to. But I believed we could have that again if these things weren't getting in the way. Things like fighting... Things like Damien.

It seemed unfair to be so unforgiving when I had been holding another man's hand just days ago, when the only reason I knew about Liam's fight was because my old lover told me...who was also my husband's friend. He wasn't innocent, but neither was I. "I'm not going anywhere, Liam."

He angled my head, so our eyes were locked on each other. His expression was the same as it had been on our wedding day—the first time. His gaze was filled with deep love, as if I was the most important thing in the world to him. Sometimes he screwed things up, but his heart was in the right place. I knew he loved me...from the bottom of his heart. "Baby, I love you." His arms circled my petite body, and he held me close, squeezed me like he never wanted to let go. He lifted me from the floor and held me against him, my feet dangling in the air.

My face moved into his neck, and I closed my eyes. "I love you too."

I LAY BESIDE HIM IN THE DARK, THE LIGHT FROM THE BEDSIDE clock providing a subtle shine to his face. I was in his t-shirt, which was a million sizes too big. It was more of a blanket, but that's what made it comfortable.

His arm was hooked around my waist, and he held me close, our heads sharing the same pillow. His pretty eyes were on me, the only soft feature he possessed. His fingers rubbed against the soft skin of my back, caressing me like a giant trying to tenderly caress a rose. We hadn't said much since I'd forgiven him. When he knew he'd won me over, he took me to bed and apologized in other ways.

"Baby?" His hand moved to my stomach, his fingertips grazing over my skin.

I lifted my gaze to meet his look. "Hmm?"

"How did you know?"

I hadn't expected this conversation to arise. There had been so much drama that I assumed it would be overlooked. Normally, I would just tell him the truth...but it would destroy Damien and affect his newly restored friendship with Hades. So, I covered his ass. "I changed my mind about watching your fight." Damien was loyal to me when he called me and told me what was happening. Maybe he'd encouraged Liam in the first place, but he'd clearly had a change of heart. He was loyal to me, so I would be loyal to him.

Liam accepted my explanation as fact. "Sometimes I think about quitting altogether...for you."

"That would mean a lot to me if you did." I felt bad asking him to give up his passion, but I didn't want my husband to be bruised every time he came home, to do all this damage to his body and pay for it later in life.

"It's all I've ever known," he said quietly. "It's something I'm proud of. I've worked hard to be at the top of my game, but I understand why you want me to stop. I'm committed to it, but I should be committed to you more." He stared at me for nearly a full minute before he continued. "So, I'll do it."

I inhaled a deep breath when I heard his statement. It was what I wanted, and he loved fighting so much that I knew this was hard for him. It was an incredible sacrifice, but he did it for me. "I don't want you to resent me…"

"I won't."

It was too good to be true. "Are you sure?"

"Yes." He answered without hesitation.

"But what will you do?"

He considered the question for a long time. "We could try to have a family again…"

Last time we tried, it ripped us apart. And while I wanted to start a family, it didn't feel like the right time. Liam and I were still rocky, and bringing a child into this marriage didn't seem like the smart decision. "I'm not sure if I'm ready right now, but I'll think about it."

His eyes showed his disappointment, probably because he knew he was the cause of my hesitation. But he didn't voice that sadness. Instead, he cupped my cheek and caressed my skin with his thumb. "Whenever you're ready, I'm ready."

I'D JUST PARKED IN THE PARKING LOT AT THE HOTEL WHEN MY phone rang.

It was Damien.

I stared at his name for a while before I finally answered. "Hey..." He probably wanted to know what happened between Liam and me after the blowout last night.

He didn't say anything back for a while. "You alright?" His deep voice was filled with the same intensity he always reserved for me, as if I was the only person in the world who made him this on edge.

"Yeah...I'm fine."

"What happened?"

I didn't want to answer because I felt pathetic for forgiving Liam so easily. "He apologized...and I forgave him."

Damien was quiet.

"Thank you for telling me. I told him I showed up on my own, so he has no idea it was you..."

"I don't care if he does know."

I kept the phone to my ear and stared at my reflection in the rearview mirror. Even when we sat in silence, I could feel so much for him. It was like he was sitting right beside me in that car, his hand on mine.

"I just wanted to check on you."

"Thanks..."

After a long pause, he hung up.

But I didn't get out and walk into the hotel. I just sat there for a while... staring at my own reflection.

19

DAMIEN

I sat at my desk and did nothing.

I had shit to do, calls to make, but I sat there and stared at the paperwork on my desk. I was exhausted because I'd headed to the lab after Liam and Annabella left. Shit needed my attention. I'd called Annabella in my car before I'd stepped inside the bank. My thoughts had been on her all night, worried about the fight she was having with her husband. A part of me was afraid he would hurt her. I'd seen firsthand how all logical thought left his brain when he got angry. And apparently, he'd touched her before...

The thought made me insane.

I was eager to hear from her for another reason...to know if she'd left him. She took off her wedding ring and said their marriage wouldn't survive. I wanted to know if that was true...for my own selfish reasons.

But she'd stayed.

She stayed with a man who made false promises, a man

who forgot about her the second he was enticed by something better, a man who lost his temper and grabbed her. He loved her, but that wasn't good enough.

I knew Hades was outside my door before I saw him. His footsteps were heavy and quick, as if his hands were closed into fists because he was livid before he even saw me. We had gone our separate ways last night, and I'd left before he could punch me in the face. He called me hours later—but I ignored him.

I knew what was coming. Thought sleeping on it would calm him down.

Nope.

He barged into my office, his tanned skin red because he was furious. The door slammed into the wall, and he approached my desk with large strides. He leaned over the pile of papers and slammed his hand so hard into the desk, he almost made a dent. "What. The. Fuck?" He slammed his hand again, making my pens roll off the surface and my papers slide off from the vibrations. "What the motherfucking fuck?"

I got to my feet and avoided his gaze. "I had to say something, alright—"

"Why?" He gripped his skull before he threw his arms down. "I'll never understand your goddamn stupidity. Do you try to sabotage everything I care about? Do you try to make my life difficult? After everything we've been through, why the fuck would you do this and risk—"

My temper flared, and my rage matched his. I didn't care if everyone in the building could hear us rip into each other. I didn't care about our clients sitting in the waiting area. "Because I love—" I shut my mouth when I realized what I was going to say. My temper unleashed my inhibitions, and fucking word vomit exploded out of my mouth. I clenched my jaw hard and kept my lips tightly together.

His demeanor completely changed, the anger slowly draining from his face once he'd completely absorbed my confession. He pulled his fists off the desk and straightened. His hands slid into the pockets of his slacks, and he sighed quietly.

I was glued to the spot, too rigid to move, too rigid to breathe. I didn't finish the sentence because the words were frightening, but I also didn't need to finish it because I already knew the truth. Now, it was obvious to me…really fucking obvious. I rubbed the back of my neck then dragged my hand down the front of my face.

Hades continued his stare. "Tell her."

I crossed my arms over my chest. "It's gonna cause a lot of problems with Liam…" Our professional relationship would be completely destroyed. Not only that, but we would be his enemy, and I wouldn't be surprised if he tried to ambush us both to make us pay for what we'd done. We'd lied to him, purposely misled him, and now we'd taken his wife away.

"Doesn't matter."

I turned to him, my eyebrow slightly raised.

"If that's how you feel about her, then I don't care about Liam. I don't care about the consequences."

I was shocked he'd said that. "Why?"

"Because I know exactly how it feels to love a woman."

I ARRIVED AT CHARLOTTE'S DOORSTEP AND RANG THE BELL. Our relationship didn't deserve this formality, but if I did it over the phone or through a text, she would just hunt me down until this conversation happened.

She opened the door, her eyes lighting up with joy. "Damien." She immediately moved into my chest to kiss me.

I grabbed her by the arm and steadied her. "Char, we need to talk..."

Her happiness faded. "Okay..."

I didn't even try to come inside. "It's time we go our separate ways." I didn't sugarcoat or make excuses. I wanted her to understand that those midnight text messages wouldn't make a difference, that showing up on my doorstep in nothing but lingerie wouldn't entice me. The idea of kissing her made me sick to my stomach...now that I knew how I really felt. "I wanted to tell you in person so you would understand I'm serious."

She was shocked for a couple seconds, probably because a man had never dumped her in her life. "Why?"

"It doesn't matter why. I don't want to see you anymore." I felt like shit for bringing her around Annabella. I knew how it felt to see Annabella with Liam, and I did the same thing with Charlotte when I shouldn't have.

"I don't understand."

"There's nothing to understand, Charlotte. It's over. Period."

I knew I was being harsh, unnecessarily cold, but Charlotte wouldn't stop pursuing me until she got what she wanted. She played by her own rules, wouldn't go away no matter how many times I pushed her away. "I wish you the best."

Now she was speechless, her eyes slightly wet but also furious.

I lingered for another moment in case she wanted to say something, but when silence continued, I turned around and left.

I sat in front of the fire with the game on the TV. It was just me and a bottle of scotch for the evening, the one thing that had cured my loneliness for over a decade. I was in my sweatpants, with my cheek propped against my closed fist.

The bedroom door opened, and Hades stepped inside.

I glanced at him without turning my head. "Grab a glass."

He was in jeans and a t-shirt, ditching his suit after he returned home from the office. He grabbed the decanter and filled his glass before he took a seat on the same couch as me, sitting at the opposite side. In silence, he watched the game with me.

These were the moments I'd missed the most when he'd left my life. The quiet evenings when we didn't feel obligated to say anything. The silence wasn't uncomfortable, not when we were so close. We could watch the game and not mutter a word for hours.

Hades took a few drinks and held the glass on the armrest. "Why haven't you told her?"

"I just broke it off with Charlotte."

"Alright. Then why are you sitting here?"

I watched the TV with blank eyes, not reacting when a goal was scored. "I'm not exactly looking forward to the conversation."

"Why? Every minute you wait is another minute she's with Liam." Now that he knew how I felt, all his loyalty to his client disappeared. He was on my side—one hundred percent.

"I don't even know what to say to her."

"Tell her what you told me."

"And I barely confessed anything to you." I'd never felt this way about anyone, and I only acknowledged it when it looked me straight in the face. "This isn't me. I don't do this kind of shit."

"I didn't either...until Sofia."

"Well, I never thought I would be a pussy-whipped asshole."

He chuckled. "It's not so bad."

I stared into my glass before I took a drink.

"Just do it, Damien. When you see her face, the words will come to you."

Would they?

"She'll leave him immediately. She'll be in your bed before the sun sets. And everything else...doesn't matter. Liam won't be happy, but we can handle him. I'll kill him if I have to. No problem."

"I thought you were loyal to him?"

He nodded. "I am. But not nearly as loyal as I am to you."

The solidity of our friendship meant the world to me. The moment he knew I was serious about Annabella, he was willing to move mountains to give me what I wanted.

"Sofia told me she's in the ballroom tonight—for a wedding."

I turned his way.

"It's the perfect chance to get her alone…and end up in a hotel room."

20

ANNABELLA

Now that spring had arrived, I was in charge of booking weddings for the hotel. It was a romantic place to get married, and many generations of families had their events in that very ballroom. It'd been renovated many times, but the energy from the years of celebrations was cemented into the structure of the building.

When the final glass of champagne was finished and guests cleared out of the room, I was left to clean it up with the staff. Dishes from the sliced cake were carried to the dishwasher in the kitchen, and the empty glasses were collected in a bin to be cleaned later. Unopened bottles of champagne were returned to the bar, and the leftover flower arrangements would come home with me...whatever I could fit into the trunk.

Most of the staff went home, so I finished up in the ballroom alone. I pulled the tablecloths off the round tables and placed them in the crate so they could be taken to the laundry on my way down.

I'd wanted a job that was during business hours only, but when Sofia had asked me to do this, I didn't dare say no. At first, I was bitter about seeing new couples pledge to love each other forever since that hadn't worked out so well for me. Now, Liam offered to retire because it was important to me, proving to me that I was his biggest priority.

It was exactly what I wanted…I just wished it had happened sooner.

Maybe I would still be madly in love with my husband if it had.

I pulled the tablecloth off the table and shook the fabric so the crumbs fell to the floor. Then I folded it, which was stupid because they were going to be washed anyway. I walked back to the crate to toss it inside.

That was when I realized I wasn't alone.

I lifted my gaze and came face-to-face with a beautiful man with green eyes, wearing a short-sleeved shirt that showed all the individual muscles of his forearms. He was ripped in every single place, from his wrists to his calves. A shadow was on his sharp jawline, and he was still as he watched me, like he'd been there for a while.

I inhaled a deep breath when the adrenaline passed. My hair was pinned back in a braid wrapped into a bun, and I wore a purple gown, earrings in my lobes. It was my job to look nice for the reception but also to blend in at the same time. So, I'd gone through my closet and found this in the back. I'd stopped wearing it because it didn't fit anymore. But those extra pounds had left my hips and thighs, making the fabric fall around me perfectly.

I straightened and stared at him, seeing the way he gazed back at me with equal fascination.

His eyes combed over my features, taking in the diamonds in my ears, the blush on my cheeks. Without blinking, he studied me as if I were a work of art, a painting that belonged on the wall in the Louvre.

As always, I didn't know what to say to this man. I was illogical, shy, and, frankly, stupid. I was a schoolgirl who turned silly whenever I was around the cutest boy in class. But Damien wasn't just the cutest boy in class…but the sexiest man in the world.

He clearly wasn't going to say a word, not explain his presence at all. His shirt was olive green, a perfect color for his tanned skin. Black jeans were loose on his hips, his tight stomach making the fabric flow down his body.

"What are you doing here?" I turned and walked back to the table I was working on. It was near the balcony doors along with the others. My heels tapped against the floor as I moved, the echo loud because there was nothing to absorb the sound…except our souls. When I reached the table, I started to pull off the material.

He grabbed the cloth and pulled it from my hands. He let it drop back to the table, a wrinkled mass.

I was hostile toward him, but I had no idea why. He was the one who'd called me…and saved my husband's life. But when he looked so gorgeous under the lights from the chandelier, I just became so angry…so angry that I couldn't have him. One hand moved to my hip, and I looked across the ballroom, remembering the last time we were in this place together.

"Look at me." His voice was quiet but still packed with so much intensity.

My eyes obeyed on their own.

He came around the table and stepped closer to me, looking at me so hard.

I took a deep breath when he came near, my skin prickling with the energy transferring between us.

When he was close enough for us to touch, he stopped. His chin was tilted down to look at me, his green eyes so bright, they were like stars. He looked at me like he'd never really looked at me before, like he'd missed so many of my features in the past. "I love you."

My lungs sucked in a breath of air when I heard the words leave his lips. His tone was deep, matching the desire in his eyes. I knew I'd heard it, there was no mistaking it, but instead of bringing me joy…it brought something else. I automatically took a step back. "What…what did you say?" Last time we were here, he'd kissed me on the balcony, ignoring the ring on my finger. Now, he took it a step further, crossed a line so thick, it had to be purposeful, not an accident triggered by the candlelight, the alcohol, and the beautiful night in this gorgeous city.

One of his hands moved to the table, his fingers pressing against it as he watched me. "You know exactly what I said, Annabella. I'll say it again if you want, but we both know I just said those words, out loud, and straight to your face."

I'd fantasized about this moment so many times, but months had passed, and I'd stopped believing it would ever happen. When I married Liam, I gave up all hope. Damien broke my heart, and from that moment on, I vowed I would never give it to him again. "What do you expect me to say to that?"

His eyes slowly fell, as if this was not how this conversation played out in his head at all. "You say it back."

"Damien, I'm married. There's only one man I should say that to."

"Then leave him…and say it to me."

I took another deep breath, trying to process this crazy reality. "Are you insane?"

"I just told a woman I loved her…so, yes."

I didn't crack a smile at the joke. "I gave you a chance before I married him—and you didn't want me."

"I told you that wasn't true. And I didn't love you yet. I fell in love with you…" He sighed quietly, his eyes shifting back and forth as he tried to search for the memory in his brain. "I don't know when the fuck it happened. It doesn't matter anyway. But the words tumbled out of my mouth in my anger…and that was when I knew."

"Damien…" I shook my head slightly, doing my best to keep the tears in my throat and stop them from getting to my eyes. "You're too late. I'm married to someone else, okay? It's over."

His eyes narrowed, his entire body tightening in a subtle hint of rage. "You don't love him. He's a goddamn rebound, and you fucking know it." He raised his hand from the table and placed it over his heart. "You love me. Don't sit there and bullshit your way out of it."

"I'm not—"

"We're gonna continue to sit in restaurants and hold hands like lovers? We're gonna hug like it's an adulterous affair? We're gonna act like there's not something real here? You're really going to do that?"

"I'm married to Liam, and you're seeing—"

"I dumped her. It's over. You think I came here to tell you I love you when there's another woman on my hook? No."

I shouldn't feel relieved Charlotte was gone...but I was.

"Leave him." His eyes commanded me, issuing an order that had to be obeyed.

"Damien—"

"He's a piece of shit. The second someone provoked him, he was ready to jump back into the ring—and he wasn't even going to tell you. Who the fuck does that—"

"He said he would retire—for me."

He lowered his hand, his deep breathing continuing.

"I can't just leave a marriage because you've decided you're ready to be in a relationship. I promised to be with him until death parts us. I'm not going to break that vow just because you've changed your mind. People don't take marriage seriously anymore—but I do. I won't do that to him."

He shook his head slightly. "Even though you love me?"

"I never said I loved you..."

"Annabella." His deep voice completely suffocated me.

I dropped my gaze because I couldn't take the intensity. "I gave you everything, and you didn't want me…"

"So, this is payback?" His voice rose, and it was a good thing no one else was in the ballroom with us. "You're that fucking petty?"

"No. I'm just saying—"

"You're the only woman I've ever loved in my life. This is new for me, alright? Cut me some slack."

"And if I weren't already married, then things would be different…but I am."

He sighed loudly and stared at the floor, his hands sliding into the pockets of his jeans. "Liam fucked up everything, and while I think he loves you, I don't think he'll ever understand how to be a man for a woman." He lifted his gaze again. "He says he'll retire, but how long will that last? Until there's another bump in the road? And what we have…is stronger than whatever the fuck you have with him."

It was so damn hard to listen to this man say these things, that he wanted to be with me, that we should be together. I was so head over heels, stupidly in love with him, and here he was…asking me to be his. "I promised to be with him. And until he breaks that promise, I'm here. I never really gave him a chance because I've been so emotionally unavailable because of you."

"He wasn't emotionally available when he fucked someone else—"

"I forgave him and gave him a clean slate. Constantly bringing up the past isn't fair."

"Fair?" he asked coldly. "No. *This* isn't fair." He moved closer to me, anger in his eyes. "You shouldn't have run off and married him so quickly. You wanted to get back together with him? Fine. But you—"

"And you shouldn't have let me go, Damien. We can play this game all night." I stepped back from him, my eyes growing wet. "I loved you...and I still do. I hate the energy between us anytime we're alone in a room together. I hate the fact that I think about you all the time. I hate the fact that I have to concentrate so hard not to let you into my mind when I'm with him. I hate the fact that I miss you when I don't see you for a while. I hate...everything about this." A few tears escaped, and I quickly wiped them away with my fingertips.

His anger was tamed by my emotion. "If you weren't married, would you leave him for me?"

I dropped my gaze and gave a nod.

He sighed loudly. "Life is too short not to be with the person you really want, Annabella."

"I know," I whispered. "But..."

"Don't you think he would step aside if he knew? If he really loved you, he'd want you to be happy."

I released a sarcastic laugh. "No. He'd fight to the death for me."

His eyes fell in disappointment.

"And even if I wanted to...he would kill you."

"He wouldn't, Annabella. And he would be my problem, not yours, so don't worry about it."

I crossed my arms over my chest. "I'm sorry..."

He stared at me with drooping shoulders, as if he didn't know what to do other than accept my painful decision. His eyes didn't have the same light they'd possessed earlier. Now he was empty, like the sun had set and darkness ensued.

If Liam hadn't offered to sacrifice his passion for me, maybe I would feel differently. But I knew that Liam was dedicated to this marriage, that he loved me with all his heart, and he would be devastated if I left. Once he knew Damien was the man I'd picked over him, he would feel foolish, betrayed by everyone around him...including me. He was a good man, and he didn't deserve that.

Damien stared at me for a while before he moved in close, his hand cupping my cheek and his fingers sliding between the strands of my combed-back hair. His other arm wrapped around my waist, hugging me to him.

I didn't fight even though I should. I let him take me because I didn't have the strength to stop it. I needed the comfort as much as he did. The man I loved felt the same way...but I still couldn't have him.

His forehead rested against mine, and he held me that way for a long time, squeezing the fabric of my dress with his large hand. It was right above my ass, touching me like I was his...even though we both knew that would never happen.

His fingers found the clip in my hair and pulled it free, getting my hair to come loose and fall down my back. Now, it was just the way he liked, so he could feel it with his fingertips, touch me the way he used to. His breath fell on my nose, and when we were close like this, I got lost in time...traveling back to nights when he was mine.

I wanted to stay there forever.

His hand moved up my back to my bra strap, and he squeezed me there too. He didn't kiss me, even though the thought probably crossed his mind. He lifted his chin and pressed his lips to my forehead, kissing me with his warm mouth.

I inhaled a deep breath, treasuring the touch.

He let his lips stay there for a long time, as if he didn't want to step back and leave this beautiful moment. But when he did, he pulled away and looked at me, his green eyes fixed on me. His palm brushed against my cheek, and his thumb swiped at the corner of my mouth. "I love you, Annabella." He looked me in the eye as he said it, taking the opportunity to tell me what was in his heart before he lost his chance altogether.

I shouldn't say it back. I shouldn't feel this rush of affection, this heart-pounding pain all over my body. In that moment, I knew my feelings for Damien were true. They weren't misplaced lust, confused infatuation. The love in my heart was pure…and I loved him with every fiber of my being. "I love you too…"

21

DAMIEN

I FELL ASLEEP IN THE LEATHER CHAIR, MY FEET ON THE DESK and my head resting against my open palm while my elbow was propped on the armrest. Instead of going home, I headed back to work, getting lost in drugs and money to numb the pain radiating from my chest. I didn't want to go home alone, and I didn't want to go to a bar...so I just stayed here.

A loud thump made me jolt.

Heath stood in front of my desk, wearing a long-sleeved shirt and black jeans. His tattoos were visible up and down his arms, and the smirk on his face told me how much he enjoyed catching me off guard. "Baby didn't get enough sleep last night?"

I pulled back the sleeve of my shirt to check the time on my watch. "Why are you here? It's morning."

"I'm not a vampire." He glanced around my office and checked for the black duffel bag of money that was usually waiting for him. "Where's my shit?"

I had been so caught up with Annabella that I forgot about the biggest bill I had to pay every month. "I'll have it for you tonight."

"I want it now."

"I haven't done accounting yet." I pulled my feet off the desk and straightened in the chair. Sleep was in the corners of my eyes, and I wiped it away, still half asleep. "You caught me at a bad time."

"Then should I hit up your father instead?"

This was a terrible way to wake up—to be full of rage.

He smiled when he got a rise out of me. "If you think your father is safe in your cathedral, you're wrong." He grabbed a folder off my desk and threw it down. "You have everything you need right now. I'm not leaving until I get my money." He slammed his forefinger into the surface of the desk. "You already wasted enough of my time. I'm not letting you waste any more of it."

I got to my feet and held his gaze, my hands tied behind my back as if I were a prisoner behind bars. Was this how Hades felt when he was stuck with Maddox? A helpless hostage who could do nothing but obey? It was worse than torture, having all your pride stripped away like it never meant anything in the first place. I'd been stabbed, beaten to within an inch of death, and that was still preferable to this.

If only Bones hadn't retired out to pasture like a goddamn pussy.

Heath stared at me with his ice-cold blue eyes, prepared to make good on his word if I didn't cooperate. He was still livid at the way I'd thwarted his plan, and he would make me pay for it every single day until one of us was dead.

But that person was going to be him…someday.

I grabbed the folder on the desk and pulled it to me. "It's gonna take at least thirty minutes."

"I've got time. Have one of your cronies get me a cup of coffee."

"They don't do—"

"Or you can get it." He fell into the chair across from my desk and smiled, enjoying every second of this.

I held his gaze and felt the bloodlust in my veins, the desire to give him so many paper cuts with this folder that he bled all over the floor until he died.

"What are you going to do, Damien?" He loved to taunt me. "Get my coffee? Or bury your father? If I give him back, of course…"

Days passed as a blur.

I spent my time at home, not going to the office because I didn't want to be the recipient of Hades's looks of pity. I didn't want to meet my clients and pretend to give a shit. I just wanted to be alone, to drink and watch whatever garbage was on TV.

Hades called a few times, but I didn't answer.

He texted me too. I never answered.

I was tempted to call Charlotte so I wouldn't have to be alone. It was also spiteful, because I knew Annabella was jealous of her. But if I did that, I would get involved with a clingy woman again.

I was home when someone knocked on the door and let themselves inside.

I didn't move from my spot on the couch. All I did was turn my head and see Hades enter my bedroom. Patricia never told me when he arrived because he had unlimited access to my property. He was the only person who could come and go as he pleased. Except Annabella...when we were together.

Hades walked across the room and headed toward me, in jeans and a t-shirt. His short dark hair was rigidly styled, as if he'd skipped his workout after the office and headed straight to my place. "Who's winning?"

"Do you care?" I was a soccer fan, but he wasn't.

He helped himself to the scotch and took a seat. "You want me to get straight to the point, instead?"

"No."

"Your dad talked my ear off when I came inside. He gets along with Patricia well."

"Yeah. He was really stubborn about it in the beginning, until his room was spotless, his sheets were always clean, his laundry was always hung in the closet. And he's a big fan of her cooking too."

He got comfortable on the couch and watched the game,

resting his ankle on the opposite knee. He took a few drinks before he set the glass on the table beside him.

"You aren't gonna finish that?"

He shook his head. "Trying to cut back."

"Why?"

"I've got another kid on the way…"

"Didn't matter when Andrew was born."

"Well…time to grow up."

"Fuck, that sounds terrible."

He leaned forward and rested his forearms on his thighs. He stared at the floor for a while, the light from the fire blanketing his skin in a distinct glow. "Sofia told me what happened."

The room filled with tension, with discomfort that neither one of us could ignore. "And how does she know?"

"Anna told her."

I wondered exactly what she said.

He continued to stare at the floor so he wouldn't put me on the spot. "But she didn't say much about it. Sofia asked, and Anna just said you guys couldn't work it out. Didn't give any details."

Now I had to fill in the blanks.

After a few minutes of silence, he lifted his head and looked at me. "So?"

"You're gonna interrogate me?" I took a deep drink of the scotch, letting the fumes enter my nose at the same time.

"How many times have you interrogated me?"

Touché.

"It's been four days. I've given you your space."

"Well, I'm sure you already figured out that she shot me down."

"Yeah, that's obvious," he said. "But it's not obvious why."

I put the drink down and decided to get this inevitable conversation out of the way. "I told her how I felt—and she wasn't happy about it. I told her to leave Liam, but she refused."

"Why?" he asked, genuinely perplexed.

"Because she made a promise to him...and can't break it."

"Even though she loves you?" he asked incredulously.

I nodded.

He sighed. "I don't agree with that logic."

"Neither do I, but I understand it. She said she gave me everything, put her heart on the line, and I had the chance to be with her then. But I waited too long...and now I lost my chance."

"But you didn't feel that way about her at the time—"

"I know. But she wouldn't change her mind. She won't ditch Liam just because something better came along. It pisses me the fuck off...but I also admire her for it. She's nothing like me. She keeps her word. She's loyal, far more loyal than you and I are."

"But she's showing her loyalty to the wrong person."

"I agree with that."

He faced forward again. "We could kill him."

I released a sarcastic laugh. "No."

"I could do it. Make it look like an accident. When he pulls up to an intersection, we'll have a semi—"

"Hades, no." That would only hurt her. "The only reason I've been sticking my neck out for their relationship is because I know she cares about him. She still loves him. And I'm not gonna kill someone she loves just to get what I want."

He gave me an incredulous look. "That's not the Damien I used to know."

"Well...I guess I'm different now."

He turned to the TV and chuckled.

"What?"

"Looks like you're pussy-whipped now too."

I couldn't believe this shit was happening.

"What are you going to do now?"

"What do you mean?"

"You just going to give up?"

"I don't see any other option."

He turned back to me. "If you love a woman, there's always another option. Liam is a loose cannon. Put him in a bad situation, and he'll fuck up everything on his own. Remember how quickly he changed his mind about death fighting? He was about to jump into the ring on the spot."

"He gave up fighting altogether."

"What?" He leaned back against the couch. "He said that?"

I nodded. "Told Annabella he would retire for good. So, I don't think that's gonna happen."

"Damn..." Hades was probably annoyed that this affected his business, but he didn't voice that.

"There's nothing I can do. Just let it go."

Hades turned quiet, sinking into the sofa as if the conversation had really expired. He watched the TV passively, thinking about something else. Minutes passed, and I drank my scotch while he relaxed in my living room, probably out of words. Then he leaned forward again and turned to me. "Hold on."

I took another drink until the glass was empty. Then I set it down for good, cutting myself off.

"What was the fortune the gypsy read to you?"

I hadn't thought about my experience in the purple tent for over a decade. My memory was watered down from all the booze over the years, the concussions to the head, and the broken bones. The thought of her suddenly made me turn cold, because I knew how much his fortune had changed my best friend's life. It'd nearly killed him, because once he found the woman he was doomed to love forever, it almost destroyed him. All his priorities changed overnight, and he wasn't the same powerful man anymore. He became a slave to his queen. Fuck, I refused to let that happen to me.

"Damien?"

"It's been so long...I can't quite remember."

"Well, try."

I searched through the fog of my murky brain and came up with nothing. "Hades, I can't remember. It was about a woman, but I can't remember exactly what."

"Why do I have a feeling Anna is the woman she was referring to?"

"Fuck, I hope not."

"We have to return to Marrakech. Tomorrow."

Jesus, were we really doing this? "Maybe it's better not knowing."

"If that were true, yes. But you do already know...deep down inside."

I sat with my father in the dining room. "I'll only be away for a few days. You won't even know I'm gone."

He took a few bites of his soup before he responded. "Then why are you telling me?"

"In case you need anything, you'll call instead of going to my bedroom."

"I don't go to your bedroom anyway. Too many damn stairs." He grabbed the saltshaker and poured it into his soup.

I sighed. "Father, you really shouldn't—"

"Stop sounding like your mother." He dumped even more salt into the soup—just to make a point.

I let it go. "Anyway, I just wanted—"

"Ooh, lunch." Catalina entered the dining room, wearing a sundress with a cardigan even though springtime had just begun and it was too cold for that. "What are we having?"

Father's eyes lit up for her in a way they never did for me. "Sweetheart, what a nice surprise."

She leaned down and gave him a big hug before she took the seat across from me. "Thought I'd stop by."

"You gonna say hello to me?" I asked, noting the way I missed any kind of affection.

She waved—like a smartass.

Patricia brought a cup of soup and a panini and placed it in front of her.

"Ooh, this looks good." She grabbed the shaker and dumped a bunch of salt into her food.

Father smiled proudly.

I rolled my eyes.

"What's new?" Catalina took a few bites, the steam rising above her face.

"Your brother is going to Marrakech today," Father said. "He'll be gone a few days."

"You are?" she asked excitedly. "Are you going to the bazaar?"

"Actually, yes," I answered.

"Oh my god, I've always wanted to go." She set down her spoon and stopped eating.

That was never a good sign. "No."

"Oh, come on," she said. "Let me tag along."

"You walked in here and didn't even say hi to me."

"So? You know I see you." She grabbed her spoon and took a few more bites.

"Forget it." I didn't want to drag my little sister with us. She would tease me forever for seeing a psychic.

She pouted her lips like a begging child. "Please. Pretty please."

"Take her," Father said. "If she's gonna go, I'd rather you take her than someone else."

She grinned in victory.

I sighed in annoyance. "I'm just making a stop in the bazaar and leaving—"

"That's all I want to see anyway." She moved her empty soup bowl to the side then grabbed her panini. "I'm excited. I want to see the fire dancers and the cobras. Ooh...and the camels! Cute."

I dragged my hands down my face in frustration. I was a drug lord and a money launderer, and I still had to babysit my little sister. Hades would be thrilled about this.

She scarfed down her sandwich. "I'll hurry up and pack and meet you back here." She got to her feet and kissed Father goodbye. "And if you try to ditch me, I'll kick your ass." She flipped her hair and stormed out.

Father returned to eating like nothing had happened, but this time with a smile on his face.

Catalina hugged Hades before she grabbed her bag and headed out the front doors to the car waiting outside. "Come on, let's head out. Party time!"

Hades turned to me, his eyebrows high. "Why is she coming?"

All I could do was shrug in response. "Because she's a pain in the ass."

"This won't be a problem?"

"She and my father ganged up on me."

"Alright. Are you gonna tell her what's going on?"

"I don't know…she wouldn't believe us anyway."

Hades knew exactly where the purple tent was because he'd been there so many times over the last few years, but we took our time because my sister wanted to see the sights. Most of the men there stared at my sister like a piece of meat, and one even tried to grab her.

Second

We handled that so fucking fast.

Now I was glad she'd come with me instead of a group of friends. She was heavy baggage that I didn't want to carry, but at least she was safe this way. After we handled the guys who tried to grab her, everyone was too scared to mess with her, so they left us in peace.

She bought a couple things—and of course, I had to carry them.

When we made it down the quiet alleyway and spotted the purple tent, we'd finally reached our destination.

I turned to him. "Stay out here with her."

He nodded in understanding, knowing she shouldn't be left alone.

"What's that?" she asked, pointing to the single purple tent that stood alone.

"Nothing," I said. "I'll be right back." I headed to the tent and heard them talking behind me.

"Why is he going in there?" Catalina asked.

"It's a fortune-teller," Hades explained.

"Ooh…I want to go next."

Their voices died away when I opened the flap and stepped inside.

The woman with the scarf around her head and neck was there, smelling her scented oils and laying down cards like it was a round of solitaire. The tent was small, so she knew I was there, but she didn't look up to greet me. "One fortune per person. No exceptions."

She recognized me?

I approached the table and stood there, inhaling the musty smell of dirty drapes and humidity. I glanced around at the assortments of pots and other decorations, noticing the way it looked exactly the same as the last time I was there. Then I looked at her and examined the odd cards. She flipped one over, revealing a fanged cobra. Another had nothing but angel wings.

She didn't acknowledge me again.

"I'm not here for another fortune. Just want to hear my original."

"If it's that important to you, you should have written it down." She looked down her long nose and continued to play whatever game she was playing. Cards flipped before they were returned to the pile sitting in her hands.

"I was twenty-one...and didn't take it seriously."

"That's not my problem, Damien."

Bumps formed on my arms when she knew my name... without even looking at my face. Now I wanted to turn back because this woman was the real deal...and whatever she said would change my life.

But I had to know.

I drew out a few bills and dropped them on the table.

She finally pulled her gaze away from her work and examined the cash. "I want everything in your wallet—and I know exactly how much is in there."

I pulled out the rest of the cash and placed it on the table before I took a seat.

She grabbed all the cards, shuffled them, and then started over.

"Well?"

"I'm refreshing my memory. It's been a long time since I read your cards." For ten minutes, she played with the cards, flipping over the various animals and symbols that represented something to her. "No…" She kept working, trying to find the words she'd said to me before.

I'd walk out of there right now if I didn't know how serious this was, that she wasn't a hack. I'd witnessed Hades fulfill every single prophecy. I knew this shit was real.

She flipped over a few more cards before she sighed. "Ahh… there it is." She stared at the arrangement for a minute before she pulled all the cards toward her into a massive pile. Then she inserted them back into the deck. "You will be a rich man, Damien. Very rich. You will have more money than you could ever spend in one lifetime."

Her words started to jog my memory, and the past returned.

"But you will be alone. And you will lose many people you love on the way. One woman will love you for you, not your money or your power, but you'll lose her. And once she's gone…she's gone. Your life will be filled with regret, mistakes that can never be undone." She held my gaze as she finished.

It was like a punch to the stomach, a knife to the artery. I inhaled a deep breath and felt the nausea form in my stomach, making me want to puke up the lunch we'd had when we arrived. Despair like I never felt before weighed me down, made me sink so far that I thought I would never rise again. She said I would lose loved ones along the way…and I had. I lost Hades for a year, and that was the most painful experience of my life.

Until this.

She watched me with her fingers tight around her cards. "You got what you wanted, Damien."

When Annabella had rejected me, it was painful, but this was worse…because it was so final. Hope still resided in my heart, that Liam would fuck up sometime in the future and I would get my chance. But now, I knew she would never be mine…and I would return to my empty bachelorhood, bedding models that didn't mean a damn thing to me.

Sympathy filled her gaze. "I'm sorry."

"There has to be something I can do." Hades was able to break the curse. Could I do the same?

She shook her head. "For as long as she's married, you'll never have your chance."

I sighed loudly. Annabella was committed to making this marriage work because she was filled with so much integrity. Nothing would shatter that. It was obvious how much she loved me, but even that wasn't enough.

"I'm sorry."

I didn't rise from the chair because I didn't have the energy. I was weak, so fucking weak. But I couldn't stay here. My fortune had been read…and the consequences would haunt me forever.

Knowing I could never have her back wasn't the worst part. It was knowing that she truly loved me...for me...and I would never find that again. She was the only one. Wordlessly, I got to my feet and left the tent. I pulled back the purple flap and stepped into the firelight from the torches and bonfires.

"My turn." Catalina darted into the tent, excited.

I didn't stop her because I didn't have the stamina. She was in such a hurry that she didn't see the devastation on my face.

Hades let her go too and walked up to me. "Should we stop her?"

I shook my head. "I've never gotten her to listen to me her entire life. That's not gonna change now." My hands slid into my pockets, and I stared across the bazaar, the warm breeze moving over my cold skin.

"What did she say?" His hand moved to my shoulder, offering support.

"That only one woman will love me for me...and when I lose her...she's gone. I can never get her back."

He gave me a gentle squeeze. "I'm sorry, man."

"I said there has to be something I can do, but she said no. As long as she's married, I have no chance."

His hand slowly slid from my shoulder until he dropped it to his side. "As long as she's married..."

I lifted my gaze to look at him.

"I think you just found a loophole."

I stared at him in silence.

"As long as she's married... What if she's not married?"

"But she is, and she's not going to leave him—"

"And what if he leaves her?"

"Not gonna happen." Liam didn't work his ass off to get her back just to throw her away. He might make mistakes, but he wasn't going to walk away.

A slightly victorious look came into his eyes, as if he figured out the world's toughest puzzle. "But we could make it happen."

22

ANNABELLA

Liam still trained every day to keep up his size and strength, but he didn't mention fighting again. He seemed to really retire, and there was no resentment directed my way. It'd only been a week, so maybe that would change.

After my last conversation with Damien, I'd constantly felt sick. It was so painful to hear him tell me he loved me...and not be able to reciprocate with everything that I had. It was hard to believe we'd been apart for so long when these feelings were so rampant.

Why didn't he love me when I could still love him?

Why did Liam have to betray me in the first place?

Why did I marry Liam when I should have just waited?

So many fucking mistakes...all over the place.

Liam asked me if something was wrong a few times, but I lied and said I was under the weather. I considered telling him the truth, but that didn't seem necessary when I chose him in the end.

Now that Damien had told me he loved me, I wasn't sure how we could be in the same room together. It was already difficult enough, but now with this...it was a nightmare. I didn't ever want to be a cheater, so I would never consider an adulterous affair, but being around him was still hard... when I loved him in the way I should love my husband.

Liam sat across from me at dinner. "How was work?"

Sofia didn't question me about Damien after I'd told her what happened. I'd picked Liam, so there was nothing else to say anyway. But the environment was still tense, because I feared Damien would show up for lunch with Hades...and I'd have to look into his beautiful eyes and see the way he loved me. "Fine. How was your workout?"

He stabbed his fork into his food and took a few bites. "Brutal, like always."

I kept my eyes on my plate.

Liam continued to watch me. "I gave up fighting, but it still seems like you aren't happy." His tone dropped with his melancholy.

I closed my eyes when I felt responsible for his sadness. "It's not you, Liam."

"Then what is it?"

"I just..." I didn't want to say the truth and start a war. "Just stuff at work... I don't want to talk about it." I lied to my husband and felt like shit for it.

"You don't have to work. It doesn't matter that I'm not in the ring anymore. We can afford it."

"I know, but I like working."

"You like working more than staying home with me all day?" he asked, taking a pause to chew. "I know you said you aren't ready to start a family, but we could still practice."

A smile broke through on my lips. "As nice as that sounds, I need more purpose in life."

His eyes suddenly fell, as if those words meant something to him. "Yeah...I know what you mean."

SOFIA CAME INTO MY OFFICE AT THE END OF THE DAY, HER long coat stretching over her stomach and stressing the closed buttons. "We're going to dinner. Would you like to come?"

I looked up from my desk and stared at her. "Who's *we*?"

"My husband and I...and Damien."

I didn't want to keep doing the same thing over and over, spending time with Damien and suffering through the heat between us. Now that I knew how he felt, he dangled our possibilities in front of me, whether it was intentional or not. "I already have plans...but thank you."

Sofia shouldered her purse and lingered. "Your plan is to never see Damien again?"

"No...I just don't think I should be in those situations anymore."

She gave me a disappointed look.

"The wound is still fresh, you know?"

She nodded in agreement, but her eyes showed a different story. "Alright. I'll see you tomorrow."

"Goodnight." I watched her walk out before I returned to my work. I could go home whenever I wanted, but I kept finding things to do because I wasn't anxious to head back to my place. Damien was constantly on my mind, and it was impossible not to think of him around Liam. A part of me wished that Damien had never told me, that he wasn't so arrogant to assume I would leave my husband for him at the drop of a hat.

Nearly thirty minutes later, someone stepped into my office. Their footfalls announced their presence.

I looked up to see those deep green eyes looking into mine. I dropped the pen I was holding and inhaled a deep breath the second I felt his presence. It was like a disease infecting my cells. It entered my body, and the symptoms showed just seconds later.

A pizza box was in his hand, and he set it on my desk. "I thought you'd appreciate the leftovers." He was in his suit and tie, as if he'd left the office and headed straight to dinner with Hades.

I didn't open the box out of defiance. The enormous desk was between us, and I was glad such a solid piece of furniture formed some kind of boundary. As long as I stayed in my chair, he couldn't get to me.

He slid his hands into his pockets and continued to stand there.

My stomach betrayed me and growled loudly.

A subtle smile moved over his lips.

I still refused to take a slice. "In case it wasn't clear, I didn't join you guys for dinner because—"

"You're avoiding me. I know." He pulled his hand out of his pocket and rubbed his fingers through the hair at the back of his neck. His chin tilted to the floor, and he sighed before he lowered himself into the white armchair facing my desk. "But I don't want you to avoid me."

"I have to…"

His green eyes studied mine, so intense that this desk didn't seem thick enough to keep me safe. "I would never put you in a compromising situation, Annabella. You've made your stance on adultery clear."

I felt more at ease, but not much. "You should feel the same way about adultery too."

He rubbed his hands together. "I've been with married women before, so I don't share your morality. But I respect you for it."

I shouldn't expect anything less. He was a drug lord and a notorious criminal. Why would he respect something like marriage, especially when a woman was throwing herself at him?

He continued to stare at me. "I don't want it to be this way…"

"I have no other choice."

"Nothing has changed, so why does it—"

"Exactly," I said with a sigh. "Nothing has changed, so it needs to change. I can't be around you without wanting you. I can't look into your damn eyes without wishing you were mine. I haven't been physically intimate with you, but I've been with you emotionally every single day... It has to stop." My hands covered my face for a moment, and I breathed through the emotion before I dragged my fingertips to my lips. I closed my eyes for a few seconds before I looked at him again.

His expression didn't change.

"How am I supposed to make this marriage work if I'm still hung up on some other guy?"

"Exactly."

I shook my head slightly. "We aren't having this conversation again..."

"But it's a valid point. Why force a marriage that's not working?"

"Who said it's not working?"

"Liam," he snapped. "The guy was going to go behind your back and jump back into the ring. He's had one foot in and one foot out—just the way you have. Neither one of you has been one hundred percent committed. So, call it quits and move on."

"He is one hundred percent committed. He wouldn't have retired if that weren't the case. He made a huge sacrifice... and I need to do the same."

His expression showed how much he disagreed with that. "If you tell him the situation, he might bow out."

He couldn't be more wrong. "You don't know Liam the way I do. If I told him what happened, he would hold me tighter. He would move us to France or England so we could start over away from you. And honestly, that's not the worst idea."

His eyes narrowed in pain. "He's not worth it, Annabella."

"I don't want to keep talking about this, Damien. I picked him—end of story."

He inhaled a deep breath. "But you picked the wrong man."

"You should go..."

He didn't move. "What are you afraid of, Annabella? You think, if you choose me, I'll just hurt you?"

I never allowed myself to think that far.

"I can't promise you marriage and kids, but I can promise you that I'm committed to us, that I want to be with you in any capacity. Don't pick him just because he's the easy choice. You're better than that."

"That's not why," I whispered. "You don't understand what marriage is. If you sleep with married women, then you obviously have no respect for the institution. It's a promise, a lifelong commitment, and I already made it. This isn't some random guy. This is a man I was already married to, whom I have a history with, and despite what he did, I still respect him and love him. I can't do that to him... I just can't. You need to respect my decision. I know you're used to getting whatever you want, but not this time."

He released a sigh so big, his nostrils flared. He massaged his knuckles and bowed his head, processing the rage that coursed through his veins. "I would respect your decision... if we weren't so fucking in love with each other." He raised his head again and looked at me with fury in his eyes. "That's the problem, Annabella. You love me in a way you don't love him anymore. And I love you in a way I've never loved anyone before. Why don't you understand that?"

My eyes started to water. "I do understand that...more than you know."

His eyes filled with sadness.

"You really should go. Nothing will change my mind."

He didn't rise from his seat. "I want to tell you something."

"Damien—"

"Listen."

I ran my fingers through my hair and glanced at my phone, relieved that Liam hadn't texted or called.

"Remember the night I told you Hades and Sofia were soul mates?"

"Yes...on the balcony." As if I could ever forget.

"You asked me how I knew that...so I'm going to tell you. This story is ludicrous and unbelievable. Anyone else would think I'm batshit crazy, that I made up this story just for attention. But I know you'll believe me."

Now that he had my full attention, I listened.

"Hades and I went to Marrakech for his twenty-first birthday. We met a gypsy there who read our fortunes. The woman said Hades would only love one woman all his life... but she would never love him back. It was punishment for the crimes he committed...for killing his father. We both thought it was horseshit. But every prophecy she made came true, and when Hades met Sofia and fell in love with her on the spot, he knew it was real."

"If that's the case, how does she love him now?"

"Because he had to break the curse...which he did."

This did sound like a fable, a story parents told their children at bedtime.

"It took him a long time. He suffered a lot to make it happen. But he did it because...the gypsy said she was his soul mate."

It was one hell of a story, and I was paralyzed by the tale.

"Do you believe me?"

Normally, I wouldn't. But if two powerful men like Damien and Hades believed it, it was compelling. Drug lords and criminal bankers didn't believe in bullshit like that...unless they lived it. "What does it matter if I believe you or not?"

"Because the gypsy read my fortune too...and I want to share it with you."

Now my heart sank as a shadow of fear crept over me. It was a curve ball I didn't expect.

His green eyes shone with sincerity, as if this was the most serious conversation he'd ever had. "Annabella, do you believe me?"

"I trust you," I whispered, the words coming out of my mouth all on their own. "So, yes..." I got lost in those green eyes, fell so deep into our connection that I would believe anything he said.

He didn't say anything for a moment, but the affection in his gaze showed how much that meant to him, that my unconditional trust was everything to him. "She told me only one woman would love me for me, that she wouldn't care about my wealth or power, but I would lose her...and she would be gone for good." He rubbed his palms together. "I think she was talking about you..."

If that was the case, then there was no hope for us, ever. And that disappointed me...even though I'd made it clear that I intended to be with Liam for the rest of my life. It was terrifying to think that this was meant to happen, that we'd never had a chance to be together anyway. "Then we need to move on."

"Hades broke his curse. Why can't I break mine?"

"But is it really a curse? Did she say that?"

"No, but it seems that way."

"No. It seems like you took me for granted, and now you're suffering the consequences." I shouldn't be petty right now, but I was resentful that he took so long to fight for me, that he waited until I was married to another man.

His eyes showed his pain. "She said as long as you're married, we have no chance."

"That's obvious. That's the only thing dividing us. And no, I won't leave Liam."

"What if Liam leaves you?"

It was a stupid suggestion. "He wouldn't. Not now. Not ever." I knew Liam made mistakes, but his love for me was obvious. We could be in our fifties, and a twentysomething could throw herself at him, and he wouldn't leave me for a younger woman. "I know you don't have a very high opinion of him, but he's more than the mistake he made. The only reason I knew he cheated in the first place was because he told me himself. He's not gonna let me go, not gonna trade me in for someone better. He's committed...as am I."

His words came out as a whisper. "I don't believe that."

"Did the gypsy say we were soul mates?" Was that why she'd told him this story in the first place?

He held my gaze for a long time. "Would it make a difference if I said yes?"

My heart started to race in my chest. If his answer was yes, it would complicate everything. It would make me question my loyalty to my husband. Because if I was destined to be with someone else...then everything wouldn't be in black-and-white anymore. "Yeah...I think so."

He rubbed his palms together as he continued to stare, his answer on his tongue. But he kept his mouth shut, breathing loud in the quiet office. He stared at the floor for a moment, drawing out the silence.

"Damien...is that what she said?"

He closed his eyes for a moment before he lifted his chin. He didn't open his eyes as he answered. "No."

Disappointment ran rampant.

He finally opened his eyes and looked at me. "But that doesn't mean I don't love you from the bottom of my heart, Annabella."

"Even so...it makes a difference."

"It shouldn't. Because I could have lied to get what I want, but I won't. I won't lie to the woman I love...and that's pretty fucking strong."

23

DAMIEN

HADES SAT NEXT TO ME IN THE BAR, HIS DRINK UNTOUCHED IN front of him. He ordered the scotch but never drank it, probably just to keep up appearances. But he was cutting back on the booze…on Sofia's orders. "Why the fuck didn't you lie?"

"Because I couldn't." I held the glass close to me, gripping it like a lifeline. "Would you lie to Sofia?"

"She's my wife. That's different."

"Whether she's your wife or not, you wouldn't lie to her."

"Or I would have lied and told the truth later. Because if you waited long enough, you would fight and she would forgive you. But at the end of the day, you would have what you wanted."

That was probably the smart thing to do, to say we were soul mates and confess to the truth later. But I couldn't look her in the eye and deceive her. My relationship with her was pure—fucking holy—and I couldn't tarnish that. "It's done, so whatever..."

Hades shifted his gaze across the room, staring at the wood paneling on the wall with a scowl on his face.

"She won't budge." I thought if I got her alone enough times, she would cave. How could she be with Liam every night when she felt this way about me? It was impossible not to think about her when I was with Charlotte, even if she was a supermodel. "Says we shouldn't see each other anymore because it's not fair to Liam."

"I think staying married to him isn't fair to Liam," he said sarcastically.

"I agree, but I guess he doesn't care. She told him she was in love with another guy and that didn't change anything. That's devotion. So, I guess I understand why she's so committed to him...even though I don't like it."

He shook his glass, the ice rolling with the movements. "We could entice Liam to fight again."

I shook my head. "Leave it alone."

"You're just going to give up?" he asked incredulously. "Did I give up on Sofia?"

"Sofia wasn't married to some other guy. Different situation."

"But Liam is a tool. We both know it."

"He's not all bad..."

He gave me an incredulous look. "Did you tell her that he

was going to fight behind her back until you talked him out it?"

After a long pause, I shook my head.

"Are you fucking kidding me?"

"I'm not a snitch."

"But he's not your friend. You're trying to take his woman, and that means you have to play dirty."

"Nothing ended up happening, so it doesn't matter. She would have forgiven him anyway."

"Maybe…but who knows?"

"I waited too long to tell her. If I do it now, it's pointless. He already retired from fighting, so he made the grand gesture. She doesn't live in the past, so she's not gonna hold that against him."

"Man, this woman is infuriating."

"A bit."

He finally caved and took a drink.

"Good thing I'm not a snitch…"

"She'll know the second I get home anyway, so whatever." He finished the glass and turned it upside down, so the bartender knew he didn't need a refill. "How about we encourage Liam to fight again? I know exactly what to say to entice him. We'll get him in the ring, convince him to keep a secret from Anna—"

"No."

He turned back to me.

"I'm not going to sabotage the relationship she's working so hard to fix."

"Who gives a shit? You just tried to hire Bones to kill Heath. Don't sit there and pretend you're a good guy—"

"I'm a good guy for her, alright?" I snapped. "I'm not gonna do that shit, okay?"

Hades finally let it go. "Crazy. Never thought this day would come."

"Neither did I."

"So, what now?" he asked. "You're really just gonna move on? Let her go? Forget about her?"

I couldn't imagine myself doing any of those things. But what other choice did I have? "Yeah…I guess."

24

ANNABELLA

A WEEK PASSED, AND I DIDN'T HEAR FROM DAMIEN AGAIN.

Hopefully, I'd ended things...for good. It was time to move on and stop thinking about him, to be devoted to the man who was so devoted to me. I'd made my bed, and I had to lie in it.

We had dinner together like we did every night then watched TV on the couch. My arm was hooked through his with my face pressed to his chest. When we snuggled like this together, I loved feeling his size, feeling the strength of his biceps and every other muscle. And his smell was divine too.

It made me drift off to sleep.

Liam turned off the TV then picked me up.

I was aware of him carrying me to bed, his powerful arms holding me like I was weightless. He set me on the bed a moment later and pulled off my bottoms.

I thought he was getting me ready for bed, like when a

parent put their child to sleep.

But he took off my panties too.

He dropped his sweatpants and moved on top of me, his thighs separating mine before he slid inside me. My shirt was still on, so he pulled it up so the bottoms of my tits were visible. He started to rock inside me, doing all the work because he knew I was tired and ready for bed. He was a manly man, so he wanted sex every night, every morning, and any moment in between.

I lay there and enjoyed it, my nails deep in his back. My ankles couldn't lock together because he was too wide, so my knees hugged his hips as I felt his large length move inside me. I moaned as he rocked me, knowing he would make me come like always, even when he was doing the least amount of work. His hard muscles rubbed against my clit, making me reach heaven every single time.

His face was buried in my neck, and he rocked me gently, pressing me into the mattress over and over.

My nails dug in, and my breathing became deeper, harder. My toes curled because I knew the threshold was on the horizon. Ecstasy was just heartbeats away, when the pleasure would make my brain cells flatline. It was coming quicker and quicker...and then it hit me just right. "Yes..." My nails sliced down his back, and I whimpered as it felt so good, as my mind left my body and went somewhere else. "Damien..." I closed my eyes and felt the cramps begin in both feet because I was clenching my toes so hard. It was so good, an explosion that sent me deep into space. All I could do was feel...feel this carnal goodness.

Then Liam stopped.

I finished anyway because I was too far gone. My eyes were clenched tightly shut, and my head rolled back once the pleasure began to fade. I could hear my own breathing, feel my pussy loosen its hold on Liam.

When he didn't resume, I knew something was wrong. He hadn't finished even though I knew he usually followed me immediately. I opened my eyes and looked at him, wondering if he wanted me on top instead.

But I was met with the most ferocious look I'd ever seen.

That was when I realized what I'd said…what flew out of my mouth.

His blue eyes burned into mine with such savagery, it might set me on fire. They shifted back and forth, looking at me with sheer disappointment…and unbridled aggression. He wasn't hard inside me anymore. He went limp like a fish out of water.

I had no idea what to say.

He took a deep breath and closed his eyes, as if he was doing his best to holster his anger, to not say or do something he would regret. Then he got off me.

"Liam—"

"Shut the fuck up, Anna." He grabbed an outfit from the closet and quickly dressed, throwing on denim jeans and a black t-shirt.

"I'm so sorry—"

"I don't want to hear it." He grabbed his wallet and phone and marched out of the bedroom.

I ran after him, in just my t-shirt. "Let me explain—"

"Oh, you've explained enough." As he walked down the hallway, he deliberately knocked over a vase of flowers so it would shatter onto the floor. He knocked paintings off the wall, pictures of us from our wedding day. He demolished everything in his path on the way to the door.

I ran after him. "It just came out. I didn't mean it."

He turned around at the doorway, looking at me as if I was an opponent in the ring. "I accepted the fact that you had feelings for him, that you still loved him, but I don't accept this goddamn bullshit. I don't think about anyone else when I'm with you, so how dare you—"

"I wasn't thinking about him. It just came out—"

"I've fucked women in the ass, chained them to my bed, had more threesomes than I can count—but I don't think about that shit with you. I only think about you." He pointed his finger in my face, his hand shaking uncontrollably. "Yeah, I fucked up in the past, but I didn't do this. Go fuck yourself, Anna."

Tears streamed down my face. "Liam, please don't go."

He ripped the front door open and stormed out.

"Liam!"

He reached the sidewalk, crossed the street, and then disappeared down an alleyway.

I was in only my t-shirt, so I couldn't chase after him. But even if I did, I knew it wouldn't make a difference. He was too far gone…and I was the only one to blame.

25

DAMIEN

"What do you think about the first guy?" I sat beside Hades in the first row of the fight. We'd spent the evening examining all the different fighters we could recruit next. There were some good ones, but none like Liam.

Hades shook his head. "No."

"The third guy in the death match?"

He shook his head again. "He got lucky because the other guy tripped."

It looked like we were out of ideas. We made a couple bets and paid up with the ring announcers before we left the basement. We got into the industrial elevator and rose to the casino floor.

It'd been over a week since Annabella and I had last spoken, and I was doing my best to respect her wishes and leave her alone. I did my best to persuade her, but it was pointless. She'd made up her mind, and I couldn't make her go back on her word. She was too honorable—and that made me want her more.

The doors opened to the casino floor, and we passed the poker tables, the sounds of chips in play audible. The closer we got to the bar, the more we could hear the music from the speakers. Women danced in cages, and topless women carried trays of drinks to customers.

"You want to get a drink?" I asked.

Hades shook his head. "No. Sofia was pretty pissed at me when I smelled like scotch the other night."

"Since when did she start caring about your drinking problem?"

"Since I went in for a checkup and found out I have high blood pressure and liver damage."

"Oh shit…"

"It's not a big deal, but Sofia flipped out. Started crying… said I won't live long enough to see our sons grow up."

"Her concerns are valid. I'll make sure you stay sober."

"I guess I shouldn't have told you."

I glanced at the bar because I thought I saw a familiar face. The guy looked just like Liam, but it couldn't be him because he wouldn't be here at midnight…and he wouldn't have his arm around some other woman.

Hades noticed my sudden change in mood and followed my gaze. "That looks like Liam."

"It does." I stopped walking and continued to stare. "But it can't be."

Hades stood beside me, his arms crossed over his chest. "No, that's him."

"Then what the fuck is he doing?"

"No fucking clue."

I headed to the bar with Hades behind me. I moved past the line of stools until I reached him. He stood beside a woman in a short dress with his arm around her waist. His hand reached down, and he gripped one ass cheek. "What the fuck are you doing?" I was angry, but I was mostly delirious. My mind couldn't process what I was looking at. Annabella said she wouldn't leave him, so there was no way he was there as a single man.

He turned at the sound of my voice, the smile on his face showing how drunk he was. "Hey, it's my boys." He reached his hand out to shake mine.

I pulled away. "Liam, what are you doing?"

Hades stood there, still as a statue.

"What do you mean?" Liam asked. "I'm having a drink with..." He turned to the woman he was still holding. "Sorry, sweetheart, what's your name again?"

"Belinda." She smiled like she wasn't the least bit offended he didn't remember her name.

"That's right." He snapped his fingers.

That was when I noticed he still wore his wedding ring.

"I'm glad I've run into you," Liam continued. "I want back in the ring. And death fighting only."

Hades exchanged a look with me.

Belinda threw up her arm and cheered.

"What happened with Annabella?" I asked.

"Who?" Liam asked, being a dick on purpose.

"Your wife." Both of my hands tightened into fists because I was livid he disrespected her like that. He was out catching tail, and she was home, probably worried about him. "Did you guys have a fight? What's going—"

"Excuse us for a moment." Hades grabbed me by the arm and pulled me out of earshot. "What the fuck are you doing?"

"What?" I asked, completely lost.

"Unless she left him, which I doubt, he's still married...and he's about to cheat on his wife."

"Yes...which is why I'm about to beat his ass."

"Let him."

I cocked an eyebrow.

"Let him," he repeated. "Let him destroy his marriage."

I stared into his face, finally understanding how I should play this.

"This is exactly what you want. He fucks this woman, and it's over. We know Anna won't stick around after that."

I glanced at Liam, who returned to his cozy conversation with Belinda. His arm moved around her waist, and he leaned down and kissed her, groping her right in the bar like no one else was there. It made me see red.

"Problem solved."

"And I'm just supposed to leave and pretend I didn't see anything?"

"Exactly. He's not gonna remember that conversation we just had."

"But I will..."

Hades narrowed his eyes on my face. "Please don't tell me you're gonna try to stop him."

"It'll devastate her."

"Not your problem."

"It is my problem," I snapped.

"Even if you stop him, you aren't doing her any favors." He pulled out his phone and started to record Liam making out with the woman while groping her ass. "Getting Liam home and cleaning up his mess is even worse, and you know it. He's gonna cheat. And even if you stop him now, the damage is done. Let him dig his own grave." When he got plenty of video, he returned the phone to his pocket.

"What are you going to do with that?"

"Nothing. But it's evidence if we need it."

I turned back to Liam and watched him stick his tongue down the woman's throat. "I can't just leave..."

Hades sighed.

"It's one thing to tell her he was gonna cheat, instead of her having to listen to what Liam did with this woman in the back seat of his car. Far less painful. And I want to rip out his eyeballs and tongue with my bare hands."

"I can understand that part." He clapped me on the back before he walked away. "Have fun."

I turned back to the bar and returned to Liam.

He didn't even notice me.

"Belinda."

She turned at the sound of my voice.

"Leave," I commanded. "Now."

Liam tightened his grip. "Get your own. Are you still with that sexy model?"

I punched him so hard in the face, he landed on the surface of the bar.

No one blinked an eye over the confrontation because bar fights were a dime a dozen.

Belinda bolted.

Liam took a second to recover from the unexpected hit. He gripped the edge of the bar and righted himself, his face already bruised. He turned back to me, the rage brewing. "You want to die, asshole?"

I grabbed the back of his head and slammed his face into the bar, making his nose explode with blood. "You sneak out of the house and fuck some other woman when your wife is asleep? That's the kind of piece of shit you are?" I slammed his face down again.

Blood got everywhere and dripped to the floor.

He righted himself and turned to me, blood streaking down his chin. "I'm the piece of shit? At least I don't say another woman's name in bed..."

I was about to hit him again when I changed my mind. I heard what he said, let it sink down into my bones. Beating him bloody wasn't fair when he was this intoxicated anyway. I'd like to beat him at his own game—and destroy him. "What are you talking about?"

He grabbed his glass of scotch and poured it down his face to clear off the blood. Then he wiped away the liquid with his forearm. "She came and screamed out some other asshole's name. Fucking bitch..." He leaned over the bar and rested his head on his arms, breathing through the painful memory and the beating I just gave him.

I moved to the spot beside him, where Belinda had been. My palms started to sweat because I suspected I knew what name she'd said, what she'd shouted when she was screwing her husband. Maybe he was between her legs, but I was the one making her writhe.

"I've given her everything... I sacrificed everything for her." He raised his head and stared straight ahead. "And then she does that?" Both his hands tightened into his fists as he stared at his own knuckles.

"What name did she say?" My curiosity shouldn't matter right now, but if she'd said my name, Liam would be ripping me to pieces right now.

He slowly turned to me, his blue eyes now arctic fire. "Damien, actually..."

I held my breath as I met his look, waiting for him to realize that wasn't a coincidence.

But he never did. "She told me she was still in love with this other guy. I wasn't happy about it, but I accepted it. But I thought things would get better...until she screamed this fucker's name in bed." He gripped his skull and growled, sounding like a bear deep in the woods.

I wanted to tell him it was me...so fucking tempted. But that would affect Annabella as much as it affected me, and it might be easier to say nothing at all. Just let it go. "Going out and getting ass isn't the solution, Liam."

He slammed his hand into the bar so he could get another drink. "Tonight, it is."

"You'll regret it in the morning."

"I doubt it," he said quietly. "I'm back in the ring too. I'm not gonna give that up if she's not gonna give up this guy." He downed the glass in a single gulp before he turned away. "Now, if you'll excuse me...I have pussy to find."

I grabbed him by the arm. "Liam, go home."

He twisted out of my grasp. "No."

"You're really going to do that to your wife?" I moved in front of him and blocked his path. "This is exactly where you were when she lost the baby. Shit got tough, and you got going. You're gonna make the same mistake?"

His eyes narrowed. "How did you know that?"

Adrenaline spiked. "You told me."

He was still suspicious, but that quickly faded away. "She'll never know, so what does it matter?"

I knew he was drunk, but that still sent me to the brink in rage. "You're really not going to tell her?"

"The second she said that fucker's name, she gave me a get-out-of-jail-free card." He started to walk away. "So, I'll do whatever the fuck I want. I'll fuck who I want. I'll pay for who I want. And I'll be back in the ring…where I belong."

I moved in front of him again. "Last chance, Liam. Let me take you home."

He gave me a slight smile. "I appreciate you looking out for me, but I'm a big boy. I can take care of myself."

26

ANNABELLA

Liam didn't come home for three days.

His phone was off.

He didn't come back for clothes or other essentials. When he'd walked into the night, he truly disappeared.

I spent my time worried sick, concerned something had happened to him, that he got hit by a bus while he was stumbling around the city drunk. I called all the local hospitals to check if he was there...or in the morgue.

He wasn't.

It was the middle of the day when he finally walked through the front door. I hadn't gone to work because I was afraid he would come to the house when I wasn't there. When I heard the front door open and shut, I hopped off the couch and ran into the hallway. "Liam?"

He tossed his wallet and keys on the table. His hair was messy like he'd woken up on the wrong side of the bed, but he was in different clothes, so he must have picked up a few things while he was out and about. He clearly had showered too, so he must have checked in to a hotel.

"I'm so glad you're home…"

"Are you alone?" He finally turned his gaze to look at me, anger still on his face. The last few days hadn't been enough space for him to cool off fully.

My face fell. "What's the supposed to mean?"

"Assumed you shacked up with your boyfriend while I was gone." He walked around me and headed to the bedroom, his heavy footfalls thudding against the hardwood. I'd returned the pictures and paintings to the wall, so the place was restored, but he didn't seem to notice.

I followed behind him. "I would never do that."

He sat on the edge of the bed and untied his shoes. "But you'll say his name in bed when your husband is on top of you?" He pulled off each shoe and tossed it aside. "You expect me to believe that?"

"If you hadn't stormed out, I could have explained it to you."

His hands came together, and he leaned forward so he could stare at the floor for a while. "What's there to explain?" He sighed before he lifted his gaze. "It's pretty clear you were thinking of someone else when you were with me."

I sat on the bench of my vanity and rested my hands on my thighs. "But I wasn't. His name just slipped out. I swear."

His expression was completely stoic.

"Liam, I'm telling you the truth. Nothing happened between

us. I don't want you to think I'm sneaking around when I'm not."

He didn't blink.

"He told me he loved me the other day." I decided to share everything, so he would understand.

A shadow passed over his gaze.

"But I told him it wasn't going to happen because I'd already made a commitment to you. That's probably why I said his name…because he was on my mind subconsciously."

He grabbed one set of knuckles and squeezed them in anger.

"But I said no, Liam. That's what happened…honestly."

He took a deep breath and let out a sigh that sounded like a growl. "Why should I believe you?"

"Because I'm still here."

He looked away, staring out the window since the curtains were pulled back.

"I can't justify what I did because it was so horrible…saying his name. I truly feel terrible about it and completely understand why you were so angry. Whenever I'm with you, I make sure I don't think about him, but when I'm alone…it's not the same story. I understand if you don't want to do this anymore. You deserve more."

He turned back to me, his blue eyes fierce. "You think I'm gonna walk away so you can run off to him?"

"That's not what I meant. I just meant… I haven't been fair to you. I'm committed to you and loyal, but my heart has a mind of its own that I can't control. I understand if you don't want to put up with it anymore. Because you're a great guy and deserve—"

"No." He massaged his knuckles. "I'm not letting some other guy have you. You're mine." He immediately turned territorial, acting like a dog that refused to let someone else play with his toys. "But I'm sick of this bullshit. I'm going back to fighting because I'm not making that kind of sacrifice for someone who won't make any sacrifices for me. And we're moving."

"What?"

"If you aren't gonna move on from this guy, then we need to move on from him. There's an underground fighting community in London. That's where we're going."

"But my job—"

He flashed me a terrifying look. "It's nonnegotiable, Anna."

WHAT OTHER CHOICE DID I HAVE? AFTER EVERYTHING I'D PUT Liam through, he had every right to relocate us. It was probably the best chance I had to forget about Damien for good, when I wouldn't have to see his pretty eyes anymore. How could you get over someone you saw all the time? Who hugged you and never let go?

I liked my job at the Tuscan Rose, and Florence was my home…but I had no other choice. If I wanted my marriage to work, I had to leave.

But leaving Damien…was so hard. I knew that was the part I

was dreading the most, walking away from him for good. When enough time passed, I would stop thinking about him, would start my family, and he would be a distant memory.

It was exactly what I wanted...

I went into Sofia's office. "Hey, you got a minute?"

She was pulling off chunks of her muffin and placing them in her mouth. Crumbs were all over her desk and papers. "Of course." She spoke with a mouthful of food and wiped her hands together before she brushed off all the pieces of blueberry that got on her dress. "What's up?"

My friendship with Sofia was something I would miss too, even seeing Hades. So, when I handed her my resignation letter, I felt so weak. I placed it on her desk, and I sat in the chair across from her. I'd convinced Liam to let me finish my last two weeks at the Tuscan Rose because quitting on the spot seemed like a terrible way to repay her generosity. He agreed...eventually.

"What's this?" She picked it up and scanned over it, her eyebrows furrowing when she realized what it said. "Wait, you're leaving?"

"Unfortunately..." My hands twisted together with unease because I was terrible at goodbyes. When I'd had nothing, Damien and Sofia were there for me. They were friends that I had to leave behind.

She dropped the paper on her desk. "Why?"

"Well...it's a long story."

"I've got all day." She pushed her muffin forward so we could share it.

I smiled slightly, thinking about all the times we'd split a pizza or a tray of brownies. "I really fucked up with Liam..."

"Oh no."

"We were in bed together a couple nights ago...and I said Damien's name."

"Oh shit." Her eyebrows exploded to the top of her face. "What happened? Did he hunt down Damien?"

"He didn't realize that Damien was the same person..."

"Wow, that was fortunate."

"But he stormed out of the house and was gone for days. When he finally came home, we talked. I told him I understood if he didn't want to be with me anymore. But instead, he said he wanted to relocate to London so we could start over...away from Damien. He's going back to fighting too. I don't want to leave because I love this city and my job, but I don't have a choice. His request is totally reasonable, and if I see Damien all the time, I'm never going to get over him. It's our only option to make this marriage work."

Her eyes drifted down as she processed everything I'd just said. She was clearly sad to lose me. She pulled her hands closer to her body and sighed. When she lifted her gaze, she gave me a look of pity. "That's rough..."

"Yeah..."

"But I understand."

I nodded. "Thanks."

"But I have to ask…is Liam worth it?"

I was quiet.

"Is he worth uprooting your life like this? When you are in love with someone else…"

My heart started to pound when I pictured leaving Damien forever. "This is all my fault. I'm the reason this is happening, so I think Liam's request is fair. The fact that he still wants to be married to me at all is a mystery. Ever since we got remarried, he's had to deal with this other guy in my heart…"

"And if he really loved you, wouldn't he step aside?"

"I…I don't know."

"If he knows you've fallen in love with someone else, he should let you be happy."

"I know, but we were married before. We both pictured us spending our lives together—"

"And then he slept with someone else. All the events were triggered by him—and him alone."

"Doesn't mean he deserves to be treated like this. He's been really understanding and patient about all this—"

"Because he's the one who fucked up, Annabella."

I hadn't expected to have a debate when I'd walked in here. "At the end of the day, I married him. And marriage is about commitment…until death. I can't just change my mind about that. I have to see it through."

That was when she dropped her argument. "Well, I'm really going to miss you."

"I know. I'm gonna miss you too."

She reached across the desk, her hand outstretched.

I placed my hand on top of hers. "I'll still be here two weeks..."

"You don't have to stay that long, Anna. But I appreciate it." She squeezed me before pulling away. "There's a ton of people who will apply for that job once it's posted."

"I know. it's a good job."

"So...have you told Damien?"

I shook my head.

"Are you going to? Or would you rather me do it?"

I didn't want to have a painful goodbye conversation. He would try to convince me to change my mind, and it would just...be terrible. "You should do it. And tell him not to call me. It'll just make it harder."

27

DAMIEN

I'D JUST LOCKED UP MY COMPUTER WHEN MY PHONE RANG. I probably would have ignored it, but since it was Sofia, I answered quickly. "What's up?" I put the laptop into the safe drilled into the floor and shut the door. An audible click sounded when the safe was secure.

"You got a minute?"

"I got all the minutes for you, sweetheart."

She chuckled. "Don't let Hades hear you talk like that."

"What's he going to do?" I sat back down in my leather chair. "I'll fight him for you."

She chuckled again. "That's romantic..."

"So, did you need something?"

"Well...this isn't going to be a pleasant conversation."

That warning was enough to silence me. Now I could feel the pulse in my ears, feel the dread in my blood. "Everything okay?"

"Hades and I are fine. It's about Anna."

Now I couldn't breathe. My throat tightened into a ball and fell into my stomach.

"She submitted her resignation this afternoon. She and Liam are relocating to London to have a fresh start."

"What?" I barked.

"She wanted me to tell you because she doesn't want you to call."

"Is she still there?"

"What do you mean?"

"Is she in the office?"

"Uh...I think so. But Damien, she doesn't want to talk to you—"

"That's too fucking bad. Don't let her leave, alright?"

"Damien—"

"I caught Liam cheating on her a few nights ago."

Sofia went dead silent.

"I wanted to see if he would come clean himself. Obviously not."

"Oh my god... Are you sure?"

"Absolutely. I have proof."

"Oh Jesus...that poor girl."

"So that asshole is putting all the blame on her so they can move. Fucking piece of shit. I've got to go."

"Damien—"

I hung up.

Hades entered my office. "Sounds like a pleasant conversation..."

"Liam didn't tell her." I walked around my desk and joined him in the doorway.

"Why do you look surprised?"

"I'm going down to the hotel to talk to her. Send me that video."

He pulled out his phone and texted it to me. "What's your plan?"

"I just told you."

"But once you tell her, she'll confront Liam. And when she does, he'll know you snitched."

"You think I give a damn?"

"And he'll know that your name isn't a coincidence..."

There was no way to hide my identity this time. The truth would come out, and I'd have to deal with the consequences.

Hades continued to study me. "Just want to make sure you're aware of the full situation. Because Liam is a fighter—and this will start a war. You have to ask yourself, is she worth it?"

I didn't hesitate. "Yes."

He held my gaze with the same intensity. "Then I'm with you."

I stepped inside her office with no preamble. I knew this was the beginning for us, so that electrified me with excitement. My fingers tightened into fists over and over, my muscles pumped with so much blood.

But I was also packed with dread...because this would hurt her.

Tear her apart.

She'd just finished stacking a pile of papers on her desk, probably finishing up all her projects before she left for good. When she saw me in the doorway, her eyes popped wide in shock, as if she'd expected me to actually listen to Sofia and leave her alone.

Didn't she know me at all?

I shut the door behind me and approached the desk.

She got to her feet, immediately combative. "Damien, nothing you say is gonna change my mind. You're just making this hard—"

"Shut up and listen to me." I placed my palms flat on her desk.

She stilled then slowly lowered herself back into the chair.

Now that I had the moment in my grasp, I didn't want to execute it. I already knew exactly how her face would look when I told her the news, that her husband was still the same piece of shit he'd already been. That was how I knew I really loved her...because I wasn't selfish. "The night of your fight, I ran into Liam at the bar at the casino. He was drunk...and hooking up with some woman."

She stilled at my words, not blinking as she processed what I said.

"I tried to get him to go home, but he wouldn't. He told me what you did and said he was free to do whatever he wanted. He said he wouldn't tell you what he did, but I thought he might feel differently when he was sober."

Still, she said nothing. She started to breathe harder, the anger and pain beginning to infect her blood. "Why did you wait so long to tell me?"

"Because I hoped he'd man up and confess."

She finally broke our contact and stared at the desk. She pressed her flat palms against the wood, the sweat leaving moisture that outlined each individual feature. "He wouldn't do that..."

Denial was the last thing I'd expected to hear from her.

"He wouldn't do that to me, not after everything we've been through—"

"Annabella, he did. I saw it."

She wouldn't look at me. "How do I know you aren't lying just to get between us?"

Fuck, that was a punch to the sternum. "Because you know I wouldn't do that shit."

"You're desperate to break us apart—"

"Shut the fuck up." I wouldn't sit there and listen to her torch my reputation when it was all bullshit. "I know you're hurt and you're lashing out, so I'm gonna let that go. But you better shut your mouth right now." I pulled my phone out of my pocket and set it on the desk. "I have a video...if you want to see."

She stared at it for a while, considering it, but then she turned the phone over. "I can't see that..." She put her hands to her face and covered her features, taking a few moments to breathe through the pain she'd just endured.

I gave her the time she needed.

She finally pulled her hands away, her eyes slightly wet like she'd let herself shed a few tears before she bucked up. "The second we hit a bump in the road, he gives up. For a man who fights to the death, I don't understand why he throws in the towel so easily." She slowly rose to her feet and took a deep breath.

I studied her, unsure what she would do.

"This wouldn't have happened if I hadn't..." She didn't finish the sentence because she was ashamed. "But I never, even at my weakest moments, would ever think of doing something like that..."

I knew that all too well.

"I just don't understand," she whispered.

"He said he deserved a get-out-of-jail-free card because of what you did. But he was drunk when he said it."

She stared at her desk.

I'd just crushed her, but I wanted to clean up all the pieces and make it better.

"Do you want to know—"

"I'd rather not." She straightened her spine and inhaled a deep breath as she prepared for what was next. "I'm sorry about what I—"

"It's forgotten."

She wouldn't look at me, her eyes down.

"What are you going to do?"

She sighed again then moved around the desk. "I'm gonna kick his ass—that's what."

28

ANNABELLA

I was blindsided.

I'd trusted Liam more than I realized because I hadn't expected this at all. It was almost too ridiculous to believe because he'd have to be an idiot not to learn his lesson. I stepped through the front door and slammed it behind me. It didn't snap off the hinges like it did with Liam, but it was still a strong enough slam to make the house vibrate. "Where the fuck are you, asshole?" I stormed into the house, my heels echoing against the hardwood floor as I made my way into the living area.

He stood at the kitchen island, still as if he was actually afraid of me. He'd just taken a pan out of the oven, and he gently pulled the red oven mitts off his hands as he stared. Instead of asking questions like an innocent person, he took the Fifth.

"Are you fucking kidding me? You come into this house and boss me around like that, when you're the one fucking someone else the last few days?"

Still quiet.

There was a picture of us on our wedding day. My long dress trailed behind me, and I looked away as he kissed my forehead. I yanked it off the wall then slammed it down onto the floor, where it shattered into pieces. "You make me pack up my life and move when you're the one getting laid at the bar? You make me feel like shit for not being over a man I never cheated on you with—even when I wanted to? Who the fuck do you think you are?" My hands moved to my hips, and I stood my ground, so furious that I would smack him upside the head if he came too close.

He continued to stay quiet, as if he was thinking of a plan to get him out of this. He finally came around the kitchen island and slowly approached me. "Baby—"

"You wanna die, asshole?" There was a block of knives on the counter, and I grabbed the big one, the one with the serrated edge that sliced through thick pieces of steak. I gripped the handle and pointed it at him. "Don't fucking 'baby' me."

He held up his hands in surrender.

"I can't believe you would do this to me." Angry tears entered my gaze, making my vision blurry. My fingers tightened on the handle. "I trusted you. I actually believed you'd just made a mistake and you were a good man. But the second our lives got difficult, you pulled the same bullshit again."

He stepped back and slowly lowered his hands, obviously afraid I might actually stab him. "Anna—"

"And you were just never going to tell me? What the hell is

wrong with you? How dare you treat me like a criminal when your crimes are far worse than mine? You were really going to let me leave my job and my life and never tell me what you did."

"I don't know what you think happened—"

I lunged at him.

"Shit." He ran back and got behind the kitchen counter.

"Don't fucking lie to me, Liam. You're only making this worse."

He finally stopped the bullshit. "How do you think that made me feel, hearing you say some other asshole's name when I was inside you?"

"How much worse would you have felt if I'd fucked him instead?" I snapped. "But I never did. He kissed me, and I said no. He told me he loved me and we should be together, but I stayed with you."

"You didn't tell me that before—"

"Doesn't fucking matter. And you didn't have the balls to tell me yourself."

He gripped the counter and bowed his head. "Anna, I was just angry about the whole thing. I had too much to drink, and I just—"

"I don't want the specifics." Hearing him actually admit it made me feel so terrible, made me want to burst into tears. I felt so stupid falling for his false promises, his sexy charm. I was the dumb girl who kept taking her cheating ex back while expecting things to be different. I'd married him because he was safe, but he wasn't safe at all. "Your decision is unacceptable. Our crimes are not equivalent. You had every right to be angry. You had every right to want your space. You had every right to want to move somewhere else so we could get a fresh start. But you did *not* have the right to fuck someone else." I threw the knife down, and it slid across the floor. "We're done, Liam."

When he saw the world burn around him, he finally softened into the man I knew, the one with the heart of gold. "Anna, hold on." He came around the island now that the knife was on the floor.

I held up my hand. "Don't fucking touch me."

"You made mistakes, and I did too. But you never gave me a real chance. You said you did, but you never did—"

"I married you!"

"But I had to compete with that asshole. If that hadn't been a problem, we'd be fine right now."

"If you hadn't cheated the first time, we'd be fine right now," I corrected.

"Anna, let's move to London like we planned and start over. A fresh start for both of us."

I rolled my eyes and turned away. "Fuck off."

He grabbed me by the wrist and pulled me back. "Please."

I twisted out of his grasp and kneed him right in the dick.

"Fuck…" He fell to his knees and covered his balls.

"We're done, Liam. I'll come back for the rest of my stuff in a few days." I walked away and headed down the hallway. I grabbed a duffel bag and stuffed it with the essentials. After

I zipped it up, I pulled off my ring and left it on the vanity—exactly where I'd left it the other two times. This was the last time.

When Liam recovered from the attack, he joined me. "Anna, let's talk about this."

"No." I pulled the strap over my shoulder and faced him. He blocked the doorway so I couldn't get out. I was cornered like a rat. "Move."

"I'm sorry, okay?" Emotion flooded his eyes. "I'm so fucking sorry. They didn't mean anything to me—"

"*They*?" My blood boiled. "Get the hell out of my way, Liam."

"You said he didn't mean anything to you when you said his name. Well, they didn't mean anything to me."

"But he does mean something to me," I snapped. "I still love him, and I rejected him so many times because I was committed to you. So, there's no excuse you can make to justify what you did. You can't pin this on me. Now, move, or I'll scratch your eyes out."

His feet were rooted to the spot.

"Keeping me here isn't going to change anything, Liam. Making me your prisoner won't make me forgive you. It won't fix this. If you wanted to fix this, you could have stayed home and screamed at me until you lost your voice. You could have demolished this entire house. You could have done anything you wanted. But you chose to leave. Now, let me leave."

His eyes started to gloss with tears. His large arms stayed by his sides, and he made fists with both hands, like he wanted to fight until his last breath. But defeat was in his veins. He knew there was nothing he could do to stop this. Love wouldn't be enough to fix this...not this time. He finally stepped to the side.

When the pathway was clear, I moved forward. I marched down the hallway, ready to leave that house and move on with my life. It used to be full of so many memories, but now those memories had been torched by his betrayal. I used to believe there was so much here, that we had something special, but now I realized that was all a lie.

We were never special.

I GOT A ROOM AT THE TUSCAN ROSE AND CAMPED OUT THERE for a few days. I didn't go to work, but I didn't need to explain why. Sofia must have learned everything from Damien because she texted me.

Take all the time you need. Your desk will be here when you're ready.

I was so lucky to have a boss like her.

But I wasn't lucky to be me right now.

I ordered room service for all my meals and charged everything to Liam's account. He left me alone for the first few days, but then his impatience got to him and he started to text me.

Baby, please talk to me.

Anna?

I know I fucked up...but we can fix it.

I got so angry about that last message I blocked his number altogether. I didn't have a concrete plan at the moment. I'd have to find a divorce lawyer to finalize the paperwork. Then I'd have to find a place to live and figure out the financial situation with Liam. But for now, I'd rather watch movies and cry into a pile of tissues.

Sometimes, I was so heartbroken by what he did that I got lost in my tears. At other times, I told myself that he wasn't worth my tears, that he only deserved my hostility and indifference. But then the cycle would repeat over and over.

A knock sounded at my door.

Liam was too stupid to figure out where I was, so I suspected it was Damien. I'd expected him to come sooner, but he probably understood I needed my space, that there was nothing he could do for me right now.

In sweats and a t-shirt with a tear-stained face, I opened the door without even looking who was on the other side.

It was Damien. In a black t-shirt and jeans, he stood with his hands in his pockets, his eyes focused on mine like they had a story to tell. They shifted back and forth as they continued to examine me, wanting to see me smile rather than frown.

Wordlessly, I walked to the couch near the TV and took a seat. I pulled my knees to my chest and watched the screen even though I hadn't been watching it minutes ago. My arms circled my knees.

Damien stared at me for a while before he joined me on the couch. He kept his distance by allowing a few feet to remain between us. He glanced at the TV. "What are you watching?"

"Not sure. I haven't been paying attention."

He watched it for a few minutes. "This is that new film with Robert De Niro." He snapped his fingers. "Can't remember what it's called...*the Scotsman*?"

"*The Irishman*," I corrected.

He nodded. "I've been meaning to see it." With one arm on the armrest, he watched the screen casually, like he hadn't told me my husband had cheated just a few days ago.

I pulled a blanket over my lap. It was the first time I didn't feel anything for Damien. That undeniable heat wasn't there anymore. Explosive chemistry, desperate need, they were all gone. All my feelings were masked by rage.

After a few minutes, he turned back to me. "You want to order a pizza or something?"

"I'm not hungry. And you don't need to stay with me, Damien... I'm fine."

"Really?" he asked, calling out my lie. "I can see the rivers of tears on your cheeks, see the redness in your eyes."

I looked away.

"It's okay not to be fine."

I looked out the large floor-to-ceiling windows and stared at the bright city beyond.

He scooted closer to me on the couch, his arm sliding around the back of my neck. He turned to me as his hand cupped the back of my head and brought my face close to his. He examined me for a while, reading the pain in my eyes like words on a page. "I'm sorry."

"Why?" I whispered. "You warned me about him. This is your time to say you were right. Go ahead, say it."

He didn't stoop to that level. He continued to stare at me with the same concern. "I didn't want to be right, Annabella."

"I don't believe that..."

"I really didn't. I wanted him to be what you deserved."

I couldn't look at those beautiful eyes anymore. I turned away, feeling the pain in the pit of my stomach. "I feel stupid...so fucking stupid." Tears burned all the way in my gut and coated my throat. I'd been crying on and off for so many days that they blurred together. Liam had hurt me this way once, so I didn't think he could hurt me again...but he did. "How hard is it not to sleep with someone else?"

"It isn't."

"Well, Liam would disagree with you..."

"He's impulsive and disloyal. The second things go to shit, he jumps ship. But if he's the captain of that ship, he should go down with the crew and the boat. That's not him. You, on the other hand, have the kind of integrity that the mafia pays a fortune to possess. You have the loyalty of the mob, of a gangster, or a drug lord."

"Is that supposed to be a compliment?"

"Damn right, it is. And it's the biggest compliment you'll ever get." His fingers gently moved into my hair, lightly touching me as he looked into my eyes. His cologne was heavy in my nostrils, and his clean-shaven jawline looked so kissable. "What happens now?"

I pulled my gaze away. "I told him we're done."

He didn't hide his approval. "Good."

"I grabbed a few things and left. But I'll go back and get my stuff in a few days. I need to find a place to live...again."

"You could always stay with me."

I refused to look at him. "Damien, I'm not in a good place—"

"That's not what I meant. If you need a place to stay, I've got something like twenty bedrooms in that house. That's all I meant."

I could rent my old apartment, but it wasn't very nice. I'd saved most of my checks since I'd married Liam, so I could afford a nicer place, especially now that I was keeping my position at the hotel.

His fingers gently caressed me. "You better take half of his money this time."

Liam had cheated on me twice now, and I was entitled to every single euro of his net worth, but I still didn't want it. "He earned all that money. I never contributed, so I don't want it."

"That's not how it works—"

"I don't want his money. If I buy a house with it, I'll think of him. If I buy a car, I'll think of him. My old apartment sucked, but at least it was mine..."

His fingers dragged down to my neck as he abandoned his argument.

"I can't believe he wasn't going to tell me...just keep it from me."

"I was surprised too."

"I guess he feels entitled because of what I did, but our mistakes aren't equal."

"Not at all," he whispered. "I understand he was upset, but… that didn't make his behavior okay."

I still didn't ask for the specifics of what he saw because it would hurt me. I knew there were multiple women, and that disgusted me. What if Damien had never found out, and I'd continued to sleep with my husband after he'd been with others? What if I'd caught something? Had to tell every partner I ever had after him that I had herpes?

I hated him so much right now.

"I can get you a good divorce lawyer."

"I'll probably use the guy I used last time…" I was going to be divorced twice, and I was in my twenties… So pathetic.

"If there's anything I can do to help, just let me know."

I stared at the carpet while the TV played in the background. I was a free woman who could do whatever she wanted now, but I had no urge to destroy those crisp sheets with our sweaty bodies. I was broken…deep down inside. "Thanks for coming by. I think I'm going to get some sleep…" I moved from his side on the couch and rose to my feet. My fingers ran through my messy hair, and I glanced out the large window.

It took him a moment to mimic my movements, to rise to his feet and walk with me to the door. Maybe he'd hoped something would happen tonight, that I would fall into his arms and tell him to never let me go.

Maybe he didn't understand I was genuinely sad my marriage was over. Genuinely hurt Liam had done that to me.

I opened the door so he could leave. "I'll see you later."

He stared at me for a long time, staying on this side of the door because he didn't want to leave. He tried to think of something to say, but nothing was forthcoming. "I'm here if you need anything." He didn't try to hug me before he stepped into the hallway, giving me the space I obviously needed.

I didn't look at him again before I let the door close.

29

DAMIEN

"What now?" Hades sat next to me in front of his grand fireplace, drinking water instead of his usual scotch.

"Not sure." His sobriety didn't stop me from raiding his liquor cabinet and enjoying whatever he couldn't imbibe. "When I saw her in her hotel room, she looked dead inside. She was genuinely hurt by what he did."

"Can you blame her?" Sofia asked, holding a sleeping Andrew in her arms. "She was committed to that marriage. She wanted it to succeed. She wanted to believe Liam was the man she thought he was."

"Motherfucker." I swallowed the profanity with a drink.

"You mind?" Hades asked, nodding to his sleeping son.

"He's one," I argued. "And he's asleep."

"You're in my house," Hades threatened. "You play by my rules."

I rolled my eyes. "Alright...*Father*."

Hades gave me a glare but let the conversation drop.

"She's been at work all week," Sofia said to dissipate the tension. "She's quiet but seems to be okay."

I hadn't called or texted her because I could tell she didn't want me to. Maybe I was stupid for hoping she would jump into my arms the second Liam was gone, that she would fuck me right on that couch in her hotel room. Liam was out of the picture, but that didn't mean I would get what I wanted so easily. My fantasies warped my reality, and I could think clearly. "Did she say anything about filing for divorce? Finding a place?"

"She did find a new apartment. Signed the lease," Sofia answered.

I hoped it was better than her old place. "Did she move out?"

"I don't think so," she said. "But she got all the paperwork from her lawyer."

"Good." That meant it was almost over.

Hades turned to me. "I think I'm going to take him back as a client. What do you think?"

I didn't want to deal with Liam more than I had, but I wouldn't mind watching him get his ass kicked in the ring—and getting paid for it. And if he did death fighting, that would be even better. "Fine with me."

"He never figured out it was you, so why not?" Hades asked.

"Fucking idiot." I couldn't believe it. How many Damiens were out there?

"Did he ask how she even knew what he did?" Hades asked.

"Not sure," I said. "She didn't say."

"He must not have asked." Hades took a drink of his ice water. "Otherwise, he would have connected the dots. You're lucky Anna continues to cover for you."

"I told her she doesn't need to." I didn't care if he came after me. He may be larger than me, but I was faster.

Hades watched me. "I think it's best for everyone if he doesn't know. We can continue to milk him for millions, and he'll have no idea that he's making his wife's lover richer."

"Ex-wife," I corrected. "And she's not my lover."

"Give her time," Sofia said. "She's getting divorced a second time. That's rough."

"She wouldn't have gotten divorced a second time if she'd just listened to me," I said bitterly. I'd warned her about him so many times, tried to convince her this was a stupid decision. But she was too hurt to think clearly.

"Be patient." Sofia gently rocked her son as she looked at me. "She loves you. She just needs time."

30

ANNABELLA

I walked up to my own front door and knocked. The folder was tucked under my arm, and I wore a dress with a denim jacket on top. Springtime was here, and while the sun was shining, it was still a bit chilly.

Footsteps sounded on the other side, and the door opened a moment later.

Liam stood there, his eyes defeated, his frame weak. His chin was covered in a thin beard because he'd stopped shaving, and that brightness to his blue eyes was gone. It used to remind me of the sunshine reflecting off the blue waters of the ocean. Now they were gray, lifeless.

I almost felt bad for him…almost. "Can I come in?"

"It's your house." He stepped aside so I could enter. "You didn't even need to knock."

My heels clapped against the hardwood as I stepped inside. The house was silent, abandoned. It was as lifeless as a vacant house, feeling almost haunted. I passed the table where I used to leave my keys and purse and entered the living area. It was an open room, the kitchen and living room one spacious area.

Liam followed behind me, in sweatpants and a t-shirt. It didn't seem like he'd showered in days.

I opened the folder and pulled out the papers. I laid them out on the counter.

Liam didn't look at them.

"I just need you to sign these. I'll grab the rest of my things and be out of your hair." I opened the drawer and found a pen before I uncapped it and set it on top of the papers. It rolled slightly until it came to a stop.

He stared at me as if I'd said nothing at all.

"Liam." I felt like a mother berating her child.

He crossed his arms over his chest. "I'm not signing those again."

"For what it's worth, I hoped I would never sign these again either. But here we are..."

He released a painful sigh. "No."

"Liam, I can get this divorce without your signature. It'll just take a lot more time and work on my part. After everything you've put me through, the least you can do is make this easier for me. I'm just as devastated as you are...even more so."

He bowed his head. "Baby—"

"Please don't call me anymore."

When he sighed, his nostrils flared. "Please work this out with me." He raised his head and looked me in the eye. "Let's move and start over. Let's have a clean break. This was a recipe for disaster, and you know it. I was constantly competing with another guy—"

"And I was honest about that from the beginning. I didn't hide any of that from you. That doesn't give you…" I took a deep breath and closed my eyes to harden my emotions. When I opened my eyes again, I was calm. "I'm not having this conversation again. I've made my decision, and you can't change it. Please sign these papers so I can collect my things and leave."

"Anna—"

I grabbed the papers and prepared to leave.

"Okay." He grabbed my wrist and stopped my movements. "Fine."

I returned the papers to the counter.

"But shouldn't we talk about the specifics?"

"It's the same as last time. I didn't change anything."

His eyes narrowed. "Anna, take the money—"

"Never." I didn't want anything from him, anything to make me think I needed him. "I don't need your wealth. I already have a nice apartment and a good job. You made that money doing something I never approved of. If I take it now, it would be hypocritical. I won't take a single euro that you had you beat someone for, that you killed someone for." It was blood money.

He looked defeated once more, but he made was no argument.

I held the pen out to him. "Sign where I placed the X's."

He stared down at me for a long time before he looked at the pen in my grasp. He studied the writing implement for minutes, breathing deeply and evenly, before he took it and pressed the tip to the page—and added his signature.

I walked away so I wouldn't have to watch him. My echoing heels couldn't block out the scratch of the pen against the paper, and the sound of the scrawl was heavy on my ears. I turned down the hallway and headed to the bedroom, where my clothing hung in the walk-in closet. It was the last time I'd ever be there, and I couldn't stop the tears that welled in my eyes and streaked down my cheeks.

I knew Liam loved me, but he'd still hurt me.

Maybe love didn't mean anything... Maybe it never meant anything.

I MOVED IN TO MY NEW APARTMENT AND HUNG UP MY CLOTHES in the closet. I was missing furniture, so all I had was a mattress on the floor in my bedroom because I'd sold my old stuff when I'd moved back in with Liam. It was empty and lonely, having this place all to myself. I was starting over, again, and I didn't feel motivated like I did last time.

A knock sounded on the door.

"It's open." After Liam signed the papers, he didn't contact me again. Once his signature was permanently in ink, he knew there was no going back. He wouldn't be able to convince me to take him back again. The only reason he was successful the first time because I was heartbroken over someone else.

Damien stepped inside. His t-shirt fit his thick arms in the sexiest way, his sculpted muscles visible even through the fabric. He wore black jeans, so he was dressed completely in shades of shadow. He took a look around the empty space before he looked at me. "I like it."

"It's much nicer than my last place."

He walked past the large windows in the living room and approached the kitchen, where my unpacked boxes sat on the counter. He looked at the fridge and the appliances before he moved down the hallway and examined the bathroom and my bedroom. "It's in a better neighborhood too." He walked back to me and glanced at the folder sitting on the counter, which held my finalized divorced papers. He must have assumed what the contents were because he stared for a long time before he looked at me again. "Need help unpacking these things?"

"It's just clothes and stuff. I got it."

He leaned against the counter and crossed his arms over his chest, staring at me longer than the average person would. "What about your furniture?"

"I ordered a couple things. They'll be here in a few weeks."

His eyes lingered on my cabinets, taking in the features of the apartment even though he probably didn't care about the details. "How are you?"

I pulled the packing tape off the box so I could get the lid open. "I'm okay. I've been better, but you know...whatever." I was still in so much pain, haunted by what Liam had done behind my back. Emotion caught in my throat, but I swallowed it.

Damien continued to watch me, his eyes sympathetic. "It'll get easier."

"I'm broken by what he did, but—"

"You aren't broken, Annabella." He placed his hands in his pockets. "You're bruised...but those bruises will heal. I promise."

"I don't know..." I pulled out a few hangers and carried them to the closet in my bedroom. I hung up my stuff and knew he was behind me, following me into the bedroom. "I'm just over it."

"Over what?" His deep voice reached every corner of that room, filling it with heat and energy.

"Men." I turned back around and faced him. "I'm just done with it."

His face remained stoic, but his eyes filled with emotion. "Not all men are like that, Annabella. If you don't believe me, think about Hades. You think there's anything Sofia could ever do to break his loyalty? She could sleep with another man, and his response would be to murder the guy...not sleep with another woman. Don't let Liam's stupidity ruin the reputation of every other man."

"But Hades and Sofia are soul mates. The rest of us...are just people."

"Love is love—regardless of the intensity."

"Well, I know Liam loved me, but he still stabbed me in the back." I walked back into the kitchen.

"Not all men are like Liam." He grabbed me by the arm and forced me to turn around. "I'm not like him, and don't you fucking dare think I am. I would never do that shit. If I'm committed to a woman, I give it one hundred percent."

I pulled my arm away. "How do you know? You even said you've never been serious with a woman."

His eyes showed his offense. "I don't need the experience to know what kind of man I'd be. Once I fell in love with someone, I knew exactly who I was. No matter had bad things get, I don't sniff around. I'm loyal…just like you."

Hearing him talk about love made me want to push him away. "Damien, if you think you and I are just going to get together because Liam is gone, you're wrong. I need time. I need space. I'm not in the right place—"

"That's fine, Annabella. I can wait."

"I don't want you to wait," I whispered. "I just want to be by myself for a while…"

His eyes filled with pain even though he tried to cover it.

"He hurt me, you hurt me, and then he hurt me again… I need a break."

He took a deep breath before he whispered his response. "I won't hurt you again, Annabella."

"Liam said the same thing."

His temper flared like a bomb exploded. "I'm not Liam!" His voice suddenly grew loud, his anger a gushing volcano. "And

I hurt you to protect you. I hurt you because I'd only known you for a short time. The situation is totally different now."

"And you don't want to protect me anymore?"

He took another deep breath. "I haven't thought that far ahead yet…"

"This was never meant to be, Damien. I wanted you when you didn't want me. And now you want me, and I don't want you."

He shook his head slightly. "I know you don't mean that. You're upset, you're traumatized, and you need space. I got it, alright? I'll give you as much space as you want. Just don't lie and pretend you don't love me—because I know you do."

I dropped my gaze. "I just don't want you to expect anything."

"I don't," he said quietly. "I'm a patient man. If all you can offer right now is friendship, that's fine. I can be a friend." He dropped his arms and departed from the kitchen. He stopped to look out the windows that overlooked the city, the sunset leaving beautiful splashes of red and pink. He stared for a while before he turned back to me. "You know where to find me." He focused on me as he waited for a response, hoping I would say something to numb the pain I'd just inflicted. He clearly wanted an embrace, the affection that we used to share, that we used to be addicted to.

But I couldn't do it. "Goodbye, Damien."

31

DAMIEN

Liam looked like shit.

His eyes were permanently gray, and his strong shoulders sagged from the weight of his grief. He wasn't the powerful man with the bright-blue eyes. Now, he was a ghost of the man he used to be, still wearing his wedding ring even though the divorce papers had been filed.

I'd seen them sitting on Annabella's kitchen counter.

He stepped into the ring and tightened the wraps around his hands. He was in just his trunks, his body slicked with oil so the punches would slide across his swollen muscles. He had been eager to get back into the ring when Hades had approached him, but he'd rejected death fighting.

As if there was a chance he could get his ex-wife back.

That train had left the station.

The horn blared, and the match began.

Hades wasn't as interested in the match because the stakes

weren't as high. And Liam was so miserable, he didn't believe he would win anyway. "She'll come around. I've been divorced, so I understand why she's so cold."

"Not the same thing at all."

"Divorce is painful, even if you want the divorce. She was dedicated to that marriage, determined to make it work. The fact that Liam betrayed her the same way, for the same reasons, just makes the sting more potent." His hands were together as he watched Liam and his opponent move around the ring and battle it out. "She's not gonna jump into bed with some other guy."

"I get that. But I don't appreciate the way she pushed me away."

"Just give her time. She'll come around."

I bowed my head in frustration. "I just can't believe I've wanted this woman for so long, and now I can't have her."

"For now." He turned to me. "Do you really want Liam's leftovers anyway?"

I narrowed my eyes.

"You don't want Anna when she's still thinking about Liam, whether her feelings are positive or negative. Let her work through this, come out the other side, and be ready. When you guys were together the first time, you were the only thing on her mind. It won't be that way again if you force it."

"Yeah...I get it."

Liam channeled all his rage into the fight and beat his opponent, knocking him out cold to the sound of cheers from the men. He raised both fists in the air in celebration, but his face was still blank like none of this really mattered.

"It looks like you benefit the most from all this." I watched Liam head to the gate so he could join the rest of the crowd and walk back to his locker room in order to shower.

Hades gave me a slight grin. "I'm not ashamed of that."

When we got to the locker room, Liam was already gone.

"I guess he just wants his money so he can go home." Hades shut the door and walked with me to the elevator. We got inside and watched the metal doors shut before we rose to the top floor.

The casino was in front of us, loud music playing and naked girls everywhere. We walked across the room.

"I bet he went to a whorehouse." The second things got rough with Annabella, he turned to pussy. Why would his actions be any different now?

Hades stopped when we were within sight of the bar. "Looks like he just wants a drink."

Liam sat alone, his fingers around his glass as he stared into the dark contents. His face was bruised from the punches he'd endured, but he didn't seem to be in physical pain...just emotional pain. He seemed genuinely heartbroken by what he'd lost, but that made him even more difficult to understand.

"All he had to do was keep his dick in his pants," I said bitterly. "I don't understand him."

Hades continued to stare at him. "He's just too impulsive. He loves her, but his behavior is driven by something else." He pulled his phone out of his pocket and glanced at the screen. "I need to get home. You'll talk to him?"

"Why the fuck would I talk to him?" I didn't feel bad for the son of a bitch. He'd brought this on himself...and hurt a woman who didn't deserve an ounce of pain. The turn of events was fortunate for me, but that didn't make me hate him less.

"Because he's your client."

"No. He's *your* client."

"Damien, come on." He patted me on the shoulder. "He's out of the picture with Anna. You got what you wanted. No reason to feel anything for him anymore." He winked. "You won." He walked off and exited the casino.

I sighed and turned back to Liam, who looked utterly devastated. He wasn't pressing up against a naked woman or buying someone a drink. He was just alone...because he wanted to be alone. He wasn't angry anymore.

There was an open spot beside him, so I joined him. It was a quiet night at the bar because the regulars preferred to sit at the poker tables. The rest of the guys were still down at the fights, watching the rest of the matches.

He didn't look at me, as if he didn't notice I was there.

I got the topless blonde's attention and ordered a drink. I

took a sip of the scotch and turned to him, forcing myself to extend some kindness. "You fought well tonight."

He didn't look at me, staring into his glass. "It's strange. I used to want to fight more than anything. Now it means nothing to me." He swirled his drink before he took a sip. His nostrils flared as it burned his throat down to his stomach.

I couldn't bring myself to show him pity, to say I was sorry about what happened. "You'll get back into it."

"Maybe...maybe not."

Hades would just coerce him if he didn't want to.

"You want a ride home?"

He shook his head. "I hate that house."

I didn't need to ask why.

"This divorce seems to be harder than the first one..."

Still didn't feel anything for him.

"I don't know why I fucked it up so bad. I don't know why I lost my temper. I don't know why..." He bowed his head and rubbed his hands over his short hair. "I don't know why I had to throw away the only person I actually care about..."

I didn't get it either.

"I love her so much. But why would she believe that?"

She shouldn't.

He turned quiet and stared at his drink awhile.

I let the silence pass and had no response to his sadness. I just wanted him to get back to work and move on. Listening to him complain about his despair seemed stupid when he wasn't even the victim.

He finished his drink then asked for another, not even looking at the pretty waitress.

"Things will get better."

"No, they won't," he whispered. "I've lived without her before…and it was terrible."

Then he should have learned his lesson.

"When she looked at me like that…" He shook his head. "So angry. So upset. I felt like shit. When she knew what I'd done, the hurt on her face was indescribable. I hate myself for what I did to her…when I heard her tell me what I did."

I stared into my glass.

"I just…" He suddenly turned quiet.

I continued to stare at my scotch.

Then his head slowly turned my way, his blue eyes burning into my face for the first time.

I met his gaze.

He stared at me for several heartbeats. "You were there that night…"

My palms started to sweat, and my heart began to race. I watched his mind work to connect the dots, to deduce what had happened right under his nose.

"And she knew about it…because you told her."

I gripped my glass and took a deep breath.

"And you told her...because you're Damien." He stared at me without blinking, rage slowly creeping into his features. He knew exactly who I was, finally understood this wasn't a coincidence. The past six months seemed to play across his mind, remembering all the times Anna and I were together and he'd assumed it was harmless. But now he understood I was the guy who'd fucked his wife...who'd stolen her heart.

He squeezed the tumbler in his hand until the glass shattered in his fingertips, the shards exploding across the surface of the bar. His knuckles turned white as his fingers closed into a fist. The vein down his forehead thickened and throbbed, the tint of his fair skin making him look as red as a tomato.

Adrenaline spiked in my blood, but not from fear. A part of me wanted this to happen, to look him in the eye when he knew I was the man who'd fucked his wife, who'd claimed her heart and never let it go. She would be mine soon enough, and he'd have to live the rest of his life knowing he was the reason Annabella was sleeping with another man.

I didn't sugarcoat the truth or connect his assumption. This moment was bound to happen, and now I was relieved the truth was out in the open. I didn't have to pretend to like the guy. I finished my drink and left the empty glass on the table. "She was always too good for you. You know it." I slid off the stool and got to my feet. "She's better off without you. And she'll be better off with me." I turned my back and walked away. Fighting him when he was drunk was cheap. Not my style.

He got off his stool and yelled after me. "I'm going to kill you, Damien!"

I stopped and turned around.

He stood there, his arms hanging by his sides as his veins thickened with blood and adrenaline. "I'm gonna crush that skull with my bare hands until your brains explode. And I'm going to make Anna watch."

I stood still in the middle of the floor, the distant sound of moving chips on my ears. The deep bass of the music was loud, the women in cages dancing despite the lack of rhythm. I didn't see anyone around us, no men crossing the path between us. All I saw were those blue eyes. "That's the difference between you and me. I would never use Anna like that. That's why I deserve her—and you lost her."

THEIR STORY CONTINUES IN FOREVER...

Order Now

Printed in Great Britain
by Amazon